MYSTERY
IN
MONTMARTRE

MYSTERY IN MONTMARTRE

Raine Baushke

23 Leaves Press
Kentucky

To my mother,

Evelyn Jean Genson Urban

Chapter I André

PARISIAN ATTORNEY ANDRÉ Gensonné's ordered life began unraveling in June and typically for him involved a work of art.

He had first noticed the curious painting on an impromptu visit with friends to the Musée de l'Erotisme and just managed to hide his heart-pounding response.

He had returned to view it a second time and a sense of foreboding settled onto his shoulders. He didn't realize it then, but his pursuit of the painting and the woman depicted on the canvas would ultimately jeopardize his career in the art industry, and threaten his family's social position. *Miriam* had changed everything. Only nimble fingers could disentangle the resulting Gordian knot.

André now hesitated for a third time under the round red sign identifying the Musée de l'Erotisme; it appeared tasteful compared to the glowing signage in the windows. He slipped on his suit jacket and ran a finger between his neck and the crisp collar of his shirt. Trepidation tightened his stomach muscles. Returning to the Musée again implied a lack of restraint and André was always in control. His bespoke Aubercy shoes felt like lead; he was that reluctant. Perhaps a different attendant would be on duty today.

He unclenched his hands and opened the door. "Bonjour," André greeted the attendant. Damn, it was the same woman, just a different hair color. Did she ever have a day off?

"Bonjour Monsieur." She took André's entry fee. "Back again?" Her gaze lingered be low his abdomen and then lifted to his eyes. She flipped her hair back, silky pink filaments skimming the tiny butterfly tattoo on her shoulder, and she smiled wide. She winked one heavily mascaraed eye. André twisted aside and pushed his body through the turnstile.

The acknowledgement stung like he was a child and Maman had caught him doing wrong. André escaped with a brief glance at the erotic presentations on the street level floor. The ambient lighting of the displays appeared contrived in the stark afternoon light.

The Musée de l'Erotisme displayed the history of erotica and for André, one visit would have been enough. Explicitly arranged mannequins competed with glass cases overfilled with articles that depicted human sexuality (from fertility goddesses to bizarre sizes of the male and female genitalia). The narrow building contained several crowded floors of a unique collection spanning diverse cultures and ancient civilizations. André's destination was the top floor currently hosting an exhibition of contemporary art.

He hurried, anxious to ascend the stairs and disappear. On the next floor, he startled a young man and woman cuddled on a couch viewing an early-twentieth century pornographic movie. They glanced at him and then back at the screen, settling into each other. The jerky movements of the black-

and-white characters in the old film reabsorbed them. André climbed another set of stairs.

He turned the corner and saw her again. *Anne.* The small painting of a woman suspended among eclectic displays on a partitioned wall unit. One other man was in the gallery and he sidled closer.

"Nice, eh?" The stooped man's body emitted yesterday's garlic. "Nice figure for a drowned woman." Gnarled hands mimed an hourglass.

André eyes met the hooded scrutiny of the Frenchman clad in a tweedy jacket, wrinkled pants, and the rumpled air of another era. The man hovered too close in the vacant gallery. André shrugged.

"Sexy. Yes?"

"No. Yes…I don't—"

"Her hair. Aah." He exhaled a pungent sigh. André stepped away. "She's lying underwater, it should float."

André contemplated the woman whose image was imprinted in his mind. Lithe, elegant, and poised on her back, she wore a red ball gown; one alabaster arm appeared to be afloat, the other hidden. Her drawn-up knees beneath the billowy skirt faced the viewer; although one slender foot dangled from the filmy folds. Her neck bent forward aligned with her horizontally suspended body. The reflections of her skin and dress provided evidence she was underwater. The old man was right about her perfectly groomed hair.

He kept returning because the model in the painting looked like the teenager he had met in America when he was still reeling from his brother's death. He had been eighteen then. This exquisite woman was not the awkward young girl he remembered; seventeen years had passed. He still wanted her. How had the American come to model for an artist in Paris? Where was Anne now?

André noticed a small wooden plaque engraved with six letters—*Miriam*—and centered at the bottom of the frame. Had it been there before? André had viewed the painting twice before and didn't remember the painting had had a name or a signature. Who had painted it? He moved away from the old man irritated he was ogling Anne.

He descended the steps by twos. The third time was easier. He had suppressed the memories crashing like waves against a rocky shore; the first and second time he saw the painting of a presumably drowned woman. Interred . . . like his brother . . . in the sea.

He exited the Musée de l'Erotisme onto the Boulevard de Clichy. The nightclub district glowed in neon clouds of red, blue and green light when it was dark, producing a festive atmosphere, a magnet for the young and adventurous.

A chill quivered up André's back. Daytime revealed a seedy ambience and vestiges of last night's excess. No place for him—especially since Gilles Marini had performed on the American television show Dancing with the Stars. Some Parisian tourists mistook him for the likeable French-born performer. He abhorred the attention. He slipped in among others as he leaned into the summer breeze with his hands in his pockets. Hidden in the pack he left Anne behind; he couldn't justify another visit.

Thursday, June 13, 2013

"BONJOUR!" MICHEL BURST through André's office door—one hand on the brass knob, the other outstretched—like a comedian. "It wasn't there." The subdued atmosphere of luxurious textiles had softened Michel's exuberant footsteps; authentic nineteenth-century paintings hung on the walls, verification of the firm's status.

"What do you mean, it wasn't there? It was there last Friday." Lounging against his massive desk, André pushed back, muscles tightening at Michel's pronouncement. What had happened to the painting? He met his colleague midway.

"Are you sure? I saw it three time—." Michel's eyes had widened. Damn, he hadn't meant to reveal . . .

"That's what I said." Michel stuck his hands in his pockets, rocking back onto his heels. "Gone." Michel was more about personality than good looks, loose-jointed with a spring in his step. Michel didn't add up a person's imperfections and subtract them from his total acceptance. He embraced everyone as worthy of his friendship.

"I couldn't find the painting. Wanted to see it before I started inquiries. Saw lots of other...ah...ah...interesting memorabilia." Michel winked.

"Be serious, Michel."

"The menagerie at the Musée de l'Erotisme...outside your customary requests."

André faced him with his hands on his hips. "Did you ask the museum director?"

"Knew nothing. After I had warmed her up a bit with my engaging personality," he waggled his eyebrows, "she said the temporary exhibition was planned by an independent organizer."

"Not important." André turned.

"What do you really want?" Michel fiddled with an onyx Buddha. "Exactly."

"Exactly?"

"Am I supposed to find the painting? Buy it. Find the girl." Michel held his palms out. "Come on André. Give me a clue. You *are* acting strangely . . . even for you."

André wandered behind his desk where substantial windows framed a stunning view of Paris; the windows' ornate woodwork aged to an antique white. The painting was important; she was important. The young Anne hovered in his consciousness, her full name illusive. She hadn't revealed it then. What should he tell his confused friend? He had been pining for an image in a painting? His usual requests were decisive, well framed.

Michel fumbled in his pocket, rustling paper.

"Voila!" Michel brandished a wrinkled note scrawled with a name and address. "Due to my supreme negotiating skills..." He smoothed the paper against his knee. "The director provided the name of the organizer. It might be helpful if you told me more."

"The woman in the painting reminded me of a girl I met in college." He stared at the floor with his eyes half closed. "Surreal."

"Her name?"

"Anne."

"That's it? Not much." André shot him a stern look. Michel grinned and left, whistling.

"Michel. Wait." He paused in the doorway, leaning against the frame. "Something curious. The third time I saw the painting, it had an engraved plaque on the bottom of the frame. *Miriam*. I'm certain it was not there the other times." André moved toward Michel, pausing. "All of it. Find or buy the painting. Find the girl, find. . . Anne."

"Got it."

André expelled pent-up breath. He habitually guarded his privacy, exposing himself like he had with Michel was unusual. He rubbed the back of his neck; Michel was more than a colleague—and trustworthy. But compared to the twenty-five-year old, he felt old at thirty-four.

Michel's head popped back through the doorway. His hazel eyes sparkled, framed by well-shaped eyebrows with built-in energy. "Your Papa is looking for you. Can you spare a minute?"

"I'll check with him after my appointment." Michel disappeared. Describing himself as an indispensable investigator, he was always aware. What one eye missed, the other eye noticed. André could trust Michel. Closing his eyes he mediated for a few moments. Sometimes it helped.

André opened the Carpentier file and leaned back in his chair. This was an ordinary case. André had acquired a modest reputation for his work with art and cultural property crime. Seeking resolutions to complex crimes, he had an uncanny ability to assess facts, whether obvious or subtle. The challenge energized him.

His firm also represented the legal interests of museums, galleries, and businesses involved in the industry. This work included the mundane: contracts, legal counsel, and litigation, providing their baguette and butter. He slogged through these projects, like the one in his hands, anticipating the next exhilarating art case.

The family firm had an elite standing in Parisian society and his success in high profile work gave him access to the cosmopolitan subcultures of the art world. He was a trusted expert able to move among those with creativity, status, and money. More than once, the firm had been embroiled in the legal machinations involved in art theft from France's most prestigious public and private museums.

André arose as his assistant ushered Monsieur Carpentier into the small conference room. Carpentier required legal counsel that involved transferring valuable assets on loan to another museum. The bird-like curator flitted from one bit of minutiae to another while he and André arranged a preliminary contract.

"Are you sure our paintings will be safe?" the curator shuffled papers. "They represent a significant share of our collection." He hunched forward with a worried pinch in his brow.

"There is risk; however, the larger museum insured your paintings. They should be safe. Smaller museums don't have adequate security—too much access, too little money." The paintings would be safer at the larger museum than the curator's less secure one.

André put his hand over the man's wrist. "Trust us. We're adept at this." André assured the curator he had made respectable decisions on behalf of the museum's board of directors, and concluded the meeting. Papa's office next.

When they were young their father's office was a refuge for André and Pierre. Now he realized it was not the office, but his Papa that emanated trust and security. He hesitated at the open door and observed Vincent Gensonné reading in a leather side chair. Light from an Art Deco lamp cast a glow on the pages of a law journal. His earliest memories had been of hiding under the desk with his brother, pretending the cavity within was a spaceship.

"Bonjour." His father's face reflected pleasure.

"Bonjour." André met him for a quick hug. "Please, sit." The book-lined office smelled like comfort to André: a mixture of leather, aged paper, and his Papa.

"Did you get your mother's invitation for next weekend? She's expecting everyone, including Michel."

"Yes. It will be great to see the little ones—and my sisters." He had missed a couple of family gatherings, no excuses really. His upcoming thirty-fifth birthday troubled him—his twin should also be celebrating thirty-five years.

His sisters, Celeste and Isabel had produced five children between them, so no pressure for him to reproduce; although his mother worried he didn't seriously date. His father reseated himself and André sank into the adjacent chair, the leather cushion exuding a musky aroma.

His father nodded toward his desk. "I received the file on Monsieur Philippe Dubois. He wants to expand his restaurant, although there are historical considerations. With a building that age, requests for modifications trigger regulations, and bureaucracy crawls."

André agreed. "Dubois was hiding something. He asked me to meet him for lunch at his restaurant last Friday for legal advice. He's a fine chef; it's hard to get a table at Chez Philippe. Then he equivocated." André shifted and crossed his legs. "I left and he called later, inviting me to lunch again. I intended to refuse the case. Then he said workers found old murals in the kitchen during a new stove installation. Intriguing."

"Anything valuable?" Vincent asked.

"I couldn't tell. The new stoves took more space than the old ones. Carpenters removed part of a wall; they left the work unfinished behind the stoves because they found decorative paint. It could be anything—even frescoes. Or nothing."

"Navigating red tape. He should move his restaurant if he wants more space." Vincent stood and flexed his shoulders.

André nodded. "I'd be easier." The firm could expedite the system in some cases, in others, it was important to keep a steady course. "Philippe has a good reputation. He served me two exemplary lunches."

The rabbit braised with rosemary and Swiss chard—complimented by a fine wine with notes of hazelnuts and peaches—satiated his appetite for high-quality cuisine. It was understandable Philippe Dubois wanted to expand the popular restaurant. Even if he had wasted his time with evasiveness.

"I need a favor, André. The American ambassador has invited your mother and me to a diplomatic event at the embassy tonight. We cannot go. I promised to hand-deliver these documents." He indicated a folder on an antique table. "Will you go in our place?"

"Am I dressed appropriately?" André had been to embassy events requiring formal dress.

His father scanned his custom-tailored clothing. "You look fine; you will need this." He handed him an engraved card.

"You owe me." André took the proffered card and picked up the documents. The invitation read Vincent and Sophia Gensonné. He wouldn't need it; his friendship with the American Ambassador would gain him entrance.

VINCENT GENSONNÉ STACKED scattered documents, logged off his computer and scrutinized his schedule for Monday. His son's behavior had been troubling. André's demeanor usually conveyed an aura of seclusion; but today he seemed even lonelier. Was he content with his place here?

André was the fourth-generation partner in the century old firm. Throughout the turbulence of 20th century France, the business had retained a toehold, and when able, had expanded their influence and wealth.

As artifacts became more valuable—and vulnerable to thievery, corruption and speculation—the firm had turned its focus to specialization in the lucrative art industry. Decades of perseverance and achievement had cemented the firm's stellar reputation. Most would think the family had everything—everything except Pierre.

Vincent moved to the chair vacated by André remembering when André and Pierre had straddled the chair backs, the six-year old twins pretending they were horses, simultaneously tipping them backwards to dismount. Identical faces searched his for reaction. Vincent shook his finger and feigned anger, but they ran to him hugging his legs tight.

Now he smoothed his hand over the leather of Pierre's make-believe horse. He would give anything to have Pierre back. And his other son? Had André forgiven him? Regret burdened Vincent. When Pierre died, he had sent André away. Vincent wished he could rescind the poor decision made when they were all heartbroken. *Would this regret ever end?*

In front of the adjoining chairs hung a nineteenth-century painting depicting an English equestrian scene, inspiration for the boyish prank. Vincent moved to André's pretend horse, leaned across the back of the chair and contemplated the painting.

He and Sophia had feared suicide. The twins were inseparable companions and after Pierre's death; André retreated from them. He spent long hours in the bedroom they had shared, didn't eat with the family, and shunned friends. André turned eighteen without Pierre two weeks later; the family didn't celebrate the sad birthday. Vincent sank into the other chair—Pierre's horse.

After another sleepless night beside his restless wife seventeen years ago, Vincent remembered a friend who had studied abroad. Henri had regaled them with his antics at a small college in a tiny Michigan town. Hemlock College had an impeccable reputation, a huge endowment, and wealthy alumni.

Vincent reasoned André might escape the emptiness if he had to cope with a new experience. English fluency and exposure to American culture would also benefit his career. Vincent had been compelled to save him. André had gone because his father had asked him to leave.

André's absence opened a bigger hole in his parents' hearts first opened at Pierre's death. Sophia aged that fall, her face wilted with sorrow. Trees dropped weathered leaves in faded colors, yet stood erect to endure their winter barrenness, echoing missing sons. Sophia didn't talk to him about André. Shorter days and longer dark nights endured separately like railway tracks that never met.

Grief weighed down each cell and his body labored through interminable days. Spring came and some of the pain dissipated. When clear thinking returned, he was aghast. Vincent had sent his disconsolate young son away from his mother, from the rest of the family, when he had needed them most. Vincent walked to the horse-themed painting and lifted it from its mooring. He lowered it to floor and turned it toward the wall, erasing the image of two tiny horsemen.

ANDRÉ HAD FINISHED his studies and come back to France for law school. At age twenty-five he stepped into the life prearranged for the baby twins, a model son and respected man able to move seamlessly between two cultures. André wore an impenetrable casing around his emotions visible only to his observant parents. Now a decade later, others saw a cool sophisticated thirty-four-year-old man. His parents saw a scarred son. Vincent's sorrow was for the young man, his boy child who had disappeared in America. André didn't talk about Pierre or his time in the U.S. He wasn't the same, none of them were.

Vincent's body ached and his morose thoughts permeated his bones. Those bleak days intruded when he didn't expect it. His mind was a receptacle that saved everything, and spewed unwanted memories, splattering him with bits of melancholy. Would André have fared better at home with them? He pulled his shoulders back, putting the question behind him. The decision stood. Vincent walked to the equestrian painting and rehung it in its customary position. The family had coped.

When Vincent left his office and entered the street, the evening air played with his skin, fresh-smelling after a cleansing afternoon rain. The falling sun cast its remaining shafts, bathing Paris in the creamy light artists ached to capture. The sun crept lower, darkening the sky, white limestone buildings silhouetted against the remaining light. Vincent glanced up at André's darkened office window. What kind of parent banished a hurting child?

Chapter II Anne

ANNE MORGAN WAVERED at the margins of the formally dressed crowd at the American Embassy in Paris, her eyes flickering from the guests to her staff, everything appeared under control except her quivering abdomen. She combed jittery fingers through her hair, the ends tickling her collarbone. A deep breath calmed her. Adjusting her bearing she hid behind her usual well-groomed façade.

Her skills were on display for the elite members of the art world tonight. Although she appeared to be a French woman with joie de vivre, Anne was an American pretender with mush inside. Her mind cluttered with details, she was sure she had forgotten something. Soft classical music gradually filtered through her body and Anne relaxed as she wandered among glamourous people gathered in groups of two, three or many— touching a hand, smiling.

"Superb job, Anne. Everything looks great." The American Ambassador had approached her as she conversed with a pair of gallery owners. "Champagne?" he asked, offering her a slim glass.

"My favorite."

"I'd like you to meet a friend. He should be here; I just saw him." He glanced over the ballroom, shrugging. "I'll catch you later."

Champagne was Anne's drink of choice and a couple of sips could be magical. Whether it signified the better things in life, or a refined palette, or just took the edge off, she always felt better with Champagne. Now her world serendipitously tilted, musical tones in harmony with her enhanced mood. The Trio she had hired played the Two-Step in a moderately fast triple meter. But what had caused her quickened heartbeat?

Then the demeanor of a sophisticated man, back long and lean in a slim-fitting suit resonated, something about the way he moved . . . Her girlish self ached. For what? He disappeared before she remembered.

"Anne?" The curly crown of Jane's dark hair barely reached Anne's shoulder. Anne tipped her head to listen. Over the background music, the conversation levels had escalated. "Are we still serving dinner at seven?"

"Yes, most of the guests will have arrived." Responsibilities intruding, Anne resorted to her usual evenhanded manner to dispense with last minute requests by her staff. Why the momentary anxiety? She joined a group from the Louvre, her fluent American-accented French facilitating her hostess role, mingling, accommodating.

After a flurry of last minute instructions, Anne had rushed into her office. discarding jeans and T-shirt, stepping into her formal dress. A quick application of make-up and a change of shoes later, she hurried from her office, still fastening an earring. She stumbled into Jane.

"Whoa! Anne." Jane shrank against the wall, glorious hair flying around her curvy shoulders.

"I'm so sorry. Are you hurt?" "I'm okay. Do you need help?"

"No. Everything is done, thanks." Her colleague was one of those people who accomplished more than most, although she usually looked disheveled. Nicknamed Calamity Jane by her co-workers, she had just had casts removed from both of her wrists; she had tumbled down a stairway.

"You're tall in those heels. Wish I had more inches."

"Hard to be this tall, pants are always too short."

"You carry it off. Your dress is gorgeous." Jane gushed, another personality trait.

Anne floated in her black gown, close-fitting on top and narrowing to her waist with a full skirt billowing along her legs. An ebony bracelet and matching earrings accented her dress. Dressing appropriately was a hard-won trademark. She hugged Jane. "You make me feel good."

Anne had perfected her style at age thirteen, wearing tasteful well-made clothing gleaned from second-hand stores. Rummaging through crowded racks, fearful she would buy an item donated by a classmate, she searched for affordable clothing. Anne observed how the other girls dressed. Unable to buy the hottest jeans, she created her own panache. Her clothing covered a poor little girl with big plans. This event was evidence of her success, but the shy child hadn't disappeared.

Anne surveyed the elegant room filled with tuxedoed men and gowned woman, satisfied she had well-orchestrated each facet of the décor, food, and music. The art establishment, and business people involved with the industry, each vied to make connections with those who could advance their interests.

Under the rising and falling of conversation, inflated or softened by aperitifs, the harmonious notes of the musical Trio meandered sinuously around the guests. The Trio (a female cellist, a male pianist, and male violinist) expressed their music by graceful movements of their black-clothed bodies. People assembled and reassembled in a moving kaleidoscope of parrot color and black tie.

Massive tables bore huge bouquets in hues of blue: hydrangeas, iris, agapanthus, cornflower, and delphinium accented with red poppies and white wax flowers. The flowers perfumed the air like floral notes in an expensive eau de cologne. Anne had chosen the finest in French hors d'œuvre: glazed figs topped with mascarpone wrapped with prosciutto, salmon tartare. Desserts glistened on silver trays, testament to a talented pâtisserie chef. Tuxedo-staffed bars surrounded the perimeter—the servers bestowing wine and cocktails.

A waiter with an erect posture, holding a flawlessly level tray, offered her Champagne. Anne accepted, toasting him, she had misplaced her other glass. The splendor of formal events sometimes overwhelmed her, accentuating her unworthiness. People and places like this hadn't existed in her world.

Clutter overpowered her earliest memories. Rotting food smells, a molding bathroom, and the pungent odor of her mother permeated their home. Her unstable mother provided sustenance when able. But the growing Anne increasingly sought her own nourishment. Haunting the mailbox for the expected check became crucial when she was in the sixth grade. She bought food, before her hoarding mother bought more useless stuff.

The festivities and the music swirled around her, moving in closer like clouds descending in a spring thunderstorm. Her vision blurred. Dark thoughts intruded, unclean, undeserving, unwanted. Was she becoming insane like her mother? She consciously lifted her shoulders, sloughing off memories. Jane passed her carrying a load of dirty cocktail glasses. Jane was invaluable, but Anne didn't consider her a friend. Anne had failed to maintain relationships, the cost of a lifetime of secrets. Always vigilant prying eyes of classmates would discover her shabby lifestyle, Anne scuttled inside like an exposed beetle, refusing invitations that might need reciprocation.

Anne's colleague approached, shaking hands, stopping for a quick word with a server. His manner was a good fit for an ambassador. "Everyone is enjoying your party."

"Thank you. Glad I'm not paying for it."

"I'm with you. I couldn't find my friend, he was a sub, he must have left."

A guest waylaid him and he walked away, his posture dignified, intent on listening to his companion. His demeanor accommodating, he always displayed the right response. Unlike her, he probably had no shameful secrets. Her position at the embassy was miraculous even after five years. She loved her job and loved living in Paris, she intended to keep it.

By eleven o'clock the evening had dwindled to a hushed end and the fairytale scene dissolved into its component parts. After the last guests drifted away, stark light flooded the ballroom as the caterers cleared tableware and crystal.

His name exploded into her head. André. The teenage boy she met seventeen years before. The image of an elegant back and patrician head infused her with memories. Had André attended? Possibly, he had said he was a native of Paris. The name would be on the guest list. She hastened past workers disassembling the party.

"Anne, are you still here?" Jane said, directing temporary food service workers to the kitchen. Embassy staff removed tablecloths, and stacked tables and chairs, like worker ants each innately performing his or her duties.

"You've been here long enough. Go home." Jane pointed at the door.

"I want to check the guest list before I leave. Don't stay too late, yourself."

"Clean-up and wrap-up is my part of the action."

Anne mouthed thank you and left the ballroom, carrying her heels.

Clothing tossed onto her office chair in haste irritated Anne now, the only items out of place. She scooped them up, folding them over her dress hangar. Simple furnishings bathed in soft lighting—austere in quantity and luxurious in quality—embraced her. The desktop was bare; the top drawer contained lined-up pens and pencils, and compartmentalized bits and pieces, snuggled into their little boxes, nothing extraneous or unnecessary. Unlike her mother's house. She located the filed guest list.

Anne sank into her office chair, her aching legs protesting, funny how one kept going when necessary. She flipped open the folder, scanning the names of those who had been invited. Her job included managing invitations to diplomatic events, and keeping records of who accepted or declined the invitation of the American ambassador. Before entrance was granted, the names of arriving guests were matched against a final list of prospective attendees. No unknown André on her roster, although the name was common. She must have been mistaken; he wasn't in attendance.

The boy's last had alluded her at the college frat-house party. Anne had been an imposter there too. Young, naïve, she didn't understand much of his heavily accented English; she had only caught his first name. Mesmerized by an attractive boy who hadn't known her circumstances, it didn't matter that she didn't understand most of what he said. André had lifted her to another world. Odd he had snuck into her consciousness this evening. Had he been why she was flooded with unwanted memories?

Anne left the embassy long after the guests departed. She was tired but unlike other nights, she went home hopeful.

HOME. ANNE LET the warm space envelop her, her soothing décor a neutral gray palette. Ash pillows, a slate-patterned chair, and silver photo frames accented the creamy tones of her couch, walls, and nubby linen draperies. Through her bedroom door her fluffy white bedding beckoned; she soon basked in its embrace. Tiredness seeped from her bare legs.

Her mind drifted and she envisioned her mother, skinny and deflated by life's deficiencies. Mother loved her, though emotionally detached by her illness, she was unable to provide basic care. No one had nurtured her, she was as a flower planted in the first blush of spring, and not watered in the dog days of summer. Her mother's face, hollowed by her life, floated into Anne's thoughts. Anne pulled the covers over her head. Hard work had allowed her to execute a well-planned escape; she usually lived in the present, burying rising memories. Why so melancholy tonight?

Using an American colloquialism, she had pulled herself up by her bootstraps, with a little help from her teachers. The French language was too beautiful to explain the expression. Success had come from disparate directions: First, Anne had discerned her academic gifts in seventh grade and secondly, she had met André at the end of her Senior high school year. Both events had changed her life.

Recognition from teachers who praised her exemplary schoolwork became an addiction. Excelling at everything satisfied her thirst for kind words, touch. Perfection provided a measure of control, only a straight A report card mattered.

Meeting André had nourished a seed containing hope. *Hope is the color of clean.*

The nightmare came back. Anne forced herself awake, shaking. Was she losing it? Just like her mother. Sweaty in her tangled sheets, Anne stared at the ceiling. Distraught. She *had* seen André last night. Why else would she be struggling with seventeen-year-old memories.

God knows she had always tried. With high school approaching, Anne had unloaded one of the tiny bedrooms, hurling her mother into a frenzy. Change incensed her mother; a consequence of the disease dictating their daily lives. Anne persevered, cleaning everything with soapy water. The narrow window sparkled, only her singlewide bed and scuffed dresser remained in the lemon-scented space. She hung her scavenged clothes on the scarred rod in the empty closet. Her bedroom became a guarded haven.

The rest of the musty house overflowed, narrow pathways separating newspaper stacks, heaps of magazines, towering cottage cheese containers, balls of string and rubber bands, worn clothes, books, junk mail. Mother held to each item like a lifeline.

Her mother's condition deteriorated late in her senior year, without the will to move from the couch. Anne convinced her to visit a medical clinic; neither she nor her mother dared reveal the hoarding disorder. The doctor prescribed blood pressure medication; Mother stuffed the tablets into the cushions of the shabby plaid sofa. Her mother died soon after she met André; just days before she finished high school at the top of her class.

WHEN ANNE AWOKE, muffled morning traffic filtered in from outside. Clear morning light pierced the half-closed blinds, striping lines onto the hardwood. A matching Cherrywood armoire and long dresser, graced two walls. She arose and draped her legs over the edge of her high bed, dropping her feet to the floor.

Anne rearranged her nightgown, noticing her tousled self in the mirror. When she padded to the dresser, an Art Deco lamp needed to be moved one inch. Anne picked up the silver-framed photo of the Eiffel Tower, replacing it exactly where it had been, bending her face to a fresh lily in a crystal vase. The heady scent drifted, reminding her she should buy a fresh stem.

Anne wandered into her kitchen, bare countertop gleaming in morning light. If she opened her refrigerator, it'd contain only necessities, each shelf baking soda clean. The fragrant aroma of fresh-brewed coffee stimulated her, her routine included setting the timer the night before, never varied.

Opening the cupboard door for a mug, she removed one from the shelves, arranged with military precision. Cups stood at attention with the handles faced right, the other dishes following orders. She closed the cupboard door and leaned against the cabinets. Everything checked out. *My home is a clean place.*

It had been years since she had had to revert to this crazy routine. Not cured yet.

Chapter III Michel

MICHEL LA ROCHE, self-described jack-of-all-trades for the Gensonné family law firm, whistled and leapt step by step down the stairwell. The jaunty tune ricocheted off the white-tiled walls of the Métro station, and descended onto the crowd. Although he was investigating per André Gensonné's personal request today, he considered himself a handyman.

Before André had pulled him out of a Paris gutter, he did various small jobs for money. Michel still did odd jobs for money, but now that included investigating criminal motives, causes or culprits involved in art crime. He now worked among the elite. Next week he would guard valuable paintings traveling between museums. He loved his work—especially the firm's unexpected requests. He would also lasso the moon for André. Or find the painting he desired. Or find the woman.

The Montmartre address scrunched in his pocket could be either a business or a home address for Monsieur Bertrand. It was a starting point. When he scouted the Musée de l'Erotisme on Friday, Michel disembarked at the Pigalle station off Line 12. His stop would be the nearby Abbesses station today, his favorite.

"How are you two?" Michel asked a boy and girl, traveling on the Métro, with their mother. Their chatter stopped and they moved closer together, and stared, the little girl clutching her older brother's hand. A few moments later, the little guy got brave, or curious.

"How did you get your hair like that?" The boy dangled his feet, grinning mischievously. He collapsed against his seat, his face turned toward his sister's head. He peeked sideways.

"Came this way." Michel shook his curly hair, waggling his eyebrows. Humidity had sprouted ringlets between his curls.

"Looks like you plugged your finger in an outlet." They dissolved into giggles.

"Better not try it, you don't want this hair." Michel bent forward towards their seat and whispered. "Your mother might not like burned fingers." Michel pulled a pack of playing cards from his pocket. The children came to his seat, sitting beside him. The disappearing card trick was always irresistible.

"Our stop is next. Get ready," their mother warned. She handed the girl her pink bag, and gathered her packages. "Thank you." She nodded toward her children.

"It made time pass and I like the practice." Michel pocketed his magic cards.

Michel never let an opportunity to talk abscond; he considered his rapport with people a tool of his trade. André's secret wouldn't last long. Michel could extract it if he had ten minutes, possibly at the Gensonné gathering this weekend. He had known André for five years and he had never talked to him about a girl. André was a private person, too private in his opinion.

Michel got off at the Abbesses station, named for the women of the nearby Montmartre abbey. Michel entered the ebb and flow of people blindly moving toward the spiral steps. The undulating ocean of bodies reached the bottom of the stairway whose stairs curved out of sight.

Then, there it was, glorious splashes of color depicting whimsical scenes of Paris. Marching bands and flying unicorns and larger than life flowers, brightened the underground space lining the stairway. For more than two hundred steps, Michel traversed alongside the murals, others exclaiming over the beauty of the artwork, or ignoring it for taken-as-granted background. The crowds flowed toward street level, and then they all burst through the iron and glass Art Nouveau entrance.

Michel surveyed the colorful palette before him. Paris never failed to enthrall. He had been a poor kid from the south of France, and did not experience Paris until five years ago. Visiting many of the districts since then, he had discovered each arrondissement had its own character, its own mood and its own mysteries. Montmartre was on the hilly part of town outside the main city. Cobblestone walkways wound picturesquely, up and down stairways, and through narrow passageways that opened onto hidden streets. A blind turn often hosted a surprise: ivy climbing a wall, an overhang awash with honeysuckle.

Michel understood the city's grittier passions; he had almost succumbed to them when he ran with degenerates, intent on destruction. Overcrowded, Paris housed an undulating multitude of disgruntled citizens primed to revolt— whatever century it was. He loved her aesthetics, her resilience over time, and the way springtime in Paris caused amnesia. Surrounded by her majestic buildings and engaging avenues, one forgot the bad stuff.

Montmartre had been an art haven for penniless painters and artisans a century before, but now it drew millions of visitors; hundreds claimed the streets today. Michel headed for the Place du Tertre. The square was at the center of an interchange of goods and commodities, geared toward tourists. Artists (with the proper legal permits) set easels and enticed people with caricatures and paintings. Crafts people peddled their wares.

Most Parisians despised the crowds Michel loved; he was one in the sea of humanity floating around the old village. The shops and bistros around the Place du Tertre rubbed elbows, jostling for space, and the rich pungent aromas of the world's coffees wafted through the throngs. Kingfishers sang, teenage girls cackled and street musicians harmonized. The rich cacophony was song to Michel's ears.

The musicality of Paris beat the hell out of the deafening silence of the arid hill town, where he grew up. He had worked away his childhood at his father's boulangerie. The houses, stores and church were all limestone-gray, and there was no greenery. He and his friends hung out beneath the three windswept plane trees in the dusty square. The leaves—faintly green underneath the dust—showed little color unless it rained. It didn't rain much. Nothing for a kid to do in the dying hill town. Michel had chosen the magnificent city and never looked back.

Sure, he had had a stumble in Paris, but thanks to André—and Sophia, André's mother—Michel had survived his ordeal and now considered himself lucky, plus he depended upon the Almighty.

Michel navigated the uphill slopes of Montmartre; it was hot—even for June. His muscles strained his thighs on the uphill, and his toes pushed against his shoes on the downhill slopes. Sweat tickled his scalp. He found the address on a plaque, attached to a curving stone wall clamoring with ivy. An enormous dark green door guarded the front of the dwelling, the doorframe strong-arming the encroaching leaves. Michel rapped on the door, the dull thuds bouncing off the heavy wood. No answer. He banged it harder and it opened a few inches, revealing a semi-dark cavern defended by a person-shaped hulk.

"What do you want," rasped an unseen male.

"Are you Monsieur Bertrand?"

"What do you want?" The rasp deepened.

The impenetrable green door moved a centimeter. Michel stuck his foot in the crack before it started to close, the man pushing against it. His pulse quickened, as his heartbeat kept pace with his burst of words.

"Monsieur Bertrand." Michel wasn't sure whether he grunted, or said yes. "Did you organize an art exhibition at the Musée de l'Erotisme? A couple of weeks ago?"

"Why?"

"I'm interested in a painting. It disappeared." Michel kept his foot in the door. "Did someone buy it?" Nothing.

"Are those top-floor artworks for sale?"

"Go away," the grating voice like a snarl through gritted teeth.

"Let's go to your favorite bistro. I'll pay." Again, no answer. The silence thwarting Michel's patience, he slowly edged his foot out of the space between the doorframe and the door—but not all the way.

"Give me some time. To get ready. Take your big foot out of my door."

Michel did what Bertrand asked, and slouched against the ancient wall. He scratched his back along the rough stones, observed the quiet street...and waited. Changing positions, he sat against the building with his knees close to his chest, watching a procession of ants. The ants were like dressed-up Catholic school girls in a procession to crown Mary, first encountering his foot, then changing direction, curving around his toe and back. One ant broke ranks and ascended his shoe; it sped up, when it got to his ankle. He slapped it before it dashed up his pants leg. Bertrand continued to stall.

Michel had enough experience in negotiating to know, it was better to let Bertrand think he had an advantage. He could wait. When he worked in the boulangerie, or hung out in the hometown square, he had experienced the inch of time. He could entertain himself with the Catholic ants.

Michel's stomach growled intermittently before the green door finally opened. The man who slid out was somewhat seedy, in an arty kind of way. His elegant head topped by a dusty red beret, jerked to the right to indicate their direction. Moving with a bony grace that appeared ageless, he pulled his shoulders forward as if he wanted to cover his veiny ears with them. Michel strolled beside Bertrand, noting the friendly nature of the neighborhood. Everyone they met nodded at the older man.

When Michel and Bertrand entered the nook-in-the-wall bistro, it smelled like onions caramelizing in his Maman's kitchen, and stale cigarette smoke. Heads turned as they navigated through the tables, all eyes following Michel. Bertrand acknowledged the locals; the server greeted Bertrand by name.

"What are you drinking?" Michel asked. He pulled out a chair at a corner table for Bertrand, and sat in the adjacent one.

"Blanc." Bertrand's eyes warily surveyed the room, and then him. He ignored the chair and jerked his own across from Michel, his back to the room.

The comfortable ambience of the room was conducive to exchanged confidences among friends. Bertrand's bearing indicated stubborn resistance. Michel pursed his lips against an involuntary smile; he suspected neither of them were as tough as they pretended.

Michel ordered a pitcher of white, and waited for Bertrand to finish his first glass. When Bertrand poured his second glass, Michel ordered another jug. Bertrand sipped this wine in watchful silence, but the alcohol had tempered his prickly manner.

Michel contemplated his companion, noting a tic quivering below his eye. "How do I purchase artwork from the Musée?"

"The Musée has information."

"I'm interested in a particular unsigned piece. It's missing."

"Don't know what you're talking about."

"Who would?"

"Not me."

"I'll describe the painting. To refresh your memory."

"Didn't see the final exhibit." The tic picked up its pace. Bertrand audibly swallowed, his Adam's apple wobbling like a turkey's gizzard.

"You'll remember it." Michel refilled Bertrand's glass. "I'm hungry, let's eat first." Bertrand exhaled, his bony chest slightly caving.

"Georges will bring the daily first course." A small serving of eggplant caviar cake appeared in front of them. Michel savored each morsel.

Michel ordered the smoked herring marinated in oil with warm potatoes, and his companion chose the veal in a white sauce. When the main course arrived, he sampled the fish. "This food is amazing," he said. Bertrand ignored this and Michel's small talk, but a self-satisfied air surrounded him. The silence between them expanded and finally, all adjacent conversation stopped. Were the locals listening?

Georges cleared their plates, watchfully observing Bertrand, glancing at Michel and back to Bertrand, his face serious. Michel requested chocolate mousse for himself, and lifted his mobile eyebrows toward Bertrand.

"Tarte Tatin." Bertrand drained his glass. The murmurs of others in the café now nudged against the quiet at their table. The tasty dessert rivaled the previous courses.

"Coffee?" Michel asked. Bertrand nodded, Georges was already approaching with two cups; Michel had the feeling Georges didn't like him.

Michel eyed Bertrand as fragrant steam drifted. Bertrand eyes were focused on his cup. Michel stared until he was compelled to look up, and they visually locked eyes. Michel waited. He counted the ticks of the man's watch that beat in tune with the tic on his face. One. Two. Three. Four. Five.

"The subject was a woman floating underwater." Michel paused. "Entitled *Miriam*."

Bertrand's reaction was subtle, the tiniest movement from beret to waist, revealing he was aware of the painting. Bertrand had revealed himself. How much could Michel push?

"Do you have any family in Paris?" he asked. Bertrand shifted in his chair.

"A daughter." Bertrand's face softened, the tic imperceptible. "And two. . ." he hesitated. His tired eyes scrutinized Michel's face. Michel grinned, it was hard for him to maintain an adversarial stance, especially against this kindly old man. Bertrand's lips cracked open a bit. A smile? Bertrand's face was less somber.

"And two granddaughters, Nicole and Simone."

"How old?"

"Three and five." He appeared contemplative. His faded brown eyes changed color, deepening to a chestnut-brown, and a real smile crossed his lips, transforming his face. "They're delightful girls. Simone, she's the funny one. She wants to be a painter like me. But she wants to paint lines on the street. She makes me laugh."

Hmm. Bertrand was a painter; perhaps he had painted the missing artwork. The wine, food and conversation altered Bertrand who now appeared likeable. Bertrand stood, his knee creaked, and he leaned on the table before straightening his spine.

"I sat too long," he said. "Knee stiffened up." Limping toward the door, the old Frenchman now appeared shrunken. Michel followed him outside, and then handed him his business card.

"My client will pay well for the Miriam painting. Contact me."

Chapter IV Monsieur Bertrand

Sunday, June 16, 2013

MONSIEUR JEAN-PAUL BERTRAND paced outside his home. Sleepless for hours, he was waiting for sunrise and time to pass. The ivy-covered stone wall with the substantial green door usually provided solid reassurance, but home didn't feel as safe as it did.

In the early light his beloved ivy drooped as if saying I'm sick, leave your easel and palette inside. He wished he had never met Maximillian Broutin, the man had stolen his peace of mind. He obsessed over his careless mistake, it was the end for him. He couldn't paint. He grappled with the door with weakened arms and slipped into his home.

He had procrastinated for two interminable days, but he must contact Maximillian. The young man from the law firm probably suspected he had painted *Miriam*. His nemesis should be responsible. His legs trembled and unsteady fingers struggled with the pushbuttons of the old wall phone. It was ringing. Would Maximillian answer?

"Bonjour." Maximillian said, voice hard. Bertrand sucked in his breath.

"Bertrand here, come get the painting. Now." He hung up. He didn't own the wretched painting. Maximillian did. The lunch meeting with Michel la Roche had been a warning. Someone wanted *Miriam*, someone rich if he had interpreted the law firm's engraved card correctly. He must get rid of her.

The hammered thuds came too soon. How did he get here so fast? The thick green door reduced Maximillian's pounding fists to dull thumps. When Bertrand cautiously opened it, Maximillian shoved him aside and rushed past him, halfway into the room. Maximillian was a wiry well-proportioned man who wore a skin-hugging black shirt that clung to his muscled torso. Tight jeans encased legs that looked like they usually gripped a motorcycle seat. He had a dangerous sexy aura that appealed to some women but frightened Bertrand. A predatory danger to others, men like that could be violent. He didn't want to test his theory.

Bertrand's legs shook and his left knee caved slightly affecting his balance. He closed the door and caved against it.

Maximillian spun—advanced on Bertrand and stopped—two inches from his face. "What do you want?" Maximillian demanded. Bertrand pressed his back flat against the door and lifted his head, staring into Bertrand's rough eyes.

"Take the painting. Now." Bertrand choked past his closing throat. He pushed past him and strode to the far end of the room, his mind churning a treadmill of circling thoughts like mice feet that never stop. He was scared, he needed a hole to hide in. "Take it away. I can't keep it. If you don't . . .I'll leave it in the street." Bertrand was behaving irrationally as if he was demented.

"Shut up." Maximillian shouted. He stomped to the painting and back to Bertrand. "You're involved in this."

"No. Please. No. I'm not. My daughter, my granddaughters. Please. I'm afraid." He collapsed in a heap.

Maximillian kicked Bertrand's ribcage, the pain thudded through his torso shocked him. *Was he going to die?* His thinning skin had compressed against bone and split, his body went limp. Maximillian stalked back to the brown paper-wrapped painting, seized it, stabbing his finger in Bertrand's direction. "You're a liability!" He stashed the painting under his arm and retreated stopping just short of the door and whirled around.

"Are you stupid? Why did you hang it in the museum? I hid it for five years. I asked you to keep it temporarily. You flaunted it in plain sight." Bertrand cowered in the middle of the room. Would he ever leave? Maximillian came back, looming over Bertrand. "I said, are you stupid?"

"No . . . I . . . I . . ."

"How long did you leave it in the museum?"

"T-t-two weeks. I couldn't keep it here, at home. I thought . . ." Maximillian's exasperated roar blasted his eardrums.

Maximillian stormed toward the entrance and then slammed the enormous green door hard with his free arm. The heavy door inched shut with a soft thud.

The mice continuously ran the treadmill. Round and round the questions spun off like pieces of sawdust. *Why was I so stupid?* For an old man, he had dodged most available vices. He made one bad choice, one mistake and . . . doomed.

Bertrand couldn't sleep, he couldn't eat, and he couldn't paint at the Place du Tertre where artists like him created keepsakes for tourists who visited Montmartre. He had labored a lifetime at the edges of the art world eking a modest living from his work. He earned just enough to support his wife and daughter, Charlotte. Powerless against the urge to paint, he couldn't escape the pressure: pulling, pushing, sucking.

He had always done the right thing, had preserved his integrity until that irresistible offer just when he needed extra cash for Charlotte's wedding. More money than he had received for any commission or painting, it paid well for a reason. Maximillian demanded secrecy, tell not one person of their transaction. If he had been honest with himself, there was something fishy about the deal. Why had he listened to the brute?

He had painted the woman in an underwater scene five years ago. He never forgot the interlude when his talent emerged from obscurity. In his entire career, he had never reached great success; *Miriam* was his most impressive achievement. He was reluctant to let her go. However, Maximillian had commissioned and paid for the painting. But *Miriam* had elicited magic upon his talent, his latent genius emerged. After *Miriam*, his paintings exhibited a light unbeknownst to his earlier works.

Once he relinquished it Bertrand hadn't seen Maximillian or the painting until he had pounded on his door with a package under his arm. Maximillian had said he needed a place to store the painting for a short time. Bertrand refused. He had nowhere to hide it. Maximillian had compelled him, threatening him with exposure for his part in the crime. Crime? What crime? He was afraid to ask.

The management of the Musée de l'Erotisme had commissioned him for a collection of contemporary erotic art for a four-month show. Supplementing his earnings over the years, Bertrand had organized small exhibitions for fellow artists in the Montmartre area. It had augmented his income in the lean years. Though the extra money was not crucial now the old fear of poverty lingered.

The Musée de l'Erotisme exhibition opened about the same time Maximillian reappeared with *Miriam*. Why not hang the painting among the other artwork? It was unsigned, no one aware he had painted it. Only out-of-town tourists visited the museum, his second mistake.

The painting drew too much attention and it had to go. Two other potential buyers had contacted him before the lawyer's hack Michel came snooping around his neighborhood. Bertrand had organized the event so he took the painting home. No one would question him. But fear haunted him.

The phone rang again, a latent courier of bad news. He had ignored it all afternoon. He snatched the phone, tempted to tear it from the wall. Noise, just noise.

"Bonjour." He snarled.

"Bonjour." His daughter's lovely voice quivered along the telephone line, worried, anxious. Charlotte asked why he hadn't answered the phone all day, said he should purchase a mobile. She and her girls were coming next weekend. She would pack a lunch for a picnic in the park; he was to meet them there. Charlotte's chatter hard to follow, he drifted out of the conversation. He caught scattered words.

"What did you say?" He concentrated.

"Papa. What's wrong? You don't sound good."

He lightened his voice, focusing on a school photo of his granddaughters. "How are the girls?" She told him they changed fast at their age, even in the month since he saw them. His mind wandered again and he forgot to respond.

"Are you all right?"

"I'm tired." Exhausted from lack of sleep, he was silent...too long. Charlotte said she would let him rest. However, she changed her mind about meeting him. She would bring the girls to him, they would go together to the park.

"Papa, are you worried, you sound worried?"

"No. No. I can't wait to see you and the girls." Now Charlotte was upset with him too. She didn't trust him. He groaned.

Hunger rumbled in his belly, displaced the whirring thoughts. *How long had it been since he ate?* He closed his green door and leaned against it.

He noted how the ivy crawled along the stone, the trails it made, how it matched the green shade of his door in the June sun. The living ivy leaves contained at least six variations of green light and shadow. The stems were a rich brownish green. He needed to paint. Not now, hunger caved in his stomach, he needed food.

33

He had painted the ivy-covered stone wall with its imbedded door countless times. The ivy changed from the bright neon green of spring through the red and gold hues of fall. The vignette sold well, a desired souvenir of a typical Parisian street. He lifted his shoulders and breathed in the heated air, a gust of wind swirled dried ivy leaves around his feet.

tranquil existence ruined? Bertrand turned right ambling to his favorite lunch place. The neighborhood activities—an effeminate man carrying a small dog, animated boys kicking a soccer ball—restored his disposition.

The bistro was his home away from home, his refuge from everyday hardships where he collaborated with his cronies. It was his place to think, recharge, nourish his body with pleasurable food at an affordable price. Georges approached.

"Bonjour, Monsieur Bertrand. Specialty of the day?"

"I like whatever you're serving."

"Who were you with the last time?"

Dread engulfed Bertrand. He had made another appalling mistake. He had brought the young man here, "his favorite bistro in the neighborhood." He should have taken him to an unknown place. He *was* stupid. His refuge was gone.

"A business contact, nothing important."

He sat for two hours barely noticing time passed and his food had congealed, becoming inedible. Michel would be back asking questions. Should he go to the police?

Bertrand paid for his meal and aimlessly walked the streets of old Montmartre. The village atmosphere permeated his skin, familiar cadences of the streets soothing him. Today he avoided the Place du Tertre where coachloads of tourists emptied themselves onto the square. He still painted there. Old habit. For most of his life he had painted for tourists, the income maintaining his household, providing art supplies, allowing him to paint.

Now with more monetary success he could vary his routine. Sometimes his group hired a model; sometimes he painted the Paris around him. Financially, he no longer needed the work from the Place du Tertre, He just relished the carnival atmosphere of the outside marketplace with the overpriced bistros, craft shops, food vendors and street entertainers.

The reappearing painting disheartened Bertrand. His grandest achievement, *Miriam* had been a catalyst for a new beginning. He was proficient after a lifetime of practicing his craft, his work had a new luminescence. Like the famous painters who preceded him, his use of light clarified his work.

He accumulated enough of his finer work to have a gallery showing and his pieces sold. He had earned more money since *Miriam* than in all the years prior to her. He had been distraught when he saw her again, the painting a sinister reminder of a poor decision.

Now Maximillian possessed *Miriam*. Where had Maximillian hidden her for the last five years? Why had he not disposed of her? Why had he contacted Bertrand now?

Clever wooden toys in a store window glowing with cobalt, ruby and emerald paint ensnared his attention. He entered the whimsical children's store overflowing with dolls, puppets and toy trucks, gadgets and thingamajigs grandparents would buy. He purchased a purple kite, two princess dolls and a set of watercolor paints.

"Good choice. You must have little girls," the shopkeeper said after he choose his selections.

"Granddaughters, three and five. They are visiting next weekend. They love dolls. I hope there's enough wind for a kite."

"They should love these." She enfolded each purchase in pink tissue, tied it with a white ribbon and slipped it into an opaque bag. His mood lifted and optimism replaced his worry—the first time since Maximillian reappeared. I'd be hard to wait for next weekend. Simone needed to practice her street lines.

He longed for freedom from the constraints of the *Miriam* painting. Bertrand had always been a worrier nervous about little and big things alike.

The passage of years hadn't troubled Bertrand before. His body felt ancient and he was fearful something awful would happen.

Chapter V André

ANDRÉ ADROITLY NAVIGATED the royal blue Bugatti Veyron through Paris. He yearned for the comfort of his childhood home, as destructive old memories had returned, rushing inside like a weather cold front. He was eighteen again, a lonely foreign student in an American college, wishing he was dead too. Most of the time he buried morose thoughts, but today it had surfaced. Anne's reappearance in the odd painting brought back the intermittent grief that could still paralyze him. André had invited Michel to ride with him. Normally a loner, he thirsted for company. Michel was waiting beside the street.

"Bonjour, Michel." André had opened the window as he pulled up. Michel jumped.

"Bonjour? André? Is that you? Whoa. Is this *your* car?" Michel slid in, their bodies engulfed the finely-engineered space. "Smells new. Smells expensive too."

André clenched his teeth; he should have driven the old car. Just driving for three kilometers, he had discovered heads turned, cell phones recorded photos, and other vehicles honked. Attracting this attention bothered him.

"It was a gift." André hunched his shoulders, watching for a chance to enter traffic.

"Who gives a gift like this?"

"Grand-père." André saw an opening, and zipped into the lane of moving cars. "For my thirty-fifth birthday."

"Will he adopt me?" Michel jabbed André.

"Maybe. My mother loves you. Isn't that enough?"

"Does she give cars?"

Located in the seventh arrondissement, on the Left Bank, in the exclusive Saint Germain des Pres, the Gensonné family had owned their home for decades. The Bugatti sports car was new. Grand-père had gifted him the two million Euro car; it had just arrived from the dealer, a month earlier than expected.

The car was sensuous, a combination of fine leather and restrained horsepower irresistible even to him, the reluctant owner. The suspension tight, he could feel the engine's power under his hand. The car would surge if unleashed. Not on these streets though. Navigating heavy traffic, André understood when to be aggressive, and when to let the traffic stream around him. At times the tangled traffic stopped, frustrating those behind the wheel on a busy Friday night.

Michel perceived his mood; known to be introspective, André could pensively examine his thoughts. Michel wouldn't ask questions. Until his grandfather's craggy face intruded: thick white hair, still-dark brows protruding over his eyes, commanding presence. Jean-Baptiste Gensonné had been an unusual grandfather by most standards. He and his grandfather shared a passion for paintings, and shared their careers. Those common interests entangled André in a mixture of feelings, not comprehended by his twin, his father, even himself.

Grand-Pere had asked André to take him on an errand. When asked where, Jean-Baptiste directed him to a high-end automobile dealer.

"Your thirty-fifth birthday is coming soon, a milestone. I want to buy you a car."

"If I want a new car, I'll buy my own." André slouched in the driver's seat, turning toward him. "I like this car."

"This? An old man's car. It's ancient, a clunker." His grandfather opened the passenger door of the beat-up black micro-Mercedes. "Let's look." André unfolded himself from his small seat. "My car suits me."

"Keep it then. I want to buy you a fun car. I'm an old man. I've done well. Give me this pleasure, André." His grandfather had ordered the car they selected. The delivery date was several weeks out.

Troubled, André sought his father's advice. "Grand-père bought me an extravagant sports car."

"He told me." Vincent eyes questioned his. "How do you feel about it?"

"Uneasy. . . troubled. I don't think I can drive it."

"I advised him against it, didn't think it was a good fit."

"Thanks, Papa." The Bugatti screamed exorbitant indulgence. Despite the family's position, displays of wealth embarrassed him. When he drove the beat-up micro-Mercedes, he felt better about society's uneven distribution of goods, the randomness of life's gifts.

"Grand-père can afford the gift. Enjoy it. If you can."

When the Bugatti Veyron arrived, André felt self-conscious as soon as he sank into the luxurious driver's seat. This was surreal. Undeserved. In the passenger seat, his grandfather appeared sober, brightening when he noticed André's scrutiny. "This is a remarkable car! Let's take her out on the open road. Before Grand-maman and I leave on our holiday."

"Sure, Grand-père. Thank you."

"You'll understand later."

"Later? When I have grandkids?" André teased.

"Sooner." The word was almost inaudible.

The quality of the luxury car erased some misgivings. The outrageous cost still conflicted with his sense of justness; he hadn't earned it. But he was a man. Fast cars allured men and attracted and women. Words failed to describe the ultimate experience behind the wheel. His grandparents had left on holiday soon after the Bugatti arrived, he and Grand-père not finding time to savor the sports car.

André should ask Michel what he had discovered in Montmartre, his natural reticence stopped him. He had framed his request to him as a favor, rather than a business inquiry. Now, his obsession with the woman was too personal to speak talk about in the small space. Escape would be impossible. André would talk to him later, after his parents went to bed.

"My sisters and their families arrive in the morning. I wanted to come early, before the chaos."

"Thanks for including me, I love it there."

"Thank my mother, she invited you." André softened his tone. "And you are family." He meant it, Michel belonged in the Gensonné clan.

He did need time with his parents; the painting had awakened unspecified longings. Something or someone besides Pierre was now missing from his life. His mother understood him well, sensing his melancholy, she had called twice last week. He regretted worrying her.

He had attempted to be two sons since Pierre's death, and she innately perceived it. Although he had a close partner relationship with his loving father, his mother had saved him from himself. She had lost one son; she would not lose another.

The rest of the family? His was like a paper doll family printed onto cardboard, full of happiness on the surface, guarded underneath, unable to acknowledge their grief and connect.

"Why so serious, André?"

"Thinking." André shifted his gaze from the street to Michel, who winked.

"Aah. I'll let you think. Mind if I listen to music?" Michel fiddled with the high-tech sound system until he found a jazz beat.

Where was Anne? He wanted her. Really? He wanted to find her. He wanted to ask her . . . What would he ask? He shook his head and tried to erase his boyish yearnings.

When he had first come back to France, his loved ones acted unnatural and solicitous. He maintained control of his reactions to those nuances, with an equanimity that smoothed over family disharmony. No one fought or disagreed, and other than his mother, no one talked about the deep stuff.

Except for school breaks, and short visits home, he spent his college years away. He and his two younger sisters drifted apart. André loved them; however, Pierre's death and those lost bonding years, still permeated their relationships.

He zoomed around the circular drive in front of his old home, and pulled to the end, contemplating the overgrown shrubbery lining the walkway. André envisioned his parents performing household routines, the rhythms of family. When he and Michel slipped in the door, the scene was like an often-viewed movie of his childhood. His father poured an aperitif, and Sophia had just opened the oven, and peeked inside.

The saffron walls in the kitchen encompassed the spacious room like a membrane, evoking intimacy. The aroma of rosemary and lemon drifted past them. His mother had told him food was emotion. The sights and smells of food preparation, and a shared family meal, generated feelings too deep to describe—a part of their culture.

"Bonjour, Maman." His mother rushed to him, kissing his face, smoothing his cheeks. Just a hint of Chanel No. 5 caressed her. Tall and long-limbed, she customarily wore casual skirts and classic blouses, distinctive in a time when jeans, or slacks, were the norm. She kissed Michel's cheeks, her dark eyes bright. His father greeted them each, cheek to cheek.

"Dinner is ready. Glad you're here," Sophia said. She bustled back toward the stove, an apron hugging her trim body.

"Your father has prepared drinks; get them and come back and talk."

André' watched his mother's graceful hands prepare their dinner. Her Greek heritage had endowed her with smooth olive-toned skin and thick dark hair—almost free of silver strands. Sophia wore her hair up and entwined so its abundance framed her face.

Sophia artfully arranged the simple meal of sea bass and foie gras with peaches, onto stoneware plates, and carried them to the heavy wooden table.

"Please, sit." Her hands directed them to their places. The conversation focused on family affairs. His mother was the connector, the lifeblood, the one who kept each apprised of all the others' activities.

"Wait until you see the children," Sophia said. "The girls are taller; baby Lucien is losing the chubby look."

"It's been more than a month. I hope Lucien remembers his uncle."

"He might take a while to warm up," Vincent said. "Then he'll be all over you."

"The triplets never stop chattering." Sophia arose picking up dishes, the men following her to the kitchen, hands full.

"Do they still like magic tricks?" Michel asked. "I brought some new ones."

"They'll swarm you like flies," Papa said. "Usually it doesn't quiet down until the children go to sleep."

"Vincent," Maman admonished.

"It's joyful noise."

Outside in the garden, they finished their dinner with a selection of French cheeses. Night sounds emanated from beyond the formal garden space. The subdued voices of their neighbors could be heard behind tall manicured hedges. Creatures scurried in the shrubbery, and crickets chirped. His mother left to prepare coffee.

"She's excited about the family coming," his father said.

"I am too." André stretched out his legs as Sophia arrived, carrying a tray with four cups. After serving the others, she picked up her coffee, and sat.

"Papa says you have a mystery." His father squirmed a bit, re-crossing his legs.

"In a way." Papa always told Maman everything, now she would ask questions. What should he tell her? t. Insects conversed in the shrubs, their own silence amplifying the creature noises. His considerate mother wouldn't ask again. Maman deserved more.

"I saw a painting of a woman in Montmartre. The model resembled an older version of a young girl I had met in America. At university." He sensed their expectation, their need to understand their son. Hard for him to share. Besides his normal reserve, these feelings were new. Except for Michel, he had never told anyone about Anne.

"I met her one time, my first year on campus." He stood. "After I saw the painting, I couldn't get her off my mind." He had said it. The mournful words drifted in the dark like a spoiled child whining for attention.

Until now, he hadn't admitted to himself the compulsion to find her, the irresistible pull of the painting. Why had he drawn Michel into this dilemma? Was it just Anne? His approaching birthday? Time marching without a partner. She probably lived in the United States; he would go there, search. He just needed a lead. His body suffused with heat, he sat. What an overreaction.

"It was a long time ago." He lightened his tone, his parents looked puzzled; that damned Michel was leering. "The painting disappeared." Even the insects had gone silent as if they were listening. A cricket chirped, the silence returned, warm fuzzy darkness settling over them like a soft baby blanket.

His mother didn't ask another question. Unusual, and interesting. The urge to confide in Michel tonight had passed. His Maman's question had unnerved him.

André excused himself to sleep in the bedroom he had shared with his brother. When they were young, they had often talked into the night, planning ways to tease their sisters, and scheming ways to switch places. Pierre was the creative leader; André's mind generated more mundane ideas. But he was onboard for the antics. His mother had left a lamp on, and it reflected off the glass of a faded photo of them. Arms slung around each other's neck, big grins full of crooked and missing teeth. He undressed and slipped under the covers.

In his dreams, he was young again. It was a time when kids just played, and adults took care of important things. He and his siblings often played until dark, only coming in after increasingly strident calls from their mother.

In his dreams, he was part of an identical being, one with all things, of the earth, beyond the earth, he moved in and out of the seams of time, romping with his twin brother, carefree. He awoke at three o'clock feeling complete, whole. Pulling covers over his head, he turned and slept deeply.

André savored the Saturday normalness at breakfast time. He listened to his parents' exchanges, their meshed intermingled language. They shared glances, touches, finishing each other's sentences. Time tiptoed in this house, measured by day-to-day minutiae.

"When do Celeste and Isabelle arrive?" André asked. He poured himself a cup of coffee.

"Sometime before lunch. Celeste will arrive first." His mother cleared dishes, loaded the dishwasher. "Do you want anything else?"

"No." She joined him at the table with her coffee, touched his arm.

"I'm happy you came early. Is Michel up?"

"Not yet. He sleeps late; actually, he sleeps whenever he can."

"Will he want breakfast?"

"Probably. I'll wait in the garden."

Michel wandered outside half hour later, carrying a steaming yellow coffee cup. He settled into a chair next to André.

"Home agrees with you. You look rested."

"Yes. Slept well. What did you find in Montmartre?"

"Not what I intended."

"Did you find the gentleman who organized the art exhibition? What was his name?"

"Jean-Paul Bertrand." Michel swatted a bee away. "I found him. He knows of the painting. It was subtle, but he was . . . unnerved . . . when I described it." Michel glanced around the garden. "It's pleasant here."

"It looks better now. When we were kids, it was a mess." At times the old lawn was a soccer field, the grass worn bare in front of two nets. Or a theatre. He and Pierre endured, and participated in their sisters' productions. "Four children wreak havoc on grass."

The heat intensified, bees performing gymnastics around the flowers, periodically inspecting Michel's cup. Green vegetation varied in tones of celery, kiwi, honeydew, and sage to emerald and forest green. The greenery along the sides, and a brick wall at the end of the garden created a shield from the neighbors, and a buffer from the antics of four rambunctious children.

Michel briefed André about his encounter with Monsieur Bertrand. "I'll ask around his neighborhood. He was a regular in that bistro. In some Paris districts, people live their lives close to home, everything they need is within walking distance. Someone around there knows Bertrand."

"We'll find him." André sighed. "It's not him. I want the woman."

Michel's eyes widened. "You are full of surprises this weekend. Is the real André here?"

André had startled himself. The painting changed him, creating a wish, a demand. He craved something. He shivered, chilly despite the morning sun.

"Her full name would help."

"I needed time to think; I've been blindsided, not sure ..."

"I'm listening."

"Her name was Anne."

"Yes . . . Just Anne?"

"Didn't get her last name. Wasn't important then." The rising sun warmed his shoulders, caressing him. He closed his eyes. The timid girl in a red dress, uncomfortable in her tall body, morphed into the graceful woman in a red dress, floating in water. The woman who had been represented in a painting hanging in the Musée de l'Erotisme.

Michel shifted in his chair, clearing his throat, waiting, impatiently.

"I was a shattered teenager when I arrived in the U.S. Pierre was dead." Saying the words, Pierre was dead, still had the power to stop his heart. It restarted, thudding slowly in his ears, instead of chest.

"I'm sorry." Michel squeezed his arm.

Where to start? "It was a single night, one evening. I'm sure it's happened to you. One meets a girl, and never sees her again."

"Yeah." Michel grinned, lifting his cup.

Cassette-like his mind rewound, playing memories of that night, returning despair and hopelessness, too. He closed his eyes against the pain. Thousands of miles from home, he had been a foreign student at a small mid-western college, and his twin brother was dead.

"I had just turned eighteen; I was so young, yet old. Somewhere in the twilight between child and adult, half a whole. Now alone, thrust into my future with no time to adjust. My family floundered, grieving, unsure. We all suffered.

When my father asked me to attend school in the United States, I assumed he knew best. He was our family's rock.

Papa said his partners had learned English in France; however, they were not completely fluent. Fluency would be good for my career.

I did what Papa wanted; I attended the university his friend recommended. Pierre was gone, I was in an unfamiliar country, one I couldn't comprehend, without my brother."

André had spoken slowly, remembering. Remembering the pain, the isolation. He had omitted the worst; he had researched suicide methods.

"I'm sorry. Does this make sense?"

"I'm listening."

"The culture was different; I made mistakes. My roommate was kind, helpful. No one spoke French, so my English improved." Michel gave him a thumb up. "I hid in the dormitories in the evening, and most weekends. I grieved alone. I couldn't socialize the American way. It was springtime, I had been on campus for months. My roommate invited me to a fraternity party. It was a Roaring Twenties-themed house party, even more foreign."

André envisioned the sensations of the evening. Students dressed like gangsters, flappers, and other college-student interpretations of the nineteen-twenties. Music reverberated off the walls in the furniture-stripped room, and through the gloom, he could barely see the costumed bodies silhouetted in fluctuating groups.

He waited at the edge of the room until he saw his roommate in the dark mass of partygoers. Striding toward him, André changed direction when he saw a young woman standing, wavering at the edges of the party, just like him.

"I saw a tall girl who appeared vulnerable, easier to approach. She wore a red dress and her eyes were blue, rimmed in darker blue, a violet-blue. I had an unexpected response to her; as though we were connected, kindred souls." André hesitated. He had exposed his innermost feelings for the first time.

"Have you ever met someone who interests you, even before you speak?"

"I have." Michel leaned closer.

Tears welled in his eyes. "It was a mysterious connection, unexplainable."

"Continue."

"I offered her wine. She hesitated, perhaps I'd committed another etiquette error. Then she whispered yes. We shared the wine—a gift from my parents—and talked until the party ended, sitting in a dirty corner of the fraternity house. The furniture had been removed for the party."

Michel nodded.

"I nestled her legs with mine, more than once. I wanted to kiss her, but she was nervous, skittish. She didn't tell me anything about herself, except her name. Anne.

I saved the wine bottle as a remembrance. I planned to give it to her with a letter inside, one I had painstakingly written in poor English. I longed to see her again, thought she was interested too. The next morning, I went to all the dormitories, but no one knew of her. In the four years I lived on campus, I never saw her again."

André's body felt depleted. A shard of laughter scraped past his lips, unpleasant even to his ears. "My Papa was right. I became fluent in English, with a trace of a French accent, just enough to sound interesting to women. You know the rest."

Michel sat granite-faced, as stationary as a marble statue. His friend searched for words. "You flabbergasted me." He locked his arms behind his head and rocked forward, backward. "Unbelievable! I've known you for five years. You've never said anything about this."

"I have a reserved nature. I—." Perhaps he had revealed too much.

"I came back to France, finished the law requirements, and joined the family firm. What was expected." He had rushed the last words, like a thief anxious to retreat. André absently brushing an ant from his wrist. "I've overcompensated for the loss of my brother since his death." He observed the serious Michel. "What do you think?"

"We'll find her." Michel had regained his light-heartedness.

With his hands on his hips, André rustled grass back and forth with one foot. "I was with Collette Dupris, and a group of friends, when I first saw the painting, and when I went back, it had the same effect on me. She looked like an older Anne." André glanced toward the house. "I hear car doors. The children are here, are you ready?"

"I have a pocketful of magic tricks, and more in the car."

"You'll show me up." Combined with sleeping soundly, Michel's friendship had refreshed him; it felt good to be home. "I've brought fairy dolls and video games." He reached for Michel's arm. "My story . . . I hope you don't judge my parents, or think . . .they deserted me. I came home on school breaks, they visited. Maman called every Sunday. None of us made good decisions then."

"I don't judge."

"That's why you're Michel." He turned away.

The two men skirted the side of the house. All four doors of Celeste's car opened, tiny girls spilling out. They rushed to André and Michel, screaming their names in high-pitched little voices. In identical blue dresses, the three-petite-dark-haired five-year-olds moved like flitting butterflies, curly ringlets askew. The girls leapt into their outstretched arms. André and Michel juggled the wiggling children. and greeted Celeste and Dominic.

"It's good to see you, André," Celeste said. She kissed the cheeks of each man, artfully dodging her girls.

"You look vivacious, as usual," André said. Dominic collected an armload of pink belongings, closed and locked the car doors, then greeted them.

"Bonjour." His quiet voice blended with the chattering. After André and Michel set the girls down, they ran inside to seek their grandparents. Dominic was a good match for Celeste; his steadfastness checked, and balanced, Celeste's high spirits. The four adults loitered behind the rambunctious children.

Before they reached the front door, Isabel and Christophe's car rolled up. Two boys jumped out when they spied André and Michel. They raced to the men, Lucien's chubby legs churning to keep up with his older brother, Corbin. Michel tossed the lead boy in the air, and handed him off to André, before he picked up Lucien.

Lucien pushed his hands against Michel's chest. "Down," he said.

"Yes, sir." Michel set the squirmy eighteen-month-old down. Lucien toddled off and fell over, pushed himself up, and started again, comically lifting his feet higher.

Isabelle regally unfolded herself from her seat; her husband sprinted around the car, and grabbed her hand, raising it to his lips with a flourish.

Michel turned to André. "I love your family." Pierre would have liked Michel.

Chapter VI Maximillian

MAXIMILLIAN BROUTIN WAS an opportunist; it was innate, the way he defined himself. Virtue? Vice? He had worked it both ways; he was good—sometimes—and bad when necessary, whatever it took a scrappy poor kid to endure on the streets.

He had taken advantage of opportunity, or just taken advantage, of everyone, managing to disappoint them all: his mother, his siblings, his so-called friends, the funny old priest who tried to set him straight. And his father? Papa was a part-timer who was around just enough to propagate nine kids, eight of them before Maximillian.

Good-looking and aware of it, Maximillian worked on his trademark appearance: an insolent swagger, black tee shirt, closefitting jeans. A look that drew women, invariably the wrong kind. Lean and sexy, his greatest asset was his nearly black eyes. He had perfected a useful technique, peering into another's eyes and lying, telling them anything—to get what he wanted. Not evil, just a bit bad around the edges. Like a bruised apple, Max was good on the inside.

Until about six years ago. Who could blame him? How often does an ancient rolled-up canvas drop into your life?

IT HAD STARTED around 2007. It had been before the world financial crisis in 2008, the reason he still had the damned painting.

Maximillian couldn't find the frame shop mentioned by a couple of unsavory men lurking in the Place du Tertre. He combed the street a third time and spied a peeling board with faded lettering. *Frames* had been scrawled high above a narrow door with a cloudy yellowing window. He had passed by a couple of times. Maximillian pushed the rickety door open and entered; his pupils took time to adjust to the gloom. In the shadowy recesses of the workshop, he noted heaps of canvases, frames, wormy planks and fresh-cut wood, folded cloth, old canvas liners stacked willy-nilly throughout the space. It smelled musty, a perfect place for rats; anything could hide in that mess.

"I heard you sell art abroad," Maximillian had said.

"Heard where?" the proprietor asked. He smoothed a few hairs over his head. He had a pointy nose and chin and appeared to peek over his piled-high clutter.

"The streets."

"You heard wrong."

"I guess I did. Merci." Maximillian scooted towards the door, spooky place, a good place to leave, quickly. Before he reached the door, the proprietor hollered.

"Wait. What are you selling?"

Maximillian's innards contracted. Should he risk it? What if the bloke was legitimate? He turned toward the proprietor. "The artist is Elisée Maclet."

"The painter of Montmartre? Early in his career? Or later." The man's eyes gleamed.

"Don't know much about art," Maximillian mumbled. Revulsion shimmied up his legs. The scrawny man's eyes appeared evil in his narrow face. He should have fled; instead, he had made a deal with the rat, now six and a half years ago.

Maximillian had frequented the underbelly of Montmartre for weeks to find someone who handled illegitimate art. The man who owned the frame shop had promised Maximillian big money if the Elisée Maclet painting was concealed enough to get it out of France.

Apparently, rich Asian businesspersons coveted French art. They had unlimited money and asked no questions about provenance. Maximillian must disguise the painting; maybe he could find an artist to paint over it, a good artist. Rich people didn't buy bad artwork. It was the beginning of an uneasy association.

So, Maximillian had hunted for a painter. He investigated men who existed at the edges of the art game, the ones who made money under the radar. Slinking in and out of shady establishments, snatching information from overheard conversations; Maximillian eavesdropped on the sensory language of the streets. It took some digging, but he learned a little about stolen art.

He lurked in the Place du Tertre, observed artists for days stretching into two months. Anguished about whom to approach, he had finally chosen Monsieur Jean-Paul Bertrand. His talent appeared better than most of the painters who sold tourist art.

"Bonjour Monsieur," Maximillian had said. The artist glanced over his easel.

"Bonjour. Like what you see?" Bertrand spread his hands, palms out.

"I like your style." Maximillian stilled the tremor in his words. "I want something else." He wiped his sweaty palms on his pants, heartbeat galloping. Should he do it? If he acted on this, he crossed another line in his petty criminal career. Scanning the square, everyone seemed focused on him. Greed won. Maximillian narrowed his eyes. "I have a proposition.

Good money. Can we meet in private?" Bertrand's head bobbed, assenting.

The two men agreed to meet the next week. Maximillian had commissioned Bertrand and paid a deposit. Bertrand had agreed to create a painting on blank canvas that the rat would then frame. The painting must be a good one.

It had taken six months to embezzle the money. His employer counted the money in the cash drawer each day before he left. No one counted it again the next morning. Maximillian was the first to arrive so he often pilfered small amounts. Combined with his savings, it was enough to pay Bertrand a substantial sum to paint a picture over the Elisée Maclet. Bertrand was an anxious man and that alarmed him. However, he said he would take the job and Maximillian didn't want to find another artist.

Bertrand finally finished it. Maximillian had counted the weeks, dreaming of the big payoff. When would the nervous painter complete the commission? He was at Bertrand's heavy green door half an hour after Bertrand called. The painting perched on the easel six feet from the door, an overhead light illuminating the canvas. And it had been ornately framed.

Bertrand had executed a stunning painting of a graceful woman in a dark red gown who floated on her back. She was underwater in the sea, her body reflected in the top surface of the water.

"Do you like it?" Bertrand had asked him.

"Not what I expected. Thought it'd be a head, or flowers or something."

"You said you wanted a professional painting, didn't care about the subject."

"Yeah. Don't know . . . It looks good," Maximillian said. The finished painting was worthy of a discriminating buyer. The painted woman was captivating; he noticed the nameplate on the bottom of the frame. "Who's *Miriam*?"

"I . . . it needed a title since it's unsigned." Bertrand's nervous eye twitch bugged Maximillian, time to escape from the apprehensive old man, made him nervous too.

"Why *Miriam*?"

"Aah... Aah. The Biblical story. Miriam saved her brother Moses from the Nile. It goes with the water theme."

"Rip it off." Anger flared, heating his face. Great. A religious nut, no wonder he was nervous. Took him long enough too. Ready to deliver the painting, he wanted his money. Maximillian raised his voice. "I said, take it off." Bertrand jerked toward the easel.

"Yes. Yes." Bertrand bent over the lower frame, tapping gently against the plaque. Damn, Shit, Hell. The old man barely moved.

"Hurry up!" The plaque clattered to the floor. Bertrand swooped it up and slipped it in a side pocket of his baggy pants. Maximillian handed the old man a fat packet of cash. He'd better not expect more for the frame. He paced while Bertrand wrapped the painting in brown paper and tied it with rough twine. Damn the man was slow; it had taken forever to paint *Miriam*. Shit, now he had called it *Miriam*.

THE RAT HAD scampered out of the agreement a short time after Maximillian delivered the finished painting to the frame shop. Maximillian had gone back to the frame shop after a week, anticipating piles of money. Instead, he got trouble.

"Get the painting out of here," the rat had said. "My buyer got paranoid, scared it'd be too hard to get out of France."

"It's not stolen." Maximillian charged toward the little man who backed up, anticipating danger. "It's been hidden for decades. It's not on a watch list." He spat at the ill-tempered little man.

"He doesn't care. Too risky. Art is easier to steal than fence. If it's too recognizable, no one wants to touch it."

"I didn't steal it."

"Then sell it on the legitimate market."

"Do you have another customer who might buy it?" Maximillian asked.

"Money dried up. Bad economy. No one is buying much now, even the rich ones. Now get out."

Maximillian had no choice but to take the painting and his greed and leave the shop.

DURING THE LAST five years, he had bided his time, waiting for another opportunity. The hiding place had been flawless; Maximillian had hidden it behind the stove (between partially finished walls) in his employer's business. His boss began an expansion; and he felt compelled to move the damn thing, couldn't cart it home.

Living in a minuscule apartment with his girlfriend left no room for *Miriam*. Émilie kept him on a tight regimen, nothing came in unless something went out. He had met Émilie and relentlessly pursued her, his greatest exploit. This opportunist knew when he had something good, and Émilie was good.

His life had been troublesome before he met Émilie, beginning with his name. Who named a baby Maximillian? The youngest in a too-big family, Maximillian had to scrap to be noticed. The Montmartre streets were his playground. He recognized the best place to pilfer a baguette, pluck a tourist's pocket and put the boot to a kid to get his pocket money.

The aromas of the streets invigorated him, avoiding dog poop became a game, avoiding the stinking bodies of vagrants, protection. Their plight could easily be his. Maximillian inhaled the bread aromas from boulangerie that fanned the early morning commuters. He could distinguish the fragrance of tiny blooms hanging over steep stairs amid the scent of an over-perfumed dowager. A street kid, he recognized when it smelled wrong, not the nose kind of smell, the feeling kind of smell.

Except for the petty thefts, he was a pretty good person. The end kid of nine, his parents gave up on discipline by the time it was his turn to get some; a delinquent teenager, his minor misdeeds went unpunished. If he had to define himself, he was an opportunist.

Loving Émilie had liberated him; she provided structure and worth to his life. She had created a home for him—not just a place to sleep and change clothes—but a real space for normal living, where one could get ahead.

Life had picked up for him despite the bad choices littering his early years. He clawed his way to the highest position in his company, avoiding trouble in the streets. Conceiving the painting escapade before he met Émilie, he just couldn't give it up, too much invested—money, time, hope—maybe greed. But he had more to lose now than he did then.

When forced to move the painting from its five-year hiding place, he sought Monsieur Jean-Paul Bertrand, the man complaisant in the deception. The old artist had refused. Maximillian threatened to expose him and Bertrand changed his mind, said he would keep it for a while.

Then the idiot hung it in the Musée de l'Erotisme. It had hung there for two weeks when Maximillian got a call from Bertrand.

"Come and get the painting. Now," Bertrand had said, breaking the connection. The crazy old man hung up on him!

Maximillian had retrieved *Miriam* from Bertrand's house with a few threats to the nervous creep. What would Maximillian do with it now? The painting was problematic; it held a mystical quality, a luminescence that drew people. In the museum, it announced itself to the world, *here I am*.

Maximillian's only option right then was to stuff it behind clutter in his employer's back room. He couldn't leave it there. He would sell it before he lost his nerve; maybe the stars were in his corner. This could be his break. The first year after the commission, Maximillian had relentlessly pursued a buyer, paying Bertrand so much had eaten away at him. It wasn't fair. Then the hellish recession hit, money was tight. Even the unscrupulous stopped spending.

Happy living with the sexy Émilie, he ignored the painting. It was messy business; *Miriam* mysteriously liked Chez Philippe, the building owned by his employer. Maximillian had found the rolled canvas there between the walls, after workers opened them up to install new stoves; the canvas had been hidden there for decades, if not longer. After the failed sale to the Chinese businessperson, Maximillian re-hid the disguised (now framed) painting deep inside the same wall—left open when murals were discovered. After a short time with Bertrand and a fling at the Musée de l'Erotisme, *Miriam* was again at Chez Phillipe—in the tiny storage room.

He would get rid of it; he was tired of being underestimated. *I will make money on this deal.*

"I DON'T KNOW the best way to tell you. We are . . . we are having a baby," Émilie said, sobbing, curled like a cat on their bed. "I was careful."

"What?" A sonic boom hit him. He loomed over her, rage firing in his gut, exploding. He lost control. Maximillian took two steps and hit the wall. The crunch of his knuckles reached his ears before the pain reached his brain. Émilie coiled into a fetal ball.

"Damn." He shouted across the small space. "Babies are liabilities. What will we do with a baby?" She put her arms over her ears. He thrust aside the ecru linen curtains that defined the bedroom area of their studio apartment, stomping out.

Running down the stairs, he was out of breath when he got to street level. A shockwave hit him, slamming his body backward, back to his childhood with too many people packed into a miniscule apartment. He wandered around Montmartre, despising his freelance father, hating his jumbled childhood apartment. Émilie had lovingly established their household—his first real home. How could he give it up for a smelly baby?

He tramped for hours until the warm light of a bistro beckoned. Taking a seat, ordering a beer, lifting the heavy glass to his mouth, he saw other solitary men swallowing their alcohol alone. He plunked the glass down, sloshing the amber liquid. The last two years loving Émilie had been his best. Just one baby couldn't be much trouble; it wasn't nine. He had wanted to be a father, someday, a better father than his father had been—wouldn't take much. He left the bistro, still sober, and ran home, clamoring up the stairs, much faster than he had descended hours before.

Heart pounding, he entered their home. She was still here. Maximillian exhaled; Émilie still lay on their bed, silhouetted behind the sheer curtain.

Émilie had a knack for home design and their tiny studio apartment showcased her efforts. She could make a little go a long way, frequenting second-hand shops for the basics in furnishings, giving new life to old things. She handcrafted flair with crayon-colored accessories: orange curtains, red and yellow pillows, green and blue dishes, an out-of-the-ordinary purple vase. Émilie had even splurged on two primary-colored landscapes purchased from the artists in the Place du Tertre.

The striking note was simplicity, the minimalist nature of the well-designed space. The main room included a bedroom area hidden behind a floor-to-ceiling curtain that matched the ecru walls. The tiny kitchen was part of the harmonious arrangement. Red bowls, green baskets and yellow towels complimented the décor.

Émilie's hadn't moved, still curled in the same defensive position. He ripped his fingers through his hair, mad at himself, and went to her. Maximillian pulled her close, spooning her body, nestling her against himself.

"We can—I can do it. I'm sorry." He kissed her ear and wiped her spent tears with the sheet. She snuggled, remaining silent. He held Émilie as his mind searched; they had options. Healthcare was good in France, and they could get by on his salary. He'd have to earn more for a bigger place, but It'd be hard to give up this apartment. They had created a child in this nest, but there was no room for a baby. Hell. The word baby was hard to fathom. Babies were noisy; they stank. They took a lot of room.

He still had the painting and now he had more incentive. A chunk of cash would buy a bigger apartment and some security. His eyelids were heavy but before he dropped off he thought about the baby. What would his child look like? Beautiful like her, or dodgy like him?

The late morning sun streamed between the orange curtains and cast pure light into the apartment; the scent of warm herbs awoke him. Émilie had purchased buttery croissants. She had scrambled eggs: dusted with dill, infused with scallions and topped with a bit of Gruyere. Strawberries sprinkled with ultrafine sugar glistened in two bowls. She could use a few ingredients to originate a culinary masterpiece. He stretched, savoring the morning and anticipating brunch. Émilie cooked well, but he was the professional.

Chapter VII André and Michel

ANDRÉ STOOD AT the tall ornately framed windows of his Paris office contemplating the street and the intricacies of the *Miriam* painting, particularly its disappearance. He often stood here, zoning into deeper thoughts, or meditating away unwanted ones, high above people going about their daily routines.

Family expectations had dictated the direction of André and Pierre Gensonné's lives. They were twin scions, golden boy descendants of multi-generational French attorneys, and their family history intertwined with the fate of other elite Frenchmen of the 20th century. The twins would join the family business when the time was right. On his desk rested a forever-young photo of him and Pierre on a boat, their tousled sun-lightened hair blowing in the breeze, toothy grins, identical eyes.

Pierre had bailed through death, and André had carried on the legacy. Obligations weighed heavily when he was young, but André had accepted his role. His guilt ensured it.

André would have fit the family mold despite his legacy. Carrying the art gene inherent in his lineage, he especially identified with his gruff grandfather when it came to art appreciation.

André loved museums as a young child and his grandfather exposed him to great works early. The two spent hours together. His grandparents' home contained many priceless pieces; although his own parents leaned toward a more kid-friendly home, museum and art festivals were part of his, and his sibling's education.

André had a propensity for complex situations. He resolved multiple issues related to art and cultural property crime, the process stimulating him. If he had chosen his own profession; he may not have found this appropriate fit for his skills.

France's rich history and unique place in the Renaissance created unparalleled attitudes toward art criminals and their crime. He was adept at putting the intriguing pieces of the puzzle together. French history, French culture and an unwieldy governing system intersected in a crossroads of unusual attitudes toward art criminals and their crime.

Several stories below him, Michel wove his way along the street, greeting a pretty girl, stooping to pet a dog. Michel considered himself an amateur magician; he also had a mystical connection with people and animals. He was headed for the office along his usual zig zag route. His was a natural charm that came hard for André.

Michel knocked on the frame of his open office door. "Bonjour." He rambled in. "Want to go to Montmartre? Find Bertrand?" Michel brushed André's sleeve. "But you can't wear the fancy suit."

"I have a lunch meeting with my father and grandfather. "Two o'clock too late?"

"I'll meet you downstairs at two."

"I'll wear jeans."

"Jeans are good." Michel gave André a high-five and bounded through the door; his personality kept their staid office lively. André resumed his position at the window.

Worldwide, it took constant effort to retrieve lost and stolen artifacts. Little progress occurred because some countries perceived art crime to be victimless. Other countries placed more importance on their cultural heritage, dedicating money and other resources to art crime agencies.

The extensive global list of missing and stolen artifacts testified to how easy it was to steal from the world's museums and private collections. Many couldn't afford security. If a thief didn't have good connections to fence what they stole, it was hard to make money. It was almost impossible to sell well-known art.

Non-professional crooks without networks had a tough time, often destroying paintings, giving them away or discarding them, to avoid detection. Professional thieves moved stolen artifacts easier. From a criminal standpoint, ten percent of the value of a stolen painting was better than zero, so artifacts continued to disappear.

Michel entered the street again and waved. André acknowledged him, although he wouldn't see him here. Perhaps an afternoon in Montmartre with Michel would jolt him out of this pensive mood. He sat at his desk. An open report contained preliminary information about an art stash hoarded in an apartment by an elderly German art collector in Munich. The artwork dated to the Nazi era in Germany. Investigators would determine who rightly owned the pieces. Sixteen hundred items had been recovered; he hoped he would be able to view some of those pieces. What a find for the art world.

Artifact retrieval fell into two categories: Either the piece vanished into the underworld and the chances diminished over time, or it was located fast. Law enforcement had to choose. They could concentrate on apprehension, and prosecute criminals, or use limited resources for the main goal, retrieving the lost art. The focus usually centered on the art; it was irreplaceable.

The risks for art thieves were minimal. Penalties were light. These factors ensured art crime was the third highest crime, behind drugs and illegal arms sales. The big picture was complex, law enforcers had to maneuver between degrees of legality, criminality and judgment. André thrived on the intrigue.

He checked his watch and pocketed his mobile. His footsteps muffled in the plush carpeting, André left the subdued atmosphere of his firm whose reassuring ambiance was designed to evoke confidence. His place was here, entrenched in the male hierarchy of the family firm. It had been enough. Why did he thirst for something else?

The compulsion to find Anne wrung him dry, consumed him. Maybe she was dead. Anne probably didn't exist; perhaps he had conjured her at the fraternity party. Despite his exhaustive search, she had never reappeared on campus. He had often thought of her then as he struggled with grief and depression.

Now he just had to get through lunch with his partners. André anticipated their luncheon meetings but now he just wanted to resume the search for Anne.

He had made reservations at Le Grand Véfour in the heart of Paris, a favorite eatery of his grandfather's. The restaurant resided under the arches of the Palais Royal on a picturesque Parisian street. One of the most beautiful restaurants in the city, it had opened for business in 1784. His father and grandfather both entertained clients there, although he preferred less formal places.

Past diners included Napoleon and authors Victor Hugo, Sartre, Malraux, and Collette. The menu was classic French haute cuisine; its reputation well deserved, he had never experienced a mediocre meal.

Jean-Baptiste and Vincent Gensonné awaited him in the foyer. "How do you like your new car?" his grandfather asked. "Impressed any women?"

"Is that why you bought it? Thought I needed a woman?"

"No." His grandfather slapped his arm, laughing. "It was merely a gift."

"Quite a gift, Papa. André drove it to our house last weekend. His envious brothers-in-law and Michel were salivating," Vincent said.

"Thanks Grand-père. I appreciate the car." The men acknowledged the Maitre d' hurrying toward them.

"Good. I wanted to give you a special birthday present. One you won't forget." One he wouldn't forget. Odd. André noticed a slight hunch to his grandfather's back—he must be over eighty—though he was still had a vigorous manner.

"Bonjour," the Maitre d' said. He greeted the three distinguished men by name, escorting them to a prized table and recommended an aperitif. Whenever André entered the familiar dining room, it impressed him it could belong in the Palace of Versailles, with its gilded and mirrored walls. Despite its prestige, the atmosphere welcomed guests.

Jean-Baptiste Gensonné held the fine dry Champagne aloft, and toasted his son and grandson. "Santé!"

"Santé, to family." André and his father Vincent reciprocated the toast. "Let's talk business later. Tell us about your latest case," Jean-Baptiste said.

"Papa." André dragged his name, his brows raised. Vincent shrugged. "There is no case, no client. I saw a painting. It disappeared."

"Are you looking?" His grandfather asked.

"Yes, to no avail. Yet. We should choose our food." The waiter lingered near Jean-Baptiste, awaiting instruction.

"We'll order the main course, please complement them with other courses."

"Yes, Monsieur."

"Your chef's specialty is fish," Jean-Baptiste said. "Do you recommend the Dory filet?"

"One of our best, served in a thin crust of vegetables, with asparagus salad and Argan oil."

"I'll have the filet." He laid the menu aside.

"The roasted monkfish, zucchini, and almond cream dish." André pointed at his selection.

Vincent ordered the oven baked red mullet, served with artichokes and broad beans in vinegar with orange tree and savory honey.

"We had a fantastic vacation in Bregenz. Grand-maman chose the city for our Austrian holiday, on the Bodensee in the Alps." Jean-Baptiste's face was darker; he must have sunned.

"Did you rest?" André asked.

"Some. We did relax on the beach, and climbed the foothills. We went to a classical concert in the waterfront arena. Grand-maman wants to go back when Bregenz hosts its music festival." Jean-Baptiste said he was refreshed and ready to work. André studied his animated grandfather, essential to the firm and still vital. Despite the hunch, he appeared healthy, perhaps more rested after his holiday.

The three declined the decadent desserts of Le Grand Véfour in favor of the renowned les fromage. André relished the dynamic conversation and the exquisite surroundings. He had missed Grand-père, however, Michel waited.

"I'm going to Montmartre this afternoon with Michel." André stood and when his grandfather did too, hugged him. Near the entrance, the chef bid him Au revoir.

"My compliments, our lunches were outstanding." André hastened to his office, changed clothes and phoned Michel, agreeing to meet him in the lobby.

"I thought you'd backed out on me." Michel raised his comical eyebrows alternating them like no one else could, a unique talent. "Hmm… That's casual for you, but you still look too good." His eyes swept up and down André's body, appraising André's stylish jeans, white shirt and fine leather shoes. "On you, a ratty bathrobe looks like haute couture. Let's go, it'll be late when we get there." They hurried toward the Métro.

"How was the famous, or should I say infamous Le Grand Véfour?"

"The food was excellent. It's great to have Grand-père back. The years are showing though; my grandfather seems older."

"You have wealth in family. I don't know another family like yours. You are fortunate." They descended the stairs to the white tiled tunnels of the Métro. André didn't answer, irritated by Michel's comment, not sure why. He observed Michel's progress through the crowded station, scrutinizing people, smiling at anyone who returned his gaze—unlike most Parisians.

They boarded and André remained silent, now irritated with himself. He stared out the window, watching people board, and disembark, for several Métro stops.

"We've been to Montmartre a lot."

"One of my favorite places in Paris." Michel glanced at him, eyes shining, his body lithe, ready. "Always something happening." Michel wasn't upset at his reticence.

André sat on his side of the coach, closed his eyes and listened to the rumbling train, swaying with its movement. Small talk often entailed discomfort although he valued Michel's company. Michel had been right last weekend when he said André had secluded his personal life. It wasn't in his nature to share confidences. The shifting Métro lulled him, his mind wandering back to his luncheon with his father and grandfather.

"Do you know why it's my favorite?" Michel startled him with a pronouncement, but didn't wait for an answer. "It's the contrast between my life at home, the dusty God-forsaken place where I grew up, and the lights, colors, sounds of this living, breathing city." Michel stopped and before André responded, he spoke again. "You've always lived in the city;

you've always had the best. Do you appreciate the magnificence of Paris?"

"We all have burdens." André's tone was harsher than he intended. They didn't speak again until they neared Montmartre. André couldn't shake his sense of foreboding, although he recognized his behavior troubled Michel.

"I'm sorry I offended you." Michel didn't appear sorry. He grinned at a woman seated across the aisle.

"You didn't." André contemplated the last couple of weeks. "I've had my equilibrium shaken by *Miriam*, by the painting." He hesitated. "There's a longing . . . I can't explain." He shuddered. "Enough! What's your plan?"

"Find Bertrand." When the Métro stopped, Michel set a quick pace. "I know where he lives." André hustled to catch the shorter man.

Michel pointed out local delights: a surprising little walkway ending at stair steps with ivy curling down the walls, flowers peeking out of hidden spots, children playing in little alleyways, silly dogs paraded by pretentious owners, and a wary toad nestling among the rocks where a wall met the street pavers.

Michel greeted everyone, including the toad. André never noticed these details. Was he immune to everyday pleasures? Was he a normal melancholy Frenchman or did his moroseness go deeper? Should he seek counseling?

Michel turned unerringly down a narrow street with high stone walls, stopping at a massive green door towering above them. Michel clobbered on the door, inviting André to thump on it too, no answer.

"Next stop is the bistro where I had lunch with Monsieur Bertrand."

Michel entered the homey bistro, pulled a chair and sat, motioning André to sit. He greeted the waiter by name, Georges, and ordered coffee. André respected Michel's ability to accumulate data, including names, and retain it, hallmarks of an effective investigator.

"Bonjour, Monsieur Georges, do you remember me? From last week?" Michel had asked.

"Maybe." His gaze slid from Michel to travel over André's lean frame, lingering on his well-made clothing. "Why?"

"Do you know the man who brought me here? Monsieur Bertrand? He paints. Where does he sell his work?"

"Ask him," Georges said. He turned away and then looked over his shoulder. "Or check the square where the artists congregate."

"Wait." The server hesitated. "Do you know where he paints? Do you know his daughter? He's a regular here." The waiter shifted his shoulders up and left.

"Why did my questions annoy him?" Michel asked. He half arose, settling back in his chair. "Maybe I should—." Running his fingers through his curls, he lifted his cup, waving it towards André. "Oups!" His grin wide, he swigged his coffee.

André finished his own coffee. The slide of chess pieces emanated from the corner where two men played, adding to the cozy feel of the place, like someone's homey living room. "Michel?" His friend appeared unfazed.

"I didn't establish empathy with him first. That didn't go well." Michel shrugged. "A minor slipup, not my usual approach." Michel paid the check and waited for André. "The Place du Tertre next?"

"I'm a hindrance. Without me, you can ingratiate yourself in the tempo of this place, learning more. I'm leaving. Call me tonight." He left Michel in the street without a look back.

WHAT WAS WRONG? His response to the miscalculation was irrational; Michel had sloughed it off, moving on. It was absurd a painting could shake his mental concentration. Something about the condition of the canvas tickled in his memory. The painting enticed him. Did it affect others? The artist had painted oil pigments onto canvas, unremarkable.

André strived to remember the frame: modern, traditional, old. The painting was missing, but stolen? Who would steal it?

André wandered the side streets of Montmartre and little by little comprehended his surroundings. The details of the village-like arrondissement came alive. Michel understood life and the human condition emphasizing with the individual: their frailties, impulses, triumphs, joys and fears. Michel experienced an exuberance for life that had escaped him. He was ten years older than Michel was. Had he ever been young? Did he seem old to others, or did he only feel old?

MICHEL STOOD ON the sidewalk where André had left him, observing his friend's despondent figure until it disappeared. André was miserable. Whatever bothered him was beyond Michel's comprehension. Relieved he was gone, he whistled a repetitive tune. It was hard to do reconnaissance with André. He attracted attention, sensual and brooding at the same time, intuitively humble, a lethal combination. Michel had witnessed many females vie for his attention, and though André noticed women, he was French, only Collette Dupris had a relationship with him, and it was sister-like.

Men gave him a second glance too, evidenced by the scrutiny of the waiter in the bistro. When Michel interacted with André at the office or at the Gensonné home, he didn't notice he and André were dissimilar. However, when they were in public, people noticed André, turning their heads to observe him. He possessed an undefinable magnetism within his brown hair and brown eyes, otherwise common in Paris.

Not one to dwell on what he couldn't control, Michel ambled toward the Place du Tertre, still whistling. Michel was upbeat, stirred by the beauty of a Paris afternoon in June. It sure beat the hell out of his hometown. He originally escaped his boring childhood without much baggage, though he had lost his way after he left home. Even hit rock bottom. But he had purged the past moving on without regret.

André had aided him when he first came to Paris, and he was grateful for the opportunity, especially the job, but not groveling grateful. Right. Whom was he fooling? He would do anything for André.

Michel surveyed the square, hoping Bertrand had shown up today, painting his local scenes for tourists. Threading nearer and nearer to the center of the square, Michel wove in and out of the crowds. He observed the interactions between local and locals, locals and tourists, and tourists and tourists, learning what he could, and making connections between what he understood and what he observed. Michel sometimes mingled with the crowd, sometimes melded with bystanders in front of an artist. He adopted the cadences of the street. No one noticed his eyes canvassing every inch of the square.

Michel's eyes focused on a dusty red beret ahead of him, the man under it traveling at the same speed as the throngs of people. He hauled a satchel and had an easel slung onto his back. Michel stepped back under a leafy tree to observe.

Bertrand set up his outdoor studio among many others. The spirited artist was less apprehensive than he had been the day Michel had taken him to lunch. He enticed a crowd and painted quick representations of his customers, easily responding to his fans. Michel left the shady spot, aware Bertrand might sense his presence. What was Bertrand's connection to the *Miriam* painting?

He noticed a rotund painter set up near Bertrand and edged closer, hoping to question him. "Bonjour. I like your work, Monsieur." He spoke French, scanning the painter's canvas. When he heard his native tongue, the man glanced up, nodded. The landscape came alive under the artist's talented hand. "Unless it rains, this must be a great place to spend your summer."

"It's a living," the artist said. He continued to brush quick strokes onto his small canvas, creating an impressionistic rendition of the colorful square.

"Do the same artists come every day?" Michel asked.

"It varies." He finished the painting with an illegible scrawl. Michel waited for the artist to complete the transaction. He collected his money and cautioned the buyers to let it dry, deftly replenishing his easel with a new canvas.

"What about him? Does he come every day?" Michel asked. He nodded toward the spot where Bertrand was visible amid a five-deep crowd of tourists.

"Bertrand? Used to, comes less now. He's one of the lucky ones. Finally got a break. Had some shows and sells his paintings in galleries."

Michel bought a completed painting from the artist's stock and paid him a little more than he asked.

"Merci beaucoup." Michel wedged the painting under his arm. He didn't ask for the name of Bertrand's gallery. He had Bertrand's name; he would find it.

There were hundreds of galleries in Paris. Bertrand probably existed around his home, the bistro and the square. He called André and asked him to use his technical resources to find the gallery that sold Bertrand's paintings, advised him to check in Montmartre first.

He spotted a street café with outside tables, a perfect place to loiter.

"Will you share your table?" Michel asked in French-accented English. The American girls widened their eyes and exchanged glances.

"I guess so," the blond said. The brunette with eyeglasses scooted her chair aside to give him room.

"Shall I order wine? You should sample our French rosé." He ordered a bottle from the Côtes de Provence, poured it into three glasses, and lifted his toward them.

"To Montmartre and Paris," he said. The girls lifted their glasses, giggling. "Fine French rosé from the region is a translucent peach color." Michel lifted his glass to the light to show them. He inquired about their Parisian visit, discovering they were college girls on a short-term academic stay.

"You should order the specialty of the day. Some of these café's pre-printed menus signify a mediocre meal, kind of mass-produced. They cater to tourists in this area."

"Will you order?" the blond girl asked. He crooked his finger for the waiter. Michel switched to French; he had a lengthy dialogue with him before he was satisfied.

The overhead umbrella cast a shadow between them and the hot sun, shielding the threesome from the heat, creating a private space. Michel entertained them with a card trick and when the food arrived, the women exclaimed over the exquisite presentation. A variety of tuna, vegetables and salad greens—arranged in strips of red, green, white and yellow—rested on a square blue dish. Michel soon had them laughing about his observations of people.

"Have you made up stories about the people on the street?" he asked.

"When I was little," the blond said.

"It's more fun when you're grown-up. See the man with the white tennis shoes and fanny pack? What does he want most in the world?"

"Maybe dinner?"

"He pines for a Jaguar; he drives a minivan. He desires the French Riviera with its sun and bikinis, his wife wants to visit all one hundred museums in Paris." Michel spread his arms. "What does his wife want?" The woman next to the man owned a grumpy face.

"She . . . she secretly hopes. . . he'll turn into a tall, dark, handsome Frenchman," the brunette said, her glasses slipping down her sweaty nose. Laughter bubbled from the girls. The stories evolved, each getting more creative, one-upping each other.

Michel's mobile rang. André gave him the name of a gallery and asked if he could be there soon. Michel paid the entire check, bid them good-bye, and kissed each on both cheeks. He eavesdropped, listening to their comments before he disappeared among the people and their stories.

"Why don't we have men like him at home?" the brunette asked.

"Because we're not home. Wait until the other girls hear this. They won't believe us." Michel had performed a good deed, it was fun for him too.

Michel used his mobile phone GPS to locate the gallery André found. He could have used it to search before, though he had wanted to include André and gauge his disposition.

When Michel neared the gallery, an elegant man in fashionable jeans and a long-sleeved white shirt leaned against the building, one leather-encased foot braced behind him. His arms crossed, he waited. Nonchalant.

"Bonjour."

"Bonjour. André!" He slapped his arm. "You've been in Montmartre all this time?"

"Yes. I wandered around for a while, the place worked its magic and my temperament improved. I needed to refocus; the painting held the answers. I searched for works by Jean-Paul Bertrand; it's a common name."

"How long have you been here?"

"Long enough to discover Bertrand painted the one in the Musée de l'Erotisme. Come in, he's quite good." André held the door.

The gallery displayed various artists' works in an eclectic, attractive environment, treating each representation with suitable lighting. Faint music diffused throughout the space, setting a mood that enhanced the beauty of each piece. Bertrand's work excelled here. To André's trained eye, it was unmistakable; the style and proficiency typified the painting displayed in the Musée de l'Erotisme. Each piece, though exquisite, missed one crucial component. His background and his affinity for drawings and paintings—whether oils, watercolors, charcoal or pencil—enlightened him to a possible reason. Just a suspicion, he was not ready to share it, even with Michel.

"Do you want dinner?" André asked. Twilight surrounding them, this Monday was just finishing its day on earth as Parisians joined tourists in the hunt for the best available restaurants.

"No, go ahead. I ate." Michel checked his reflection in a plate glass window. Michel ran his hands through his curls, tucked his shirt into his pants to cover a food spot on its tail, completing repairs to his toilette. André eyes found Michel's in the reflection.

"Changed my mind. Let's go somewhere casual."

"You said you ate."

"I couldn't resist some pretty girls. I joined their lunch table. Pick a place." Michel dusted the soil off the bottom of his pants and gave himself final approval in the window.

Perhaps he should examine his appearance too. He noted his reflection, turning each way. The spotless well-groomed likeness in the window indicated acceptance and turned to follow Michel.

"Let's go to Chez Philippe. It isn't casual; though the food is excellent. Monsieur Dubois can update me on his progress with the French bureaucracy; we have nudged them along. You can see the murals he discovered." André apprised Michel of the latest on the Dubois case. The streets were crowded now; Michel nodded at people, smiling. Someone asked him directions. His face open, he was approachable.

The restaurant overflowed and a line of patrons waited on the street outside the entrance. André slipped through the door. Just after he requested a table from the Maitre d', Monsieur Philippe Dubois arrived with menus under his arm for the next guests.

Dubois spotted him, motioning him forward, and displaying two fingers with a questioning lift of his bushy eyebrows. André nodded, Michel was close behind him. They shadowed M. Dubois through the crowed restaurant, (he had squeezed more tables in for the dinner trade), to a less desirable area close to the kitchen. M. Dubois indicated the table. "Yes?"

"Yes. Merci beaucoup."

Dubois recommended the grilled scallops on a bed of bean sprouts in a bright green wild-garlic sauce, recommending a complementary wine. They lingered over the exquisite dinner appreciating the ambience of the space, noting the bustling staff access the kitchen. The waiter approached carrying desserts. They ordered the homemade ginger ice cream with avocado slices and passion fruit displayed on a mango-colored dish. The dessert was a delight for the senses and the palate.

"I want to see the murals." Michel stated, fidgety like a child, he had already asked about the murals before the second course.

"I'll ask M. Dubois, if he comes back. Coffee?"

"I'd prefer to see the kitchens."

André had a disturbing sense they were being watched. He glanced around, not noticing anything unusual; he didn't recognize anyone nearby. The active staff scurried back and forth, yet something was peculiar.

M. Dubois hurried toward them, then asked if their dinner was satisfactory. "Incomparable." André placed his thumb and next two fingers together. "This is my colleague Michel la Roche. May he view the artwork you exposed with your renovations?"

"Of course, a quick look. My staff is overwhelmed right now; it is the busiest time. Follow me," he ordered, walking quickly toward the nearby kitchens. The large room was a mass of moving bodies in organized commotion. Waiters and chefs, cook's helpers and dishwashers contributed to the din. They took a hasty look before they fled back to the dining room.

"Damn!" Michel skidded to a stop outside the kitchen door. "I almost got run down in there."

"What do——?"

"I'll tell you, but let's get out of here." Grim-faced, Michel beelined through the restaurant, targeting the front entrance.

Near the Métro station, André asked Michel again about his impression of the murals.

"I didn't see the artwork, but there was one guy ... he acted ... defensively."

"How so?"

"Vibes. When we walked into the kitchen, a man radiated hostility when we checked behind the stoves. He acted more suspiciously when he caught us watching. The others went about their duties; he stood, glowering. He wanted us out of his kitchen. His uniform was of a chef or sous chef."

"You have a third eye, Michel. Let's go home, it's been quite a day." The men descended the stairs of the Abbesses Métro station for the ride home. Michel observed the other riders, his gaze lingering on the young men, many of them pickpockets that lurked in this station, preying on unwary tourists. Michel murmured next to his ear.

"The chef is familiar, it alludes me right now."

Chapter VIII Anne

ANNE DRESSED IN peach and black athletic attire for her Monday morning run, tied her hair into a high ponytail and contemplated her face in her mirror. A blemish on her right cheekbone fired red on her otherwise porcelain skin, probably stress.

Padding to her bedroom, Anne then clarified her mind with rehearsed yoga positions, connecting her body and spirit to a mindful state of awareness. The practice usually helped, today she couldn't dispel unwanted thoughts, they stuck in her mind like the beating wings of moths craving light. After three nights of fitful sleep, she yearned for an uninterrupted rest. Her sleeplessness began last Thursday, the night of the diplomatic art event at the embassy.

Anne had driven away destructive memories emanating from her former self, the little girl in a messy house. The possible glimpse of André had precipitated her childhood images, her mind reverting to hopelessness. Taking the stairs instead of the elevator, Anne chased her demons, willing them away, unsuccessfully.

Once on the wide streets of Paris, Anne disciplined her mind, concentrating on her movements and her pace, one, two, one, two, one, two.

Anne controlled her life as if a puppeteer controlled his puppet's strings. She relied on no one and unlike the dependent puppets, no one counted on her. As Anne jogged along the avenues her limbs loosened and tension dissipated. The beauty of her adopted city embraced her, substantiating her need to run as a path to healthful living. Nothing else worked.

Anne reveled in the iridescent morning, sunlight filtering through the Plane trees that transformed the lighting, creating leafy shadows. Her path changed from sunny to dark, lighter, darker and brighter, as she moved from sun to shade to leaf-filtered light and back into the sun. It was a glorious morning! She loved Paris.

The capital city of France felt safe despite its immense size, the densely-packed population providing security in numbers. She could lose herself without anyone questioning her solitariness.

Approaching her apartment, Anne saw a ramrod-straight figure stride across the front of her building. In her trademark orange clothing and matching hair, Stefania drew conspicuous attention with her unique style and self-confidence, her manner intimidating to the wimpy Anne, worrying uphill through life's challenges. She changed direction to avoid her.

Without guile, Stefania was a young woman about Anne's age, a vivid character with a flamboyant manner. Henna-red hair fashioned in a stylish bob owned her head, and at first glance, her bearing appeared haughty—an illusion. She greeted people with gusto, her flair, her open manner contrasting vividly with Anne's private nature. Anne dodged Stefania a lot.

Stefania worked at the Hungarian embassy as a Hungarian national. Stefania thought their dual embassy jobs implied the women should be friends; Anne never reciprocated friendship—with anyone. Right now, she needed to finish her run, go home and get ready for work.

"Hi Anne," Stefania said. How had she seen her?

"Hi."

"I'm thinking running. Do you want partner?" Stefania often left words, particularly indefinite and definite articles, out of her heavily-accented English.

"I need to get ready for work, Stefania." She circled around her and ascended the steps, escaping. A fit woman, she was gasping hard when she got to her floor. Stilling her thumping heart, Anne opened the door to her refuge. Escape. That was her normal response to overtures of friendship. Pitiful, she couldn't help herself.

ANNE COMMUTED DAILY with Parisians intent on earning a living. She observed early morning travelers who concentrated on their mobiles or newspapers. They mechanically stepped on and off the Métro, rarely noticing their surroundings. Many traveled long distances to work in the city, restricted to a daily routine often called Métro-boulot-dodo.

Anne viewed Paris as a visitor might, enjoyed its liveliness and splendor, delighting in its contrasts. She had discovered Paris as a student, and subsequently, discovered herself—a self that remained aloof from other humans, but in perfect accord with the vibrancy of the city.

Leaving her apartment each morning attuned to an inner timepiece, Anne assimilated everything during her residency in Paris. When the ticking stopped and her time was up, she would have no regrets. Her job at the embassy could end at any time; she would appreciate Paris in the meantime.

The Classical style, based on symmetry, simplicity of line, wide expanses and orderly buildings queued the streets and squares. The architecture stirred her. The rectangle windows became rows of eyes watching the theatrics of this historical city at the crossroads of European art, literature, culture and architecture. Graceful arches held bridges, lined squares and framed doorways. Her favorite buildings were those that met at a blunt triangular point, duplicating the triangular streets from which they rose above the people sauntering below. She discovered architectural wonders each time she walked.

Twenty arrondissements divided Paris; they spiraled out like a snail shell from the first, centered round the Louvre. She had visited many of the twenty quarters, like villages with individual nuances of cities within the city. She envisioned generations of people following their ancestors in the daily art of living in the compact city of forty square miles. Life in Paris could be cruel. At the junction of the hinges of history, Paris weathered the stresses and strains of its turbulent past. Paris was now and always, a city of tourists.

Anne was aware of the criticism endured by Parisians, that their unique identity was perceived as pride, condescending to non-Parisians, whether they were French from the countryside or foreigners from abroad. Anne now felt the same as a native Parisian, living in Paris made one special.

Located in the 8th arrondissement, the American Embassy was centrally placed between the Champs-Élysées and Chatelet on the city's right bank. More than her place of employment, the embassy had become Anne's sanctuary.

She had participated in an internship there through her university's international program ten years ago. Naïve and eager, the flight to Paris had been her first airplane ride. The excitement simmered inside long after she had finished her work in Paris and gone back to the U.S. The naivety appeared childish now that she lived in the city of light.

Her normal practice was to read a book on her commute. Almost finished with the novel *Gone Girl*, Anne was anxious to finish the novel.

"Ma'am?" Anne glanced up. The American accent was from home. A young woman sitting next to her wearing jeans, a backpack wedged between her legs, had spoken one word in

English, continuing. "Is this the Métro line to the American embassy?"

"Yes."

"I wanted to see the embassy. I'm here for study abroad."

"Be careful, you might fall in love with Paris. I was an intern, I live here now."

"Is it exciting? Glamorous?"

"A little of each. How long have you been here?"

"Six weeks. I go home in two. How did you get a job? Is it hard to work in Europe?"

"I was lucky. My college advisor had a contact at the Embassy. I received an internship, then went home afterwards. A permanent job with the U.S. State Department became available. I qualified."

"Wow. Any more jobs?"

"Not now, but openings occur. Just take advantage of opportunities." Anne resumed reading *Gone Girl*.

The young woman then spoke to a young French man. Their conversation sparked interest in the usually bored commuters. Anne shared the Métro car daily, although she didn't usually speak, she did feel camaraderie with her fellow passengers.

After her six-month internship, Anne had left Paris to finish her degree program, working odd jobs to supplement her minuscule inheritance. Her academic advisor recommended she apply for an open position at the American Embassy in Paris five years ago, one requiring proficient French and English. The job was entry-level; opportunity existed for qualified people. A dream job! Could she get it?

Now she lived in the city she had loved at first sight. Sometimes she belonged, other times she was an undeserving child. Anne overcompensated, working harder and longer than her colleagues did, wary that her past might reclaim her. Her supervisors noted her exemplary work, promoting her, rewarding diligence.

But Anne still coped alone. She held people at a distance, resisting overtures of friendship from fellow Americans in her workplace and Parisians she encountered. She craved acceptance and affirmation, but not intimacy.

André's image intruded—the teenage version. Did he live in Paris? Was he married? She had reshaped her life because he had provided a glimpse into another world. Every detail of the May evening imprinted onto Anne's mind—one magical weekend late in her senior year—the night she had met André.

Anne closed her book. "Are you getting off?" the American asked.

"Yes. Enjoy your stay in Paris."

"Thanks for the encouragement."

"Two weeks will go fast." Anne disembarked, exiting the station amid throngs continuing their commutes. Her mind replayed that weekend. When she was a senior in high school, Scott Anderson's mother had suggested Scott invite Anne to Hemlock College during Sibling Weekend. His brothers were busy with the track season and neither could go.

Scott graduated from high school in the class ahead and was her main academic adversary. Hemlock College's Sibling Weekend was an opportunity that beckoned, scary and exciting. No one would know her, or her circumstances. She accepted the invitation.

Mrs. Anderson invited her to shop for a costume for the Roaring Twenties-themed house party. They found a vintage dress and accessories in a second-hand store. Mrs. Anderson pressured her to accept a pair of fashionable jeans and two trendy blouses. After the shopping spree, Mrs. Anderson took her out for lunch. What she would give for a mother like Mrs. Anderson.

The big weekend finally arrived and she was riding in the family's maroon mini-van as Scott drove toward Hemlock College.

"You should be spurring me on, I miss the competition," Scott said.

"I miss it too." Anne shied from looking at her old friend. Inexperienced with boys, Scott seemed more grown-up than he had been in high school.

"Thanks for coming. My fraternity brothers challenged each other to invite a guest. Logan and Brad were upset it was the same weekend as a big high school track meet. Mom suggested you. Thanks for saying yes."

"I'm a little scared. What happens on Sibling Weekend?"

"The weekend is for siblings to experience college life, it's a recruitment tool. The school prides itself on multiple generations of alumni. My roommate's mother is an alumnus; she wanted one of her sons to attend Hemlock."

Anne had no experience of campus life and no expectation she would attend college. This private school was a galaxy away. Scott dropped her off at a dorm, leaving her with one of his female friends.

Friday night in the dormitory was the best night of her life, until the next night. The girls played board games and talked about boys. Excitement kept Anne awake long after the other girls fell asleep; this was just another college party for them, but for her . . . another world.

Saturday night finally arrived. The girls spent hours getting ready, applying make-up, trading jewelry, accessories. The dress Mrs. Anderson helped her choose was perfect. Instead of an awkward tall girl hoping for invisibility, Anne fit in.

Scott walked her from the dorm to the off-campus party planned outside of the school-sanctioned events. He led her inside, touching her arm.

"Will you be all right? Just a few minutes?" She nodded. He disappeared among the crowd, and left her in the alien environment of a noisy frat-house party. This was harder than she had expected, she didn't belong in a place like this.

She searched for the door, intending to sneak back to the dorm when she noticed an attractive boy surveying the crowd. Rushing pinpoints heated her skin, she ducked her head, hoping he wouldn't notice her. When his cordovan leather shoes appeared in her line of vision, she peered up—into thickly fringed dark eyes. Unlike Scott, he was taller than she was.

"Hello," he said. "Will you share my wine?" He held a dark bottle with a fancy gold label reflecting a bit of light in the murky room. Like a deer caught in headlights, she couldn't speak. "My father assumes I miss French wine." Not attuned to his foreign accent, she concentrated on the words. "I told him I'm underage here, people drink differently—I mean different than in France." When she still said nothing, he lowered the bottle. "I know one person here and he disappeared." He walked away, then hesitated, turning back. He caught her eyes watching him. "What's your name?" His tone was soft.

"Anne."

"My name is André Gensonné." His thick accent muffled his last name. André something. She hesitated, preparing to flee, until he invited her to sit. They settled in the corner with their backs to the wall, long legs stretched out, her skirt riding up. Anne tugged at the hemline.

"I don't understand college partying." André waved his bottle at the crowd. "Why is it fun to stand around a keg of beer in the middle of the woods? In the rain? That was last week's party."

"I don't know." Underage drinking was prevalent; she had often overheard her high school classmates talking about illegal drinking—apparently, it was the same here.

André produced wine glasses from a leather shoulder bag and poured the deep red wine. He swirled it, waited, swirling again, and offered his glass. Her face flamed hot. She had never tasted alcohol. Desperate to stay, she reached for the glass. Her stomach quivered, he was so gorgeous. She tasted the dark liquid, it numbed her unsuspecting tongue.

"Do you like it?" His dark eyes questioned her.

She nodded, clearing her throat; he then poured himself a glass. The wine tasted awful, Anne took tiny sips, each searing her throat. The party numbers increased—wall-to-wall people.

They remained in the corner, the crowds pushing closer. She listened, the foreign accent hard to follow. He was dark-haired with soft waves of silky dark hair crowning an elegant head. Besides thick lashes and a carved face, his nose was slightly crooked at the bridge. Thick dark brows adhered to the underlying bone, perfectly shaped. Common features, so sensual, she had never been this close to a boy. He said he was eighteen; he was more sophisticated than anyone in her world was.

He shifted closer, the warmth of his leg nestled against hers, sending wee tingles through her body, spearing her heart. The loud music intruded and he leaned in, his lips close to her ear, talking softly. Little tremors caressed her neck; she yearned to snuggle against him, yet she was petrified.

Scott had checked on her. He gave her a thumb up; she nodded and he left. Anne said little. Sensitive to her reticence, he deftly carried the conversation: his trials with English, his faux pas with forays into American culture, the countries he visited, the books he read and the music he enjoyed. André loved art museums.

She relaxed in the warm rosiness induced by the wine. She felt misty, tranquil, the alcohol enabling her to listen, less restrained than usual. Though she couldn't decipher all his words, she remembered every nuance. He was attractive, self-deprecating and funny. When the music stopped and the lights went on, the magic left.

A couple weeks later, just a week before graduation, Anne's mother died. But the evening spent with André had altered her life.

She still dreamed of that night.

Chapter IX André

PARIS WAS EFFERVESCENT, its pinpoints of fairy lights dense, the city casting a massive dome of light over northern France.

The artistry of the city flowed through him and around Collette Dupris when they left the neighborhood bistro. They walked within a bubble, intent on each other, insulated from the street. A tiny woman, her waist was so slim his hand encompassed her side as he bent toward her. Music escaping from sidewalk cafes encircled them, two Parisians in tune with each other. They shared their profession; she lived in the same building. Sometimes they collaborated on cases.

Collette had been André's friend for eight years. She was elegant—without the pretensions often accompanying rare beauty—with a classically oval face and even features. He was comfortable with her, his closest female friend. She understood his solitude.

"Do you want to come up?" André asked. She assented, and they turned toward the elevator. Neither spoke, the silence tranquil. He touched her back, stepping back for her to precede him into his apartment, ambient light from outside glowing through the window, softening the darkened room. Collette found her usual chair without turning on a light.

"Wine, Perrier, Cognac?" André leaned across her to switch on a lamp. She smelled like his mother had—Channel No. 5.

"Perrier." She sank into a leather chair, tossed her shoes aside, her pink toenails twinkling when struck by streetlight.

He poured the sparkling mineral water and handed it to her. "Anything else?"

"No. The wine at dinner made me sleepy."

He poured himself the same, turned on a Mozart symphony, volume low, settling into a chestnut brown leather chair, a companion to hers, part of a traditional-style conversational group facing the windows. Earlier he had left the two-story tan drapes open. They framed wall-to-wall glass. The Paris scene was like a night view of a postcard sold in a tourist shop.

"Remember the painting we saw in Montmartre? The evening we had dinner with our friends?" André turned toward her.

"A little."

"Do you remember it?"

"It was small—not really though. Wasn't it a drowned woman?" Collette shifted, tucking her feet beneath her.

"Yes. Did you notice any details?"

"Not any I remember."

"It disappeared. After it was in the museum about two weeks." André contemplated the bubbles in his mineral water. "Only a couple of us noticed it. It's been on my mind."

"Why?"

"The woman in the painting resembled someone I once met. I was curious about it, now it's gone, I'm more curious. Michel and I investigated some. Didn't find anything."

"Wish I recalled more." She cuddled into the chair, listening.

"Do you remember an engraved plaque? *Miriam*. Along the frame, near the bottom."

"I'm sorry, I don't remember."

"I noticed the plaque the last time I saw the painting, but not the first two times. I'm sure it was added, another curious thing."

"What else was curious?"

"The quality of the painting."

His mind had connected the bits pricking at his memory. Until he saw Bertrand's paintings in the gallery, the difference between them and the *Miriam* painting hadn't registered. The distinction was in the surfaces of the canvases.

"I know why the painting was remarkable. Its subject was unusual, and the artist's work was exemplary, but there was something else. I recently discovered the artist, and saw some of his work at a gallery. I believe the contemporary, new painting, was painted over an old canvas."

"Why?"

"Could be many reasons." Her lovely face was just visible in the reflected light. "Bertrand's other work had a luminous quality, the mark of a talented artist's use of light.

However, the *Miriam* painting was incandescent, and unusual. It had fissures in the paint, little cracks that appear in dried pigments when the work is on canvas. Either the canvas was old or exposed to extreme temperature changes. Underneath the new paint, old paint did what it does over time; it cracked in a variety of ways, adding another dimension to the art.

This painting had those fissures. It's common practice for artists to paint over used or old canvases to save money."

"A criminal act?" Collette untucked her legs.

"Not clear. In rare cases, a thief may disguise stolen paintings by painting another over the surface. There is a high risk of damage to the masterpiece beneath. If this was done, why hang it in a museum?

Art criminals can be amateurs, art is easy to steal. Thieves don't make decisions based on what's best for the artwork."

"You love it. Don't you?" Collette pulled herself upright, her eyes dark. "Love the mystery."

"Yes. It's more. I love the talent, maybe the creativity. Inspiration might be a better description."

"Inspiration of what? The artist?"

"Think about a painting you love, one of those huge Renaissance paintings full of figures and animals, food and symbolism. Most of it is religious art. The artist pulls the viewer into the scene, into his vision, using color, depth and perspective.

It's just a flat canvas or board with paint on it. If you don't believe in God, it seems—." He ran his hand through his hair. "Appreciating the majesty of the artistry, and its creator, may convert one into a believer."

"Are you a believer?"

"I was, when I was younger. However, random events change lives. I came to believe wars fought for God or in God's name confuse the natural order. France has a violent history of people killing other people. A single choice and life can end. God seems absent." Collette sat motionless, then leaned forward.

"And your love of art?" She asked. "How does it connect with a possible god?"

"When I view a painting, I almost believe." André stood. "Do you want another drink?"

"No"

André refilled his glass and when he re-entered the room, her eyelids had drifted closed. He walked to the window, the midnight sky beyond the well-lit city was mysterious tonight. *Miriam* intruded.

Why did *Miriam* hang in the Musée de l'Erotisme for two weeks, then disappear? Beyond his personal curiosity, the painting now piqued his professional interest. Other facts niggled. Monsieur Dubois and his restaurant Chez Philippe were unrelated to the mystery, however, he did meet Dubois during the same week the painting vanished.

André was the only person who had examined it. Collette didn't remember much. It was gone when Michel visited the museum. The woman could be dead, though the artist left a strange clue, her hair should drift. The artist executed an arresting painting of a woman under the sea—with a neat pageboy hairstyle.

With his proximity to the art world and its treasures, he was cognizant of well-done, if not great art. After he saw Bertrand's other pieces, he had raised his opinion of the artist. His mind wandered, contemplating Bertrand's role. The hairstyle was intentional; Bertrand was too good to make a careless mistake. Perhaps it was Bertrand's way of attribution; he hadn't autographed the painting with his usual signature.

It was imperative he talk to Bertrand, he could locate him—it was hard to hide—even in Paris. Was he complicit in a crime? Bertrand should have recognized the old canvas as historical in some way, especially notable if the canvas had a coating on it before he used it. If he found him, he would ask the model's name.

Unless a criminal had good connections, stolen art could be a burden. André had researched stolen and lost paintings on the international art crime register, scrolling for missing paintings the approximate size of *Miriam,* estimating the dimensions. The list was massive. Art theft was rampant; the punishment for criminal theft was too light to be a deterrent—and it was relatively easy to steal. Many museums and private collections carried little or no insurance on irreplaceable art.

Law enforcement tended to regard art theft as a victimless crime. In the last half century, collectors paid astronomical prices for prized pieces, and art theft rose along with those higher values. A stolen piece was recovered only ten percent of the time. Nevertheless, there was an active market for lesser-known pieces. They were easier to move into the underworld of the black market.

Collette slept, her petite frame draped in his chair. He should wake her soon, walk her home. It had never asked her to spend the night; it was not that kind of relationship. He sat down in the chair next to her, the outline of her body just visible in the darkened room; he appreciated her presence.

What about the illusive Anne? What did he want? He had a massive hole in his life now—one he hadn't noticed before. Collette was exquisite and his best female friend. He should love her, the beautiful woman who slept in his chair. He sought an illusion.

Perhaps he was selfish. Why did Collette spend her valuable time with him?

Chapter X André

BACK TO MONTMARTRE and its distinctive vibes to look for Bertrand, the paltry clues led to the village-like area outside Paris, the diverse 18th arrondissement drew visitors like sugar draws flies.

André climbed the windy stairs of the Abbesses station with its wildly bohemian artwork. His favorite was the yellow unicorns on cobalt walls, the whimsical paintings of famous Parisian sights a close second. Now twenty-first century graffiti marred the historic works. Parisians lived atop one another in the compact city filled with millions of tourists; however, scenes like the Abbesses artwork still delighted jaded citizens.

Attired in a light linen jacket over a white cotton shirt and slim dark pants, André's clothing contrasted with those dressed for sightseeing. Spilling out of the Art Deco station with a portion of the three and a half million passengers served daily by the Métro system, André caught some of their excitement.

Amid the babble of languages, André distinguished a tour guide droning in French-accented English, "Some sociologists say the average Parisian spends more than a year of his or her life underground." Was he an average traveler? Not likely.

Climbing steps and rambling through neighborhoods, André walked to Bertrand's home. Michel said to look for an enormous green door; it was a distinctive landmark in an ivy-covered stone wall. Green doors, every shape and size, appeared along the sidewalks, but not the green door. Michel must have forgotten André had accompanied him to Bertrand's place.

André recognized it when he arrived, the door looked like it could keep out sword-armed knights. He knocked hard; the dull thuds he managed didn't penetrate. He intermittently tried again, no answer. Bertrand might be painting in the Place du Tertre, or a better option might be the gallery that displayed his artwork.

But it was too quiet. Dried ivy leaves—fallen from vines growing along the wall—had piled up, pressed between the sidewalk and the doorframe. The undisturbed litter implied neglect, or the homeowner's absence. Bertrand may not be living here; he headed for the gallery.

Weather indicators had promised a hot day, but it was tolerable in mid-morning and the village hustled with activity. Coffee shops, boulangerie and pâtisserie overflowed with customers; and the aroma of fragrant coffee mingled with sugar-sweetened air lured him in.

André sat at a street-side table with his pastry and coffee. He wouldn't recognize Bertrand; he hadn't met him. Michel mentioned he wore a faded red beret; the simple description fit many of the characters roaming the area. André tossed some Euro onto the table and hastened uphill.

A group of tourists huffed up the steps and blocked his route; he bypassed them, and turned onto a narrow street, an alternate route to the gallery. Shopkeepers swept stone pavers in front of their stores, rinsed windows, and watered geraniums, some nodded at him with a "Bonjour."

Beyond the open door of the art store, a young French woman dressed in a black skirt, red striped blouse and stilettos staffed the gallery. Her attentive eyes appraised the length of him before she greeted him with a radiant smile. "Bonjour Monsieur, may I help you?"

"Bonjour. I was here last week and admired Monsieur Jean-Paul Bertrand's paintings." André swept his arm toward Bertrand's works. "How may I contact him?"

"We sell his artwork."

"I want to speak to him." André slid closer, his eyes moved from her face to her legs and back to her eyes. "Do you know him? I like his scenes of Montmartre."

"He's a talented artist." She smiled wider, her right hand stroking her hair forward.

"Do you have his mobile number?"

"No."

"A number for his daughter?" Her eyes narrowed. André pressed his business card into her hand, his touch lingering until she read it, then read him. "Please. I won't give it to anyone."

She withdrew her hands. "Charlotte Bertrand is my friend." She contemplated his face and lifted her shoulders, acceptance. "I have her phone number on my personal mobile." She hurried to the back of the gallery, her heels snapping against the tile, determined in resonance and stride. Now aware of the soothing music permeating the room, a dozen scruples crowded his conscience. He hesitated, about to call out, when she re-emerged.

The woman had written a number on a sticky memo: he hadn't even asked her name. "Please don't misuse it." She dropped the paper between their outstretched hands. They both swept down, bumping heads. She stood, smoothing her hair over her shoulder, a nervous movement. Her unease troubled him, but he wanted the number.

"Merci." André clasped her shoulders, kissing each cheek. He rushed through the door before he said anything else—or returned the paper. Another errand in Montmartre awaited.

André had planned to walk to Chez Philippe to hand-deliver documents to M. Philippe Dubois since the restaurant was near. Hotter now, Paris sizzled; heat pulsated in the sun's journey to the sidewalk, bouncing warmth back to encircle people, animals and plants. The heat magnified smells, a stench arose from areas with food or pet debris. André was grateful when he saw the restaurant ahead and quickened his pace.

Something was wrong! He sped up and then broke into a run, his jacket flaring behind him. People poured out of the restaurant, panic stricken, meandering in circles, some clutching cloth napkins, one man clasped a glass of wine in one hand, grasping a woman's hand with the other. Gawking passersby obstructed the sidewalks as fire sirens pierced the air.

André zigzagged through bodies, finally reaching the front door; his commanding presence merited him entrance. He squeezed between and around distraught patrons to find the smoke-filled dining room. "Get out! Now!" His roaring voice discharged authority. He grabbed a napkin from a table, planted it over his mouth and nose, dashing toward the back of the restaurant. Thick gray smoke billowed from the kitchen, drifting wide after it thrust through the open doorway.

Bedlam in the kitchen! More hectic than the hyperactive pace set by the staff on a busy night. Flames soared out of a giant frying pan onto the massive stovetop, arose in an orange blaze, licking and crackling toward the ceiling. The wall behind the stoves ignited, briefly displaying multicolor surfaces soon disguised in voluminous smoke.

Dubois flung huge handfuls of salt in wide swaths from a giant box wedged under his arm and screamed at the kitchen staff. "Get out! Get Out!" The tang of burnt hair overlaid the odors of overcooked food and burning oil. The scene resembled an inferno of heat escaping from the gates of hell.

"The Pompiers are here," André shouted. "Get out!" He grabbed Dubois, manhandling him through the back door, close behind the last of the exiting kitchen workers. Most raced down the street. A chef, his white uniform dusted with ash, sprinted away, a brown paper-wrapped package under his arm.

"I need to talk . . . to the firefighters." Dubois frantically tried to break André's grip, jerking back and forth to loosen his hold.

"Don't go in," André ordered. "Go to the front. Cut through next door." He dropped Dubois' arm, shadowing him, the short man's sturdy legs pumping like the rods on a steam engine, propelling him through the adjacent establishment.

They exited through the neighbor's door and hugged the storefronts amid water hoses, disoriented customers and thrill seekers. André maneuvered to the front of Dubois' building. Firefighters barked orders, rammed people back from the entrance, struggling to erect barricades against the encroaching crowd. André managed to steer Dubois toward the nearest firefighter. "Leave the premises," he demanded.

"Leave?" Dubois shouted.

André remained unruffled, holding his authoritative manner despite the dark soot powdering his light jacket. Dubois' hands had smeared sooty handprints onto his sleeve.

"Meet Philippe Dubois. He owns Chez Philippe." He moved behind the disheveled man, urging him forward; Dubois' singed hair smelled like burnt chicken feathers. Dubois glanced over his shoulder, belligerent, shrugging off André's hand.

"Leave?" Dubois roared. "Who—."

"The fire is out," the firefighter interrupted. "It could've been worse." Dubois sagged against André and adrenalin drained from his body, leaving him even more distraught.

"What do I do?" Dubois threw both arms up, then dropped them like lead weights, emanating despair. "What now?"

"Lock the doors." The firefighter's harsh monotone grated. "The brick wall behind the stoves contained the fire to the back of the kitchen. Rest is smoke damage. Call your insurance company." He turned away, still speaking. "We'll keep someone onsite to monitor."

Dubois leaned on André as he reentered his once pristine restaurant. Tears streaked tiny rivers onto his face. Dubois surveyed his dining room: chairs overturned, once tasty food congealing and precious wine still in half-full glasses. He pulled away from André, his eyes focused on his two-way kitchen door, the edges smudged with residue outlining the edges. André followed him in, sloshing through filthy water that slurped at their shoes.

Black and water-soaked plates of artistically crafted entrées, that had been minutes from their white-clothed tables, lay on the counters. Exquisite pastries and tarts swam on large silver trays. Hastily discarded white aprons littered the wet floor, black footprints staining the fabric. Evidence of flight existed everywhere, each workstation containing half-completed tasks. Dubois sank to the floor. André left him to talk with two firefighters who still roamed around the stove, poking around, inspecting.

"The brick wall stopped the fire, you were lucky," the head firefighter said. The kitchen wallboard covering part of the brick behind the stove was gone, the murals barely visible on the blackened surface. André pulled Dubois to his feet. "Find your cash receipts, take them, or put them in a safe."

Dubois only nodded.

"Where are your keys? We'll lock the doors." Dubois lurched toward a tiny office in the corner, the desk piled high, the paperwork also soaked. Probably a precaution.

André's heart constricted. The poor man faced disaster everywhere. They locked the doors, handing a firefighter a spare key; he would monitor the building tonight.

André guided Dubois to a nearby outdoor café, ordered him Pernod, waited until he sipped.

"Whom should I call?"

"My wife." Dubois stared, unfocused.

"Number?" Moments passed. "I remember my insurance company. The agent."

"Good. Here's my mobile. Search the internet. Find the number." Dubois fiddled with André's phone, sighing, returned it.

"My wife, call my wife."

"Number?" Dubois grabbed the phone, punching numbers, then sliding the phone across the table.

"I can't . . . talk."

André spoke to the woman who answered, her voice reflecting surprise at the unfamiliar number.

Mademoiselle Dubois promised to come quickly.

"Go home, Philippe. Things will look better tomorrow. You can contact the appropriate people tomorrow." Dubois slumped in his chair, white shirt soot-blackened, bow tie unknotted, dark pants wrinkled, his dirty face streaked. Dropping his head onto folded arms, he sobbed, shoulders jerking. André scrutinized the street activity. What could he say to the distressed restaurateur?

"Why are you here?" Dubois raised his head. "Did you plan to eat at my restaurant?"

"Yes. I had other business in Montmartre, so I planned to hand-deliver some documents to you, and have lunch." His beaten client lowered his head. "I'm sorry. You'll build again. Perhaps you can combine the restoration with the expansion you have underway."

André ordered two more drinks. They sat silently, until Dubois's wife arrived, the chic woman's eyes puffed and red through carefully applied make-up. She hurried to Philippe's side, wrapping her arms around him and pressed him close, despite the risk to her silk blouse and tailored skirt. "Come home. You can come back tomorrow."

It had been a short workday for Chef Philippe Dubois, just mid-afternoon, hours before he normally closed the restaurant. The couple hobbled down the street, the substantial though short Dubois leaning onto his petite wife. She appeared strong; he was in good hands.

André's body felt like a dishtowel, twisted tight and shaken out, with the wrinkles permanently pressed. The waiter approached him, offering condolences for Monsieur Dubois's loss. When asked if he wanted another drink, André's stomach rumbled. He had planned to have lunch at Chez Philippe.

"Are you serving lunch?"

"Yes. Today's specialty is pan-fried tuna with grilled polenta." The waiter's eyes lingered on his dirty hands.

"I need to wash."

"There's soap in the toilet in the back."

André ordered the tuna and chose an elegant pale rosé, wonderfully perfumed, dry but lush with character. The food and wine calmed him as he lingered at the sidewalk café, watching people interact on the wide sidewalks. What was the meaning of random events? Disasters occurring without warning? A wayward breeze wafted a gust of smoke-filled air past his table, reminding him of his ruined clothing. He must go home.

BY THE TIME André reached his apartment, desire for a shower trounced everything. He relaxed under the misting water, soaped his body, and then allowed the falling drops to erase the residue of smoke and ash. His internal instincts had responded to the stimulus at the first sight of the fire. The urge to save whoever was in the building overshadowed his own safety.

The intuitive response combined with the sound of water triggered a surge of repressed emotions that inundated him. André crumpled to his knees, remembering the day he couldn't save his brother. He managed to turn the shower off and collapsed onto his bed, memories overcoming in terrifying waves.

SEVENTEEN YEARS AGO, Pierre and André had vacationed on the French island of Corsica with their parents and younger sisters at the beginning of July, days before their eighteenth birthday. Their parents invited two of the twins' male friends to share the holiday with them. The four boys were adept sailors and proficient swimmers; Vincent and Sophia hadn't been concerned when they rented a twenty-five-foot sailboat for a day of sailing on the tranquil waters off the coast.

The boys had invited girls along for a picnic lunch for hours of swimming and boating. They set sail from Calvi Bay with calm breezes and the expectation of natural beaches farther along the coastline.

Turquoise waters lapped at the powdery sand framed by Corsica's mountainous terrain. Balmy weather promised an idyllic day. The teenagers anchored in deeper waters within sight of the beach, diving off the sailboat, using it as a base for their water activities. Three girls sunbathed in tiny pastel-colored bikinis and the four shirtless boys practiced daring dives and jumps, showing off for the females.

They lifted the anchor periodically, and sailed along the coast. In the early evening, they turned to hug the coastline on their lazy journey back to the marina.

The orange disk slipping towards the cobalt sea persuaded them darkness would soon arrive. They were close to the harbor of Calvi Bay and minutes from the marina when they lifted anchor the last time.

Everyone aboard wore their lifejackets—except Pierre. He held his in one hand; he pulled the anchor up with the other. Not able to raise it, he dropped his lifejacket to use both hands, when a large motor boat passed them. The wake knocked Pierre off his feet. He slid over the side and slipped underneath the sea.

André instantly dove into the water. The others cried for help, screaming at nearby boats, as one of the boys summoned emergency rescue via his mobile. The sun sank over the horizon, blackening the water, blotting out any chance of seeing Pierre. Other craft gathered, the paltry onboard lights flashing and bobbing across the now choppy surface.

André frantically sought his brother, diving repeatedly into the dark water, again and again. Frantic. Wild. Afraid.

Pierre never surfaced, but he couldn't leave his brother in the sea. Alone. An hour passed. André remained in the water, continuing the desperate search with emergency workers. Others aboard the rescue craft beseeched him to get onboard. Finally, a worker jumped into the water, slapped André hard, and managed to force him up the ladder. He tumbled onto the deck, inconsolable, unable to comprehend returning without Pierre.

Vincent and Sophia had been waiting on the marina docks for them, when only one son returned, his limp body supported by emergency workers. Their ashen faces and aged bodies didn't even look like his parents.

Two days later, Pierre's body washed ashore.

Chapter XI Maximillian

MAXIMILLIAN SLIPPED THROUGH the back door of Chez Philippe and peeked into the storage room just inside the building. It was still there, the top edge of the brown wrapping visible from behind stacked provisions, cast-offs and brooms. Once at his workstation, he assembled his tools: copper pots, Sabatier knives and wooden chopping boards.

Maximillian poured olive oil into his medium-size carbon steel frying pans, lit the gas burners and donned a clean apron over his pristine uniform. How would he sell the Miriam painting? Would his contacts from his former life still have access to underground art dealings?

He had already visited his old haunts, tiny illegitimate cash-only businesses that existed for three reasons: one, to sustain the owners' lifestyle, two, to stay under the table in the black market to avoid detection, and three, to evade taxes to the French government. He'd steer clear of the rat this time.

"How many Quiche Lorraine do we need?" one of his cooks asked.

"Twelve savory crusts." Maximillian dropped chopped onions into two pans, sautéing them slowly so the onions softened, and added garlic towards the end, ensuring sweetness. Meanwhile, he spread bacon for the quiches into his largest carbon steel pans and asked an assistant to continue the prep work.

The frenzied pace revealed the usual weekday lunch activity. He moved swiftly, directing his subordinates at multiple workstations, ever vigilant for excellence. Sweat rolled off his face, dropped to his chest, rivaling the dripping faces of his co-workers, the team orchestrating the final piece de résistance. There were rules to follow in his line of work, each person contributed to the whole. However, he was the master architect. He would make it big one day, and the painting was part of his plan.

"Quiche crusts ready to fill," his pastry chef said.

"Heat is too high, turn it down." Maximillian rescued the bacon from his largest pan, handing the plate and cooked vegetables to another chef, who added Gruyere and cream to finish the quiches.

An hour later, most of the early preparations were in place for the lunch trade when M. Dubois entered the kitchen.

"The restaurant is filling," Dubois said, "we'll have a full house." Maximillian acknowledged him, directing the pastry chef to fill more cream puffs.

"Take a ten-minute break," Maximillian said, "only ten minutes." He continued his grandiose scheming. He was a father now; maybe he should ignore the hazards of quick riches and move ahead legitimately.

He was an excellent chef; he could get a better job. His expertise made his employer successful; it was about time he got recognition for his accomplishments. Many fine restaurants would hire him. He was street-smart—and book smart. And he was always looking out for himself.

Maximillian had grabbed opportunity when Monsieur Philippe Dubois installed new stoves. During the renovation, construction workers removed part of the existing wall. Murals were discovered in-between the back wall of the kitchen and the brick wall that adjoined the neighboring business. When the workers saw the murals, they left the job unfinished.

Old stuff in Paris usually meant regulations and bureaucracy. Maximillian was alone in the kitchen after the restaurant had closed. He was the lowest paid and least skilled worker; and it was his job to mop the kitchen floor after the staff finished their work.

He found a dusty oblong package protruding from the space near the floor in the construction area. He grabbed it and took it home—the old place—the apartment he shared with a couple of guy friends who didn't care about cleanliness or space. Maximillian had stuffed it under his narrow cot abutting the wall.

Removing the cloth wrapping later, he discovered an old canvas that looked like a miniature bedroll. When he spread out the stiff canvas, he unveiled an oil painting. Not sure of exactly what he had found, it looked like opportunity.

His employer constructed a temporary cover over the opening, too involved with his growing business to deal with red tape. Dubois ignored the problem and over time, it became part of the background, unnoticed. As the years passed, most of the kitchen workers were newer than the stoves, and no one was aware of the hidden murals.

When Dubois wanted to expand into the space next door, he sought legal help from the Gensonné firm and disguised the mural discovery was six years old, and not more recent.

The fire had been an accident. His mind elsewhere, Maximillian had forgotten to turn the gas burner off under the bacon grease in the massive black skillet. The oil ignited spontaneously. Before he could respond, flames rose high above the pan and threatened to spread to the walls (never properly finished) behind the stoves. Maximillian ran for salt to smother the blaze and then the initial fire exploded into consuming orange tongues.

The kitchen staff panicked and mayhem followed. The fear was contagious and most fled out the back door.

Philippe Dubois burst into the kitchen, found a giant box of salt in the storeroom, and ran back to the stove, tossing swaths across the burning oil. It was too late; the flames licked and sputtered up the walls behind the stove. "Everyone get out," M. Dubois screamed, tossing the contents of the box across the burning grease.

Maximillian obeyed, remembering to stop in the storeroom for the painting before he sprinted through the door. He ran hard, chased by the piercing horns of fire trucks rushing to the restaurant. Even if he didn't lose his job for incompetence, the aftermath of the fire would close Chez Philippe—at least for a while.

The painting under his arm chafed his armpit and his heart throbbed violently, blood thumping against his eardrums. The fire had been an accident. Why was he running? He slowed to a jog and then leaned against a building, bent from his waist, his free arm braced against his thigh, gasping for air.

He must find a place to store *Miriam*, but he couldn't trust anyone, especially his unwieldy family. He had regretted every time he had trusted any of his eight siblings—except for Mimi. Perhaps she would help.

Mimi was closest to him in age, but she was the good one, even active in the parish of the Sacré Coeur Basilica. Mimi worked at the Musée de Montmartre, but he couldn't walk in there carrying the painting. The Musée de Montmartre occupied an old house overlooking the Le Clos Montmartre, the only vineyard left in the Paris city limits.

Located on the Butte, the vineyard and museum attracted enterprising tourists. The museum and vineyard survived progress for historical reasons; but the museum often faced budget constraints that caused Mimi to worry about her job. The museum had normal operating hours; however, the vineyard remained closed most of the time, available only for pre-arranged group tours. In October, the vineyard opened to celebrate the grape harvest, and sold the mediocre Le Clos Montmartre wines to raise funds for charity.

Maximillian hadn't been to visit Mimi in a while, and he had missed this section of the 18th arrondissement. He had had a lot of fun and caused a lot of havoc here. The local wine festival provided his highest weekend earnings; picking the pockets of tourists that weekend was lucrative.

Distinctive houses with unique personalities lined the hilly streets in this neighborhood, different from the long blocks of generic apartment buildings on other Paris blocks. These houses nestled within enchanting gardens in varying hues of green interspersed with riotous summer flowers. He had tossed many empty wallets in the bushes of these homes.

Maximillian reached the vineyard, the size of a small city block with a six-foot wire wall that surrounded its perimeter. Here the buildings were taller and the vineyard looked defenseless against the encroaching city.

The vineyard had been a secret garden of delights when Maximillian was a kid. In mid-October, the crisp days of autumn signaled the arrival of the biggest party in town. The annual Fête des Vendanges brought thousands of people to the Butte and the local children roamed the streets filled with food carts, art and craft vendors, and activities for all. The vineyard opened for the festival and when he and his siblings were young, they had run, up and down and among the grapevines, playing Hide and Seek and trying to avoid authorities.

When he was a problematic teenager, he and his friends had taken advantage of the influx of tourists, but they participated in the festivities too: concerts, dance performances and tastings. The festival finished with fireworks set off from behind the cathedral of Sacré Coeur Basilica.

Maximilian had met Émilie at the harvest festival two years before. He had first kissed Émilie under the fireworks; the image now reminding him of sizzling romantic nights. Last time he was in this part of town; he was a different man, exploiting everyone. Now he stayed out of trouble; his life with Émilie was worth the change. Why was he here then, with contraband under his arm?

Stashing the package behind a thick planting, Maximillian opened the door to the little outbuilding that sold tickets and gifts, handing the attendant exact change for the entrance fee.

"Where are you from?" The pleasant woman, wearing large hoop earrings, a dark strip parting her blond hair, deposited his fee in her cash drawer.

"Montmartre." She raised her brows, eyes watchful. It was a question asked of tourists and the usual response wasn't Montmartre. He followed the garden path that led to the old building housing the Musée de Montmartre.

Documenting the archeology and history of Montmartre village life, the house was the oldest in town and was once a studio for visiting artists. Renoir, among other noteworthy artists worked there. His sister loved the place. Unexpectedly, Maximillian yearned to see her.

"Bonjour, Mimi." Maximillian silently walked up to her and putting his arms around her from behind her back, kissed her cheeks. "Surprise."

"Bonjour. Maximillian. Why are you here? Aren't you working?" She turned within his arms, throwing hers around his neck. Damn, Maximillian hadn't thought this through. He would have to explain the fire.

"We had a fire at the restaurant today, everyone had to get out—fast. It began in the kitchen, burned the back wall. Not too much damage."

"Is everyone all right?"

"Yes. I need help. Monsieur Dubois let me keep something in the back room. I had to take it when the building burned. Will you store it here?"

"What is it?" Mimi asked.

"A painting. I'll pick it up soon."

"You're not in trouble again, are you?"

"No. Things are great. I have good news. Émilie is . . . we are having a baby."

"Maximillian!" Mimi ran into his arms again. "How exciting. I thought you didn't like babies."

"Things change. We don't have room in our apartment for the painting. Just store it a couple of days."

"How big is it? When will you pick it up?"

"Not too big, I have it outside. No later than Saturday." Maximillian spouted his quickly thought-up responses. "I'll be off a while, so I can find a place." Mimi agreed. After retrieving the painting, Mimi led him to a basement storage area. Perfect. He hugged her; he had forgotten how much he liked his sweet sister.

Whew! Went better than expected. Fooled her again.

Chapter XII Michel

THURSDAY MORNING AT ten minutes to eleven o'clock, Vincent Gensonné barged into Michel's office without knocking or greeting him, abnormal behavior for the formal lawyer.

"Where's my son? Have you seen André?" Vincent Gensonné stopped in front of Michel's desk, ran his hand through his hair, and planted both hands on his hips, jacket flipped open.

"Not yet. Why?" Michel stood.

"He's not here and didn't answer his mobile," Vincent stated. "He has an appointment in ten minutes. André wouldn't miss an appointment."

"He would've called Marie. What else?"

"Philippe Dubois called Marie, asked for André, said it was urgent. But Marie hasn't heard from him."

"What should I do?" Michel asked.

"I'll meet André's client. You call Dubois. We will take it from there. Call me on my mobile, interrupt the appointment if you need to." Vincent spun around, rushed through the door, and then abruptly turned back.

"Wait. André spent the day in Montmartre yesterday, looking for Bertrand. Begin there." Vincent took off again, and stopped at the door, tossed a few words back. "Call Dubois first." He was gone.

Damn. Vincent was agitated. André would notify Marie if he were running late, something must have happened. Michel opened Dubois' electronic file and called the listed contact number. No answer at Chez Philippe. Strange, it was nearly lunchtime for the thriving restaurant, also no answer from Dubois' mobile. Voice mail responded. He hurried to Marie's office; Dubois must have left a number.

"Marie, do you have—?" Michel asked, careening through the open office door. She extended a note, her head tipped toward the phone clutched against her shoulder.

"Monsieur Dubois left this number, Vincent charged off before I could give him . . ." Marie lifted her shoulders, shaking her head. "He's beside himself. André is fine." Her tone was measured, reassuring. She had worked with André for years, competent and reliable, too professional to display worry. But her hand quivered when she held out the paper.

Michel dialed as he strode back to his office. "Monsieur Dubois? Michel la Roche. I work—Whoa. Speak slower. Yes?" Dubois rattled on about a fire and André's mobile; he was an excitable man with nervous energy evidenced the night they'd eaten at Chez Philippe.

"I've got it. You've had a kitchen fire; the restaurant is closed and André was with you when it burned." Michel consolidated his rambling, listening as he chattered.

"And you have André's mobile phone." It explained why André hadn't answered, but not why he was absent.

"I'll let André know. When did he leave yesterday?" Dubois said he and his wife had left André at a neighborhood café around three.

"Merci. André will call you. He's not available. Is this the number where we can reach you? Your wife's mobile? You have lost your mobile too." He rang Vincent's personal number, and apprised him of Dubois' news.

"I'm going to André's apartment. I have a key. I'll call when I get there." Michel updated Vincent Gensonné about the Dubois call and dashed back to André's office. "Marie, I'm leaving. Vincent took André's appointment."

Leaden skies threatened rain, heavy clouds appearing like gray blankets ready to fall and smother the city. The atmosphere thick with moisture felt like they had already dropped. Michel arrived at André's apartment in record time, sweet-talking the familiar building attendant to gain access. Michel fumbled with the key, dropped it, and swore. Perhaps the automatic locks connected to André's remote would prevent entry. He inserted the key again and heard the mechanism click.

The apartment appeared to be empty, and too quiet. He checked around the living areas and sprinted for André's bedroom, found him lying on his stomach, naked, perpendicular across his bed. Michel's heart stopped, thudding against his chest walls. André's prone body appeared dead.

"André." Michel's shout blasted across the room. He dashed to the bed, grabbed André's shoulders and shook him. André stirred. He was alive! "What's wrong with you? You scared the hell out of us." André struggled to get up, twisting to sit. He hunched his back, his legs hanging over the edge of the bed, head drooping, appearing groggy or drugged.

Michel rushed to André's bathroom, grabbed a towel and his black robe. His mobile rang. He tossed the robe at André and went outside the bedroom, pulling his phone from his pocket. Vincent's private number registered on his mobile.

"He's here, he overslept. I'll check back." Michel didn't wait for Vincent's reply.

"What's going on my friend?" Michel asked. He had softened his voice. Now André sat on the edge of the bed with his feet on the sideboard, his elbows on his knees and his head held in his hands. He hadn't donned the robe —or spoken.

"Your father said you went to Montmartre. Dubois called, he has your mobile. Something about a fire?" Michel prompted. André position remained unchanged; he said nothing. "How about coffee?" Michel turned toward the door. "Put your robe on. I'll be back."

Michel slammed doors and opened drawers, looking for the coffee gear. He finally found a small French press, filled a pot with water, turned on the burner.

When he returned to André's bedroom, he was groping for the sleeve of his robe. What was wrong with him?

"Coffee's about ready." At least he was standing. "Drink too much last night?" He held the robe for André. He moved his head no. "Get beat up?" No again. Michel led him to a chair in the living room, nudged him into it and turned to open the blinds. Billowy gray clouds blotted the sun, lifting the blinds made no difference in the indoor gloom. Michel switched on two lamps.

"You want me to shut up?" Michel asked. "That would be hard. Probably won't happen." Michel left, poured the hot water over fresh ground coffee beans, noted the time, and then checked on André. He sat slumped in his leather easy chair.

Michel pressed the coffee grounds, then balanced two brimming cups, handed one to André, melting into an adjoining chair.

"Drink up. I'm hungry. We're going out to lunch." André didn't answer. He gripped his cup, staring ahead, his robe gapping.

"You can't wear that. Even if you do look good in your robe." André tasted the coffee. Michel gave André space, although it killed him to keep quiet. Should he worry Vincent or try to handle this himself? His intuition told him to get André among people. However, he was clueless. What had caused André's strange behavior? Drumming his fingers on his chair arm, he considered his choices. Vincent should know André was . . . What? What could he tell a frantic father?

When André finished his coffee, Michel took the cups to the kitchen and noticed a sack on the floor. The odor of smoke overpowered him when he lifted it. André's jacket, pants, shirt and underwear were balled up inside; André had been close to the fire. Perhaps he was in shock. Michel didn't know the symptoms, but if he couldn't get André to leave his apartment, he would have to call Vincent. Michel wrestled with the mocking demon in his conscience; Vincent expected more information.

"You need to eat. Get dressed." André's forearms felt hot as he pulled him upright, then nudged him from behind, into his bedroom. He plopped back onto the tangled sheets. Michel found jeans, a button-down shirt and underwear. This man was too orderly. Tossing them onto the bed, he left André. "Get dressed, you don't want me dressing you."

He googled shock on his mobile, "intense emotional reaction to a stressful situation or bad news." Hmm. It wasn't the medical definition of shock, although it might explain André's abnormal behavior. Perhaps the fire was the cause. Michel waited for fifteen minutes and then checked on him.

André sat on his bed, slumped forward; however, he was dressed. No shoes. Michel perused the lined-up shoes that looked like giant piano keys, choosing a casual pair and tossing them at his feet. "Put them on, let's go." Michel had an idea which might interest André, jolt him out of this. The threat of rain had turned into a downpour.

"Umbrellas, where's the umbrellas?" While he waited for André to put on his shoes, he called Vincent, rummaging in a front closet as he spoke. "We're going to lunch, we won't be back."

"May I speak to André?"

"He's . . . indisposed. I'll have him call."

"I'll cover his appointments. This is unusual, is he all right?"

"Yes. Later." Michel winced, he wasn't a good liar, and deceiving Vincent? Michel hoped he could snap André out of this—before his parents saw him.

André shuffled out of the bedroom, trailing his shoe laces. Michel handed him one umbrella, stooped over his shoes and tied the laces. He was like a giant toddler. He pushed him out of the apartment and walked beside him, hustling to the nearest Métro station.

The d'Orsay would be a good choice for lunch. Art museums inspired André's passion for paintings, and the d'Orsay had three restaurants; they could eat at one of them. André didn't speak on the Métro although he looked less miserable. His eyes brightened when Line 12 stopped at the Solférino Station near the museum. When they exited the tunnel, the now stronger wind caused havoc with umbrellas, and they joined others struggling to keep their own from flipping inside out. André's lips moved. Was it a smile?

The skirmish with the wind and rain roused André, but Michel groaned, a straggling line of contiguous umbrellas wound around the perimeter of the building, snaking away from large plate glass doors. Restless tourists awaited entry; rainy days ensured high-traffic for museums. Michel had forgotten June was prime time for the d'Orsay.

"I have a museum membership. We can enter at the door. Bypass the line." Made sense. André hung around museums more than anyone he knew.

"Great. My legs are wet." Michel followed André through the revolving doors.

The Musée d'Orsay was in the center of Paris on the banks of the Seine across from the Tuileries Garden. The Musée was originally the Orsay railway station and hotel built for the World Fair in 1900. Beautifully designed to complement the nearby Louvre, the building was itself a work of art. The transformation from train station to museum took years, but by 1986, the d'Orsay displayed art encompassing the 1848 to 1914 timeframe.

Michel and André wandered the grand central aisle on the main floor. The glass roof with its protective shades and the immense proportions of the space generated a fair amount of light despite the gray day. Exquisite sculptures occupied this majestic hall. A colossal gilded clock dominated the end of the vast gallery, visible against the backdrop of glass, one of many unusual clocks on the premises.

Michel was hungry, however, he allowed André to dictate their progress. André led them to the Impressionist Gallery and they spent more than an hour there; Michel's stomach had grumbled all morning, and it felt hollow now. Fortunately, they were near a café restaurant with a unique underwater ambience.

The Café Campana—an Art Nouveau-styled restaurant designed by the Campana brothers—lay beyond the Impressionist Gallery. The theme was a dream-like aquatic environment, too artsy for Michel. Burnished silver lamps hung over the tables and a shiny reflective blue wall enclosed one side. André understood this Art Deco stuff. When they entered, André's face paled.

"Get. Me. Out. Of. Here." André voice cracked, dangerously brittle. His body immobile, face waxen. Michel gripped his arm, apologized to the wait staff and led André out. His behavior perplexed Michel; he had eaten here with him. What had happened yesterday?

On Thursdays, the more upscale restaurant closed at 2:30 p.m., and reopened with special evening menus. The last option was the serve-yourself Café de l'Ours. The restaurant offered a simple menu of salads and sandwiches, desserts and drinks. When the men entered the café, the vast room with dozens of tables appeared full. Michel found an unoccupied table.

Michel left André and joined the self-serve line. He chose identical lunches: A Mozzarella, lettuce and tomato sandwich on hearty bread, mineral water, a Greek salad of tomatoes, cucumbers, feta and olives and chocolate mousse. waters.

Although the rise and fall of dozens of languages filled the large café, André sat motionlessly as Michel ate. The cozy atmosphere amid myriad conversations was a perfect rainy day haven. André stared over Michel's shoulder, unfocused on the pleasant scene. Managing to eat one piece of his sandwich, André left the salad and dessert untouched. Michel slid the water bottle near André's hand and he mechanically picked it up.

"Thank you . . . for coming . . .for lunch."

"You'd be there for me." Michel indicated André's uneaten lunch. "Didn't like my selections?"

"I'm not hungry."

When Michel finished eating, he covered André's hand with his own.

"What happened my friend?"

André's eyes reflected an intensity that disarmed Michel. However, Michel was determined André should verbalize his feelings. Minutes stealthily crept by, reminding him of his stint with Bertrand at the bistro. André shifted in his seat and sighed.

"There was a fire at Dubois' restaurant when I arrived, screaming people pouring out the doors. I ran in to help; thought I could save whomever was still inside. When I got home . . . in the shower . . . I remembered . . . I couldn't save my brother." André put his head onto his palms, looking down at the café table. Michel was stunned. What was the right response? André needed a professional, not him. A dozen questions clogged Michel's brain. Before he could speak, André continued.

"I was standing under the water and then, I was . . . back in Corsica . . . searching black water for my brother. I dived and dived . . . into the water. I couldn't find him; I abandoned my brother." Again, André stopped.

Damn, that's why the aquatic-themed Café Campana had repelled André. Michel remained silent. He had never heard the details of how Pierre had died, the sketchy sentences André uttered didn't help him understand, but Michel sensed it was better to listen than ask for clarification. Let André spill it out.

"I had buried those memories for seventeen years. What day is it? July first will be seventeen years since he died."

"June 27." Michel moved his chair beside André and put his arm around his friend. They sat side by side. Michel prayed André recognized he loved him; that he could overcome renewed grief for Pierre. André eventually walked out of the café without assistance. Had the Musée d'Orsay been the right choice? Michel trusted God; it was right.

MICHEL HAD CALLED Vincent. He gave him a brief update noting André needed his parents. André dozed on the Métro, awaking when the train stopped. At the station, Michel hailed a cab, directing the driver to Vincent and Sophia's home. André disembarked from the back seat like a zombie. His sloped shoulders and bowed head concealing his personality, he leaned on Michel who carefully navigated the familiar sidewalk.

The door stood open. Relief suffused Michel when they reached André's worried parents. Vincent and Sophia enfolded them in their arms. Michel pulled away, remaining close. His weary body ached, his heart bleeding for his sorrowing friend. The Gensonné family had included him in their fold since they had first met. They were family.

Her arm around his waist, Sophia led André to her kitchen, seating him near her as she finished dinner preparations. Vincent brought Michel a glass of wine, sitting in an adjoining chair, his eyes periodically glancing toward the kitchen.

"Go to André," Michel said. "I'm fine." Vincent poured a glass for André, nodding toward Michel. André walked to the couch and Vincent sat next to him, his arm resting on André's leg. A savory aroma emanated from the oven and soft music permeated the comfortable room with its timeworn furnishings.

Sophia served coffee after dinner, and then . . . and then André told his story. After the fire, and his cleansing shower, he had remembered every long-buried detail of the boating accident.

André asked his parents to tell him what they had experienced that day. They complied, although they hadn't spoken of it until tonight.

André had buried the circumstances of his twin's death and Sophia and Vincent had decided it best to nurture the rest of their children during that trying time. The girls had been much younger and they had sought normalcy in everyday life. The Gensonné family members separately grieved and had never connected in their loss. Anguish still burned inside all of them despite the years.

The evening had been cathartic for the Gensonné family. Intuitively, he hadn't said too much. Someone had guided him. He thanked his God. Michel believed He had been present.

Chapter XIII Bertrand

THE SUN SOAKED into Bertrand's skin promising a glorious summer day; Sunday had finally crept forward and his girls would arrive this morning. Jean-Paul Bertrand sat on a slatted folding chair in front of an easel, killing restless time by painting the ivy-covered stone and his green door.

The high stone wall curved out of sight obstructing his view of the narrow street, he would see them when they cleared the curve. Anticipation livened his body, his hand brushing quick, light strokes onto the variegated green leaves emerging beneath his brush. His palette exhibited a continuum of the green shades he had dabbed onto his canvas.

"Grand-papa, Grand-papa."

His granddaughters darted around the corner. Bertrand's old body creaked when he got up, hard to sit long now. Tenderness engulfed him when he saw his daughter following her daughters who skimmed along the sidewalk toward him.

"How are my babies?" His legs ached as he stooped for a hug.

"I'm not a baby, Grand-papa. I'm a big girl," Simone said. "I'm five."

"You are a big girl."

"Nicole's a baby."

"I'm not a baby." Nicole pouted her bottom lip. "I'm a big girl too."

"You're both big girls." Charlotte said, long red-gold hair swirling around her shoulders, carrying a basket and looking like her mother had when he fell in love with her. Setting the basket at her feet, she engulfed her father in a hug, kissing his cheeks. "You look great, Papa. You had me worried."

"I know, I know. I'm fine now." He moved to his easel and swiftly painted *Grand-papa's Door* over the top of the green rectangle.

"You may take this home, Simone." He handed it to her. "Be careful till it dries."

"I want to paint something," she said as she held the painting, arms outstretched. "Grand-papa's Door," she read. "It says Grand-papa's door. Thank you."

"Hand it to your mother. "I have a surprise inside." Bertrand clasped the girls' hands and waited for Charlotte.

"I knew it," said Nicole. Simone rolled her eyes. Bertrand was predictable, he usually bought them something, they had Grand-papa figured out.

"Papa, this door is heavy," Charlotte said, plunking the picnic basket, and adding the painting on top. She pulled with both hands.

"I know, I know."

The princess doll delighted Nicole, she skipped to her mother. "I love her," she said, but Simone set her doll aside when she saw the watercolors.

"Grand-papa, I want to paint."

"We'll paint later, at the park." His eyes met Charlotte's and she hugged him.

"Love you Papa." She whispered against his neck.

"I know, I know."

"You seem nervous, Papa. Are you sure you're all right?"

"Yes, ye—." He stopped. Repeating himself was a nervous habit. "Are we ready to go on a picnic? I've bought a kite."

"Yes." Both girls jumped up and down, clapping their hands. Bertrand collected the kite and painting supplies; his daughter lifted the basket.

"Let's go," he said. "We're going to the Parc des Buttes-Chaumont. Follow me, let's march." He moved his right foot. "Right, left, right, left." The little girls imitated him; Charlotte took her place at the end. She smiled, lifting one thumb and her right leg.

Bertrand and his wife had taken Charlotte to the same park when she was little. The Parc des Buttes-Chaumont was less crowded than others were. It was farther out from the city center, in the 19th arrondissement. Parisians picnicked there and walked its many trails, and unlike other parks, it was permissible to loll on the grass. A great place to paint and walk dogs. A replica of an Italian temple perched onto a cliff on the island and two picturesque bridges connected the island to the land below. Ducks and geese, and bees, birds and flowers, thrived. Simone was about to receive her first painting lesson.

"I haven't been there in ages, Papa. The girls will love it."

The Métro ride was short; they got off at the Botzaris Station, each carrying something. "This park has been here 150 years. Workers planted the trees and bushes a long time ago, and even the lake and waterfall are manmade." The girls lagged by the time they had reached the lake. "Let's stop here and eat so we can see the island."

"My feets is tired, Grand-papa," Nicole said. Bertrand set down his satchel, scooping her up, while his daughter spread a blanket.

Charlotte had packed a baguette, cold cuts and fruit, along with chocolate pastries. Birds performed flybys for handouts while they were eating. "Don't feed them," his daughter warned. "They'll eat all our food before we can." The children performed little songs they had learned at school, picking at their food, running to hug their Grand-papa in between bites. The birds continued to circle the little picnic, Charlotte was adamant. "Don't feed the birds." She was a lot stricter than he and his wife were, but Charlotte was right. The birds would signal their friends.

Charlotte repacked the food handing Simone and Nicole bread to feed the birds. "Take it towards the lake, away from the blanket." The girls ran down the grassy knoll with the birds hovering.

"Thanks for bringing them." Charlotte nodded, repacking the picnic, then sitting with him, leaning her head against his shoulder.

"Thanks, Papa. This was a good idea." Nicole wandered back to the blanket, crabby-faced, whining.

"Maman?" Nicole said. She rubbed her eyes and Charlotte pulled the sleepy child onto her lap.

"Simone may paint with you; Nicole needs a nap."

Simone encircled his neck with her arms, her skin baby-soft against his. "I love you, Grand-papa."

"Love you too, baby—err Simone. Ready?" Bertrand emptied his satchel, set an easel for himself, and a smaller one for her. "What do you want to paint?"

"The castle." Simone pointed to the top of the island.

"Good choice. That is a temple on top of the cliff. It looks like an ancient Roman Temple—copied from Tivoli in Italy." He handed her a pencil.

"What do you see?"

"A castle on a high hill."

"Use the pencil to draw the big things you see. The pencil marks should be real light." Simone clutched the pencil, drawing faint lines, concentrating; his heart ached, her innocence overwhelming. It had been a rough couple of weeks. Maximillian could jeopardize everything. Bertrand hunched his shoulders, shuddering. Nevertheless, Maximillian was gone now.

"Grand-papa, you're not watching," Simone said. "Am I doing it, right?"

Bertrand squared his shoulders banishing Maximillian's sharp face. "You're the artist, it's right if you decide it's right." Bertrand prepared watercolors for Simone, showing her how to hold her brush, holding her hand to make the first strokes. After a few swipes, he encouraged her to create her own.

She painted with her face scrunched in diligent wrinkles and changed colors by swishing her brush in the murky cup of water. Her paper wrinkled from excess water, a mass green and blue and a lot of dark brown with some blotches of yellow and pink swimming on top.

"All done, Grand-papa." She came to him, leaning against his knee, her little body warm.

"Aah, a fine watercolor." He touched her dimpled hand. "An artist finishes her painting with her signature." She printed Simone in large letters. She laid the pencil down and rubbed her eyes, smearing paint onto her face.

"Tired? He sat on the blanket and she snuggled into his lap and fell asleep. Charlotte still nestled Nicole and a peaceful silence surrounded the blanket. Why did he worry so much when he had this? Maximillian and *Miriam* seemed far, far away.

"Charlotte, do you remember our visits here?"

"Yes. Mother's favorite. We imagined we were goddesses and hid in the grottos and among the bushes. Then we climbed to the temple. I remember the steep stairway."

"It's high. When the girls wake up, let's climb it, if my knee cooperates. Your mother loved the birds here: tits, wagtails, hedge-sparrows and lots more."

"Remember the black swans? I have a picture you painted when we were here one afternoon." He nodded; it had been a memorable day.

"You revised the painting after she died. You painted Maman as an angel overlooking the park and the swans."

"We didn't come much after she died." His eyes lingered on Nicole in Charlotte's lap. "Nicole looks like her."

Charlotte was gazed at her younger child; red-gold hair stuck to her pink-flushed forehead. "I think so, especially her eyes, but she still has a three-year old baby face." She kissed her eyebrow. They sat, holding the children, listening to the birds, the breeze caressing their skin, until Bertrand's protesting knees capitulated. He shifted, waking Simone.

"Grand-papa." She rubbed sleep away. "Let's fly the kite." Simone scrambled out of his lap and her sister stirred, snuggling in closer to her mother.

"Shh. Nicole's sleeping." He pushed himself from the blanket and retrieved the purple kite. Nicole awoke and he ushered the girls toward an open space. The wind had picked up some and now the bustle of late afternoon traffic beyond the park intruded, horns honking, engines idling. Bertrand ran with the kite, attempting to help it aloft. It was windy enough and soon the kite dipped and darted in the sky. Nicole tired of it sooner than the others did.

"The playground looks like a fun place. It's time to reel it in." Charlotte had used her mother voice. He rewound the string, and soon had the kite under control. It was about time; his arms ached.

"Who can get there first?" Charlotte said. And the two girls were off. Bertrand kept pace with his daughter as the girls darted across the grass. She tucked a loose strand of windblown hair behind her ear. "Papa? You're worried about something." He concentrated on walking, determinedly ignoring her. She grabbed his arm, stopping him.

"Papa, tell me what it is. Something's wrong."

"Nothing to worry about."

"Maybe I can help?"

"I had some trouble with a commission. It's been resolved."

"I hope you come to me—if you need help." Bertrand let her hug him. "You are thinner, Papa. Why don't you come and stay with us?"

"I like painting in Montmartre. I like my home."

"I know, maybe another time."

Bertrand excused himself to use the toilet located beyond the playground. A man stood at the first urinal, so he walked beyond him to the third one.

"Bertrand. Just who I wanted to see." Maximillian zipped his pants, moved beside Bertrand, nudging his shoulder, crowding too close. Bertrand's stream stopped.

"I c . . . c . . . can't h . . . h . . . help you." Bertrand zipped his own trousers, attempting to leave by pushing past Maximillian. But he was blocked by the younger man. He looked over Maximillian's shoulder, hearing Charlotte calling.

"Papa?" Are you all right?"

"My daughter—."

"Too bad, old man. I need to sell the *Miriam* painting. I have it hidden but I need to move it." He poked Bertrand with his pointed forefinger. "You find someone to fence our painting."

"N . . . no . . . It's not our painting." Maximillian shoved him towards an open gate leading to a service area containing dumpsters and paraphernalia related to park upkeep. He pushed at his chest, nudging him against the fence and out of sight of others who might use the toilets.

"You commissioned it," Bertrand whimpered. "And paid me. It's yours."

Maximillian placed both arms around him, using his body to shove him hard against the fence. "Think about it! I need a buyer." His body pressed too close, he glared into Bertrand's eyes. "I'll be in touch." He whirled away, leaving Bertrand alone.

Bertrand's body shook. Charlotte will worry. How long have I been here? I need to get out of town. Calm down, calm down. Control yourself. He waited, breathing hard, heart racing, scared. When the drumbeat in his ears subsided and he quit shaking, he emerged from behind the building. Charlotte paced near the corner of the building, frowning. She exhaled when she saw him.

"You were gone a long time, Papa."

"I know, I know. I'm tired, let's go home."

When they arrived at his green door, the children were exhausted and Bertrand felt ancient, barely able to shuffle his legs. Bertrand motioned for them to go in and leaned his folding chair against the stone wall. He sighed and collapsed against the ivy, the leaves prickling his neck. He must leave his home, he would tell Charlotte tonight.

Chapter XIV Maximillian

MIMI HAD CALLED and she was mad as hell. It had been five days and the *Miriam* painting was still in the storage room at the Musée de Montmartre—past her saintly deadline.

"Maximillian. I knew I couldn't trust you. The painting needs to go, you told me a couple of days." Mimi had called him at home. He fled to the stairwell to talk; she must have remembered he had Sunday off.

"I'm working on it." Maximillian spoke in a hard undertone. "I had to clean after the fire. I thought I'd have a few—".

"Come get it. I mean it, Max."

"I'll come." Maximillian disconnected, he'd almost shouted, shut up. Damn painting. Five days wasn't very long, Mimi was unreasonable. He had worked too many hours, hadn't had time to look for an underground connection. He had been away from petty crime for a while, plus he wasn't motivated. Émilie and the baby complicated things. He returned to their apartment to find Émilie dressing.

"Maximillian, It's Sunday. Let's do something fun."

"Like what."

"Let's go to the park for a picnic. I can get it ready quick." She hugged his neck, kissing behind his right ear, just where he liked it. Maybe he should toss the painting in the garbage dumpster where he dumped their trash in the gaping hole every morning. He and Émilie would be fine without extra money. Except he had so much invested besides money: time, expectations, dreams.

"I guess so." Maximillian stepped behind the curtained bedroom space and flopped backwards across the bed. Perhaps, Bertrand could find a buyer. He had access Maximillian didn't. He should be able to sell *Miriam*.

"Are you ready?" Émilie pushed the curtain aside. "Maximillian . . ." She had donned a shoulder bag. "Let's go to the Parc des Buttes-Chaumont." He jumped to his feet, stepping into his jeans.

"Pick a shirt." He zipped his jeans.

"I love black T-shirts. You look sexy in them; little skinny guys turn me on."

"Wondered what you saw in me." Maximillian pulled the black shirt over his head. He grabbed her for a quick kiss. "I have an errand in Montmartre. Hard to get everything done on my day off." He would look for the rat at the frame shop before he contacted Bertrand. His operating hours appeared haphazard, maybe he'd come to the door today.

Maximillian convinced Émilie to sit at an outdoor café a few blocks from his destination. He ordered her a drink and kissed the top of her head. "Wait here until I come back. It won't be long." He walked to the place he had run from five years before. The *Frames* sign had weathered even more, and if he hadn't been there before, he would have missed it. The proprietor must not sell many framing supplies; the shop blended in with its surroundings.

Seeing the frame shop sharpened his senses, he scouted around to see who was watching, and recognized the old man he had nicknamed the rat, just approaching the door. Maximillian charged toward him and arrived as he was turning the key.

"Remember me?" Maximillian gripped his arm.

"No."

"I brought you a painting by Elisée Maclet five years ago. We struck a deal. You said if I disguised it, you had a buyer. You backed out." Maximillian grabbed his shoulders and shook him, his watery eyes still looked beady. "You owe me."

"What do you want?"

"A buyer for the painting." Maximillian kept both hands around the man's thin upper arms; he could feel his bones under loose skin. The man had aged more than five years.

"I need time." The man attempted to disengage from his grip; Maximillian was stronger.

"How much? I need a quick sale."

"A week, maybe two. It's hard to fence stolen art."

"It's not stolen. I found it."

"Sell it on the legitimate market." The rat smirked. Maximillian let him go.

"How much do you take?"

"Twenty-five percent." The greedy man presumed he had an advantage. "May not find a buyer."

"I need you to store it. I'll be back in a couple of days." Maximillian turned and moved away. He whipped back around and stood toe-to-toe with him. "Get what you can for it. I want a sale." He jabbed his bony chest. "Fast."

Émilie was still reading at the café under a tree which partially shaded her book. Her ponytailed hair gathered with a red ribbon left her pretty neck exposed. What was wrong with him? Had his greed threatened their future? Rotten and despicable, he didn't deserve Émilie.

"Bonjour." Émilie looked at him when his shadow darkened her pages. She arose, kissing his lips. "Did you finish your errand?" She slipped her book into her bag and left Euro on the table. "Time to relax. With the fire and the clean-up, you've had a hard week."

The Parc des Buttes-Chaumont had become a favorite place for them. Émilie loved it. Paris's most romantic park, it was an idyllic spot and an escape from their tiny apartment. They had climbed to the temple many times and observed Montmartre from the heights of the cliff, necking under the canopy.

"Let's visit the temple," Émilie said.

"It's Sunday, too many people there."

"Please." She put her arm around his waist. He nodded and walked her through the green haven with its wide paths carved through emerald grass shaded by towering trees, some of them planted before the park opened in 1867. The bustle of Paris had been pushed back by this oasis.

Childish laughter chimed through the relative quiet. He closed his eyes, listening to birds chattering in the trees. Sunshine saturated his skin. Something crawled down the back of his neck; he snatched it. A caterpillar.

He studied the high bridge that soared to the top of the cliff with the temple atop; it had charmed Parisians for 150 years. He had missed this park. He shouldered Émilie's bag when they reached the bridge that led to the leafy island. Olive-green water surrounded the craggy chunk of land rising above the lake. A gray stone temple perched atop the island; its long pillars surrounded a small space resembling a too-tall wedding cake.

People wandered in and out of the tiny temple. He and Émilie sat on the circular bench in the middle. Periodically, people passed across their view of Paris. They were alone for a few minutes when she moved closer.

"We should get married." She touched his leg. "The baby." She caressed her abdomen.

He studied the side of her face, the curve of her cheek. Her bottom lip quivered, but she was calm. "Why?" His eyes lost focus. Marriage had never been in his vocabulary. Women. She couldn't mean it. She didn't know him well enough.

"I don't know. It seems right." Her clear eyes met his eyes; he looked away, embarrassed, grateful she couldn't read his thoughts. Sometimes he felt she could.

"We don't need to be married. To, love." More people ascended the steps to the temple. His arm went around her, drew her closer. "Let's think about it."

"I'm sure, Maximillian."

"You don't know me, what I was like, what I am now."

"I told you what I want. I want to be a family. Now you have to decide if it's what you want." The magic left and they descended until they found an empty bench along stone railings designed to look like wood. Émilie unloaded the lunch, handed him a sandwich, and took one for herself. She placed a bunch of grapes on a cloth between them.

"You're not upset?"

"No, I knew what you'd say." She sat in the sunshine. Serene. Beautiful. What should he do? A wise woman, how was she entangled with him? He would let her make the next move. They listened to conversations sifting through the greenery before they saw the approaching people. The park was busier in the summertime, but still peaceful. No tension existed; Émilie hadn't allowed its presence.

"Let's go home." She packed the leftovers; he held his arm out to carry her bag.

They stopped at the toilets before leaving. On the men's side, three rusty urinals lined the wall under an overhang attached to the building that housed the women's toilet. He was using the closest urinal as an older man shuffled to the end one. He zipped his jeans and glanced over, recognizing the hunched figure standing at the end urinal.

"Just the man I want to see." Maximillian hissed in Bertrand's ear. Then Maximillian had scared the shit out of the nervous old man, just because he could.

He left before the quaking nervous old man did, Émilie calmly awaiting farther along the path.

THE CHEZ PHILIPPE would not open until Friday. On Monday, Maximillian hung around Montmartre thinking about his old friends, other low-lifers from his past. Then he remembered Beau. He had found him working as a waiter in a café on the Place du Tertre last April. They had laughed together about how reckless, and stupid, they were in their youth. Beau had been a cohort in the old days; time to pay Beau a visit. Like him, he had a long handle, Beauregard—a name comparable to Maximillian.

"Bonjour, Beauregard." His old friend leaned back against a pole with a cigarette pinched between his thumb and forefinger. The colorful square behind him gyrated with its parade of tourists.

"Bonjour. Beau to you. What have you been up too?" His apron tied tight around his tall slender body, Beau flicked an ash. Beau had one of those changeable faces (and gray eyes) which transformed depending on his mood or his purpose. He cracked a smile, his mobile face moving like play-dough. Beau blew smoke out of his lungs.

"Max to you. Working most of the time." Maximillian came closer, slapping his arm, affectionately. "Got a minute?"

"What do you want?"

"Information. Do you know anyone buying art? With a shaky provenance?"

"Bad business, Max."

"Yeah. I happened onto something in 2007. I want to fence it; I'll make it worth your while."

"I don't know." Beau stubbed out his cigarette. "It's not the same. When we were young, we ran like wild horses. I've got more to lose; we had no future then."

"Know what you mean. Seems like a lot goes on in this square. If you find an opportunity, let me know. Here's my number." Maximillian slipped him a paper.

"What do you have?" Beau asked.

"A painting by Elisée Maclet."

"Did you steal it?" Beau stared at him, forcing him to look at his steel-gray eyes.

"No. Found it. Just took advantage." Maximillian faced Beau. "If you can help. Great. If not, fine. Good to see you."

"Same here." Beau leaned back onto the pole. "I've stayed clean for a couple of years." Maximillian left, when he glanced back, Beau was watching. Beau had been the worst of the bunch; he hoped he hadn't changed too much. Now for Bertrand.

Maximillian perused the Place du Tertre looking for the old painter; he was not in his usual spot. He climbed to the basilica crowning the top of the Butte; the church governed the top of Montmartre and provided the best views of the city. Hordes of people visited daily. Sacré-Coeur was a new church by Parisian standards at less than one hundred years old; it contained the largest bell in France. Maximillian wandered into the nave where tourists sat in the pews gazing at the mosaic ceiling.

He had to sidestep a couple in wedding attire posing for a photograph posing for a photograph in front of the historic church. The bride's white wedding gown billowed past his legs. Damn. Émilie had shocked him with the wedding crap.

He would never wed; marriage didn't fit his image.

Chapter XV Sophia and André

June 27-July 1, 2013

S OPHIA AND VINCENT hovered beyond the open front door and awaited André and Michel. Michel's cryptic phone call had warned them something was wrong and he was bringing André home. Time crawled as Vincent paced and Sophia alternated between checking the oven and checking the front door.

Sophia finally saw them approach through the open entranceway and she reached for Vincent's hand. What had happened to her son?

André leaned onto the shorter Michel like and an older man. She gripped Vincent's hand harder and blinked fast determined to remain strong. Then André was inside and enfolded in their arms.

The four of them had eaten dinner and then talked until midnight. André shared his revived memories of the accident; he had never spoken to his parents of that terrifying night.

André was better but they had agreed healing must include his sisters. Friday morning, Sophia invited Celeste, Isabelle, and their husbands for dinner—without the children.

She began preparations early. Sophia believed food nourished the essence of the spirit and the body. Her heart ached for her son and preparing a meal for others alleviated her own pain.

Sophia had married into this prominent French family, although her genes were Greek. When she was content, she cooked, when she was happy, she cooked, and today, when her heart was broken, she cooked. Sophia measured and poured love into preparing meals for her family. Selecting the finest ingredients and using original recipes, she displayed her finest food artistry in the meal's presentation.

The three men had canceled Friday's appointments, so Michel, Vincent and André helped; Sophia delighted in their high-spirited antics.

"Michel. What are you doing?" André asked. He bent over, laughing. "Look, Maman, even I know that gadget is for dried herbs." Michel had ground fresh basil into goo using her stone mortar and pestle.

"Maman didn't cook much, so I don't know much." He carried the stone bowl to the sink. "Papa was a baker and made our meals. Simple ones, involving bread." André threw a towel at his head, he grinned and ducked.

"Wash out the mess and dry the bowl with that flying towel," Sophia said. When he set the clean mortar in front of her, she sprinkled in some dried basil.

"This is for grinding dried herbs and spices." She demonstrated. "It will be your job now." A smile flickered across Michel's expressive face. Then she shooed them away with another towel snatched from her shoulder. "Go. You and André are banished to the garden. Papa can stay." Vincent's eyes espoused his love, although he said nothing.

"Vincent? The girls will be here soon. Are we doing the right thing?" Vincent pulled her close and nuzzled her neck.

"We'll be all right. I love you, Sophia." His eyes glistened, he turned quickly and moved into the living room. A cork popped, she envisioned the sizzle of the sparkling wine. Another cork popped.

The front door bursts open. "Bonjour, Maman and Papa." Celeste rushed in ahead of Isabelle, Dominic and Christophe. "What happened? Why dinner without the children?" She kissed both sides of her mother's cheeks, leaning back to grasp her mother's forearms, questioning with her eyes.

"You'll find out at dinner." Sophia reassured Celeste, then kissed Isabelle. "I sent Michel and André out to the garden. Dominic, will you bring them inside?"

The family gathered and Sophia offered a blue stoneware plate arranged with cucumber and tomato slices sprinkled with balsamic vinaigrette reduction and dusted with goat cheese; a selection of olives accompanied the vegetables. Vincent served them white sparkling wine and lifted his glass.

"To our family." Vincent toasted. Their daughters and sons-in-law exchanged bewildered glances, their faces reflecting confusion. Children had always been included in this family.

Vincent and Sophia, Celeste and Dominic, Isabelle and Christophe and their friend Michel encircled the ancient wooden table. André sat opposite his father at the foot. Six pairs of eyes focused on hers. "Let's eat. I'm famished." Laughter rewarded her.

The old walls of the house settled around her family like a membrane protecting a vital organ. The large room was the family hub with the kitchen stretched across the back and low cabinets topped with marble countertops separating the dining area. The ell-shaped great room framed two sides of the open dining room. Heavy wooden posts supported the open spaces and various furniture groupings offered vignettes of intimacy. The front door opened onto the great room, welcoming friends and family into the warmth of the home and the subtleties of the Gensonné lifestyle.

"André wants to . . ." Sophia hesitated, swallowing the thickness in her throat. "André will tell you." She rose from her seat and walked to her kitchen. When she returned, she carried two small plates of Salmon Tartare. Celeste and Isabelle followed her and returned with other plates. Sophia had marinated Salmon belly in olive oil, lemon juice, minced chives and shallots for an hour, and then sliced the salmon into paper-thin pieces. Toasted bread accompanied the course. Sophia nodded at André.

"You're curious." André concentrated on each person individually before speaking. "I don't know what Maman told you, but I want to talk about Pierre. About the accident. I didn't remember much from that awful day. It hurt . . . to think . . . about . . ." Celeste and Isabelle reached for their husband's hands. Vincent went to Sophia, encircled her with his arms, and laid his head onto hers. Michel bowed his head. André's continued in a measured tone reflecting newfound understanding of the fateful day.

"It was an accident. We had sailed all afternoon with our friends and returned to Calvi Bay at dusk. Pierre lifted the anchor holding his lifejacket in the other hand. Another larger boat passed us creating a huge wake which rocked our sailboat. He slipped over the edge and disappeared. I dove in immediately, but I never saw him or even touched him. He was gone."

The family had retreated into themselves, into their own thoughts, stone still. The Grandfather clock in the dining room corner tapped a consistent rhythm, normally unheard.

"I came to the surface and then back under the water, over and over. It got darker but I couldn't leave him in the angry water." André paused. Sophia cried silently, tears oozing from the corners of her eye. blouse. "It seemed like hours. The night was black—the sky, the water, black."

André glanced at her, questioning. Sophia's tattered heart whimpered but she held his gaze, encouraging him.

"Someone pulled me out of the water; someone else slapped me." André's eyes darkened. "Maman and Papa waited on the dock for us, me and Pierre. But I had left our brother in the sea." Tears slipped down Celeste and Isabelle's faces.

"It wasn't your fault André." Sophia whispered. "You were just a boy."

"I know, Maman." André spoke softly, gently holding her gaze. "Now I know. I didn't then."

"When you and Maman and Papa came back without Pierre," Isabelle said, "Celeste and I were scared. No one told us anything. No one talked for two days."

"I remember when the police came," Celeste said. "They found his body. We cried, but no one remembered we were there in the hotel. We were little girls, but we realized how awful it was. Even if we didn't comprehend the finality of Pierre's death."

"I'm sorry." Sophia rushed to Celeste and hugged her, and then embraced Isabelle. "Your father and I were shattered. Not thinking clearly."

"We were sad," Celeste said.

"And so, young," Isabelle whispered.

Silence deafened the room after Isabelle's last words, each person remembering.

The pain of the intervening years descended onto Sophia's shoulders. Had she been wrong to reopen the wound? Her grieving family had lived this once. Twice was torture. Then her son spoke.

"This conversation is long overdue. Our family needs to remember so we heal. Please?" André smiled at the family gathered around the battered wooden table. "Remember this?" He tapped his wine glass against the largest dent. "Pierre tried to crack a stone on the table, thought there was gold in it." Some of them smiled. "I own some of the dents too." The silence became unbearable; Sophia's body felt empty, like the outside would cave inside. André continued.

"I had blocked the accident from my memory, but now I want to embrace his life. We need to accept his death, grieve and then remember our brother. He lived with us, he loved us, and he was fun."

Sophia rose from the table, tears streaming. Pierre was always inside her thoughts and prayers, although none of her children comprehended it. André half-stood, she waved him away, pointing to the kitchen.

Her hands trembled as she served the golden Cornish hens and baby organic vegetables that had roasted in the oven—with Vincent's help.

"About time we ate, I thought I'd ground basil for nothing," Michel said. Intense emotion changed to tearful laughter.

Then Sophia's sorrow dissipated through her pores. Her body felt delicate and pure, unencumbered and almost unrecognizable. She had carried the load for a long time.

Her three remaining children shared memories of life with the incorrigible pair of brothers. The identical twins had played tricks on all. Pierre was the playful brother and André more serious; but if his brother had a crazy idea; André helped him execute the dastardly deed. Dominic, Christophe and Michel hadn't known Pierre but Sophia observed their silent support and was thankful for their presence. The family mingled until late, hugging often and laughing freely, although a few tears lingered. All her children slept in their home that night, including Michel. What would they have done without Michel this weekend?

Sophia regretted the lost years, although she was grateful for the dissolution of fear and distrust that had shaped their family for so long. She pulled back the covers and got into bed. She had failed to reach her beloved son despite her empathy and her mothering.

Hope danced inside now. She hugged Vincent's body, spooning him close. "I love you." She moved closer. "André is better now."

"Yes." Vincent turned and hugged her. "I love you. Thank you for tonight. And for our family."

Sophia sensed the old home sigh with relief, now content their grown children and their spouses slept peacefully within.

Monday, July 1, 2013

HOPE SWEAPT THROUGH André like a wispy spring breeze as he ascended the hilly street near Chez Philippe. Usually July first heralded grief as it was the anniversary of his brother's death. Not today. The sun slipped from behind frothy clouds splattered across the deep blue Montmartre sky. His body felt light and buoyant after his awakening from buried sorrow.

Memories ignited by the restaurant fire and consumed through his family catharsis had transformed him. The painting mystery stimulated him now; he needed his misplaced mobile to call Charlotte Bertrand. His leg brushed against a pungent lavender border, a flight of yellow butterflies drifting from the purple spikes. Would he have noticed before?

Bless my mother, the words flitted and danced balletically in the shadows of his mind. Was it a prayer? How had that come in? He gave up divine favor from God as a teen. Belief in His intervention in daily life disappeared long before the boating accident. However, after Michel had rescued him; Sophia had worked another miracle.

Chez Philippe hummed with activity just five days after the catastrophic fire. Tables and chairs occupied the sidewalk in front of the restaurant and two men armed with rags and buckets were scrubbing each one. The empty dining room buzzed with restaurant staff who washed walls and polished chandeliers. The floors had been waxed and polished.

Monsieur Dubois bustled up to André. "Bonjour, Monsieur Gensonné. I'm grateful." The chef embraced André. "I'm sorry about this." He held up André's mobile. "I wasn't myself."

"I've been using my business mobile." André closed his hand over it. "Thanks. I need this one. Essential information."

"Come to the kitchen, just the back wall burned," Dubois said. "Most of the mess is water and smoke damage. We reopen on Friday."

"Good news." André followed him inside where a construction crew had pulled the stoves away from the walls and removed burned wallboard.

"What about the murals?"

"They're gone," Dubois said. He hesitated, scrunching his shoulders. "No need for concern now, eh?" Dubois winked.

André privately agreed. "What are your plans?"

"I purchased the adjoining building last year. I'll enlarge the kitchen here and here." Dubois gestured to the affected walls. "That'll almost double the dining space. Thanks to your firm, I have the permits and the construction workers begin soon. I'll remain open during most of the renovation."

"You're doing well." André patted his pocket. "Thanks for my mobile. Au revoir." Dubois encouraged him to leave via the back door.

He walked past the same area where he had prodded Dubois through last week, an uncaptured memory nudging him. What was it, something important?

André stopped at an outdoor café to make his call discovering his mobile had lost its charge and Charlotte's number was in the directory. The helpful woman at the art gallery was closer than his office; he took a shortcut.

"Bonjour. Remember me?" André greeted the same young woman.

"Bonjour. Did you talk to Charlotte Bertrand?"

"Not yet. Do you close the gallery for lunch? Will you eat with me?" André lifted his eyebrows.

"Yes, yes to both questions." She stroked her hair.

"Will you recommend a place?"

"Of course, I'll get my bag." When she returned, she flipped a sign that announced the afternoon closure.

"My name is André Gensonné."

"Nancy Legrand." She giggled like a school girl. "There's a tiny café near here, no menu. The owners bring you something delicious."

"Aah, a neighborhood café, the locals hide the best ones."

They walked one long block to the red door with Evelyn's Café neatly lettered onto the imbedded glass window. A curvy middle-aged woman pointed to a table deep within the narrow room. Pairs of people sat at more than half of the six tables lined along each wall with an aisle separating them. White linen topped tables were set with two yellow napkins and a yellow tulip. André pulled out Nancy's chair and seated himself.

"I'm intrigued," he said.

"Wait until you taste the food."

"Bonjour." Evelyn carried two glasses of white wine. Her hair was piled atop her head, curling tendrils brushing her flushed face.

"Bonjour, Evelyn." Nancy reached for the glass and tasted. "Her wine selections are exemplary."

"Yes." The wine was good. Evelyn returned with a yellow plate of four batter-fried artichokes drizzled with aged balsamic vinegar and sprinkled with minced basil. André savored the first bite.

"Good?" Evelyn asked.

"Good." They finished the appetizer, secluded amid the murmur of other diners.

"Would you give me Charlotte Bertrand's mobile number again? I misplaced my phone and it needs a charge."

She lifted one shoulder, tilting her head. "I've regretted . . . it was unprofessional. Charlotte Bertrand is my friend and her father is our client." She changed position in her chair.

André waited; he did have it stored in his personal mobile. He toyed with his wine glass.

"I'll give it to you again." She searched in her purse and pulled out her mobile.

"Thanks. Why did you give it to me last time?"

"You handed me your business card. Your name was the same as the firm's name. And I liked you." The color rose from her neck to her forehead. She read her friend's mobile number aloud.

"Maybe, I shouldn't—." Despite what he just said, he punched the number into his business mobile.

"It's okay," she said, although she absently tugged her hair. The next course arrived; a salad comprised of a red pepper stuffed with crab puree.

"Did you enjoy the artichokes?" Evelyn asked.

"Superb." André lifted his glass toward her. Evelyn bustled to the next table.

"Thank you." I want to talk to Charlotte's father about a painting, not one of those you have at your gallery. Another one." Nancy played with her fork, tracing a tiny circle. "He's a fine painter. Do you sell many of his paintings?"

"We sell more when we host a show; but his work sells moderately well in the gallery. He has attracted a following. And, an American—." Nancy glanced around, then drew closer to him. "An American businessman found our gallery. He bought six of M. Bertrand's paintings for his corporate offices. He ordered six the following year and six more this year."

The unsolicited information surprised André; the lunch had been beneficial. The food was great too. "He must be pleased."

"Charlotte is too. He's a good man, good father."

"Voila!" Evelyn carried two yellow plates with creamy Risotto encircled with thick grilled scallops. She set them with a flourish and returned to refill their wine glasses.

André toasted Nancy. "Looks delicious. Cheers."

When they finished, André paid for lunch and accompanied Nancy to the gallery, leaving her at the door with a cheek-to-cheek kiss. Within seconds, he had punched in Charlotte Bertrand's phone number as he strode down the street.

Charlotte Bertrand didn't answer.

Chapter XVI Anne

Saturday, July 6, 2013

RESPLENDENT ON THIS early July morning, the Jardin des Tuileries shimmered in the sun. Anne jogged through the gardens scattered with a few other runners, but mostly with people enjoying the park. Vast walkways of packed hard gravel crunched beneath her feet and a light flower-scented breeze cooled her skin. Parisians ambled among the plantings and lounged around the ponds, contemplating the water and the statuary.

Anne imagined centuries of history emblazoned onto these majestic grounds. The Tuileries garden took its name from the site where 16th century Parisians made tile out of the clay soil. The first royal garden open to the public, the Tuileries evolved through the specifications of multiple kings, queens and rulers. Encompassing hundreds of years of brutal French history, the gardens had evolved to this smaller version; but the gardens retained their original beauty.

Anne felt like a knee-high child looking up at giant adults when she passed the massive sculptures, statues and memorials of the outdoor museum. The Louvre situated east of the gardens stretched its window-decorated arms toward the Tuileries. Her runs released tension and suppressed undesirable thoughts, although she suspected running indicated a need—perhaps a need to escape from her past.

The dramatic statuary and symmetrical shrubbery along the structured layout of the pathways, ponds and flower gardens exemplified the vitality of Paris for her. The romantic city was the most visited capitol in the world. Anne's equilibrium had returned three weeks after the diplomatic event at the embassy, its evenness now like the tops of the manicured hedges in the gardens close to the Louvre.

Anne savored her picnic lunch in the Napoleon Courtyard as she observed people in front of the Louvre Pyramid, mostly tourists performing vacation-style antics. Irresistible pedestals had been placed in front of the iconic glass pyramid. Visitors mounted them and faced cameras, displaying angled arms to mimic the angles of the pyramid or pretending to be horse statuary. Couples balanced onto the pedestals for a photographed kiss.

A twinge of wistfulness filtered through. She had been an orphan since her mother died and had never known her father. No one else was alone. Anne tossed her unfinished lunch in a receptacle and hurried toward the entrance, joining others entering through the magnificent opaque pyramid. The glass structure occupied the space between the arms of the building blending old and new into a harmonious whole.

The glass pyramid designed by a Chinese American in 1989, at first a controversial addition to the antique Louvre Palace, was now a beloved French landmark. Anne descended the escalator into the luminous space, watching visitors pose with their hand under the glass point. She had taken the same photo on her first visit.

The vast space below the pyramid hosted a variety of shops, cafés and open spaces. It was also the entrance to the museum. Anne bought her ticket and observed the other visitors.

Anne recognized the look from earlier visits. People walked in a glassy-eyed daze, overwhelmed with 35,000 pieces of art and 380,000 objects displayed in 652,000 square feet. The mind encompassed a lot before its hard drive overloaded and crashed, leaving the eyes blank like a dark computer screen. Anne was now a resident and had time to absorb the Louvre in smaller doses.

The Louvre divided its artifacts into eight curatorial collections. Anne's favorite was the Painting Collection with its 7,500 works. Parisians loved their art, boasting one hundred well-visited museums. However, sixty-five percent of the Louvre visitors were non-local; Anne loved to watch families explore the Louvre; the acute observer saw an interesting slice of humanity.

Curators organized tours to help visitors; Anne goal was the *Masterpieces Trail*; the tour she first took as a naïve intern. It included *Aphrodite*, the *Mona Lisa*, and *Winged Victory of Samothrace*, an original Greek statue destroyed in an earthquake and put back together like Humpty Dumpty. Anne followed the detailed instructions she had downloaded.

Winding along the prescribed route, she relished the ambience of the 800-year-old Palace, in the beginning a fortress, and later home to a long line of kings, queens and rulers—some for very short periods. Anne imagined she was a woman of the great house dressed in noble clothing. Long-dead women scraped marble molecules from the floor, just as her shoes wore away the same marble. She imagined they were near her, brushing against her arms with airy touches.

Imagination had always helped her cope with her childhood. Anne fantasized she could step over the space between herself and other eras, envisioning another dimension to escape her own reality. Sometimes she pretended she was another little girl who lived in a clean house with lots of brothers and sisters.

The universal crowd in the front of the *Mona Lisa* disheartened her, but she had time to wait. The French King Francis I acquired *La Gioconda* in 1518. Created by Leonardo de Vinci on a thin poplar board, the painting was one of many well-executed artworks. Then painting became famous in the twentieth century when her photo appeared in newspapers worldwide after a museum worker stole her in 1911. The *Mona Lisa* had been lost until 1914, and made news again when the painting was stoned in 1956.

The *Mona Lisa* traveled the world in exhibits through the following decades. The painting often created a sensation even when she stayed in the palace.

Anne snaked to the front of the painting and eased to the far left of the crowd so she could take the place of those who left their viewing spaces. No one could get nearer than 30 feet of the *Mona Lisa* as it was enclosed in glass and roped off. Attuned to the reactions of others in the room, her ear sorted out English words.

"Just like pictures on the internet."

"Is this what all the excitement is about?"

"Is this it?"

Anne turned toward the doorway and in a momentary opening in the crowd, she looked up. And saw André!

Reality shifted. The people in the room disappeared and were replaced with unfamiliar people. Dressed in clothing characteristic of various historical periods, (varying from simple white frocks to elaborate purple, ruby, emerald and golden gowns), the women's apparel spanned centuries. The men's clothing equally diverse, some wore breeches and fine leather boots and others wore monks' robes. Every person who had ever stepped into the cavernous room over time was back. Anne shivered. The people moved too close, frightening her.

Her eyes met André's eyes and then he vanished.

Reality shifted again and the antique people left; the multi-cultured museum patrons usually visiting the Louvre returned.

Anne found herself in a dense crowd of warm bodies exuding a mixture of sweat, perfume and bad breath.

A tour bus-sized group of people now blocked the door where André had stood. Anne focused on the space where she saw him, swimming upstream against the flow of tourists visiting *La Gioconda*. He was gone when she reached the doorway.

Anne continued searching, scurrying up and down the substantial halls where thousands of people occupied the salons of the famous museum, a continually shifting pattern of international fads and fashion. Anne persevered for two hours, finally dropping into a seat near the main exit, examining each face. Nothing. He could have departed through the massive mall areas, and she wouldn't have seen him. Anne left when the Louvre closed at six.

Anne was almost home when it happened. Either obsessing about André had distracted her—or she was tired. Meandering along the wide sidewalk, indulging in fantasy, she strayed closer to the street. Twice, she had glimpsed André. But why now? She had lived in Paris five years without meeting him once.

Without warning, a speeding motor scooter exploded into view, traveling straight toward her. She panicked! In an instant, her adrenaline heaved her to the right. The motor scooter swerved left. Hard rubber and cold metal collided with shapely legs, slamming Anne into the pavement—and sped away. The two aboard the motor scooter left the scene.

Anne lay crumpled on the concrete.

Chapter XVII Anne and Stefania

July 6-7, 2013

A RAUCOUS SIREN screamed in the distance, the intensity increasing in volume until it reverberated next to Anne, numbing her eardrums.

Anne opened her eyes; her stinging cheek rested on hard concrete. Crawling ants dipped into a sidewalk crack and over the edge so close to her eyes the bugs were out of focus. They would be crawling over in movements. She pushed herself upright bracing her upper body with stiff arms as she gently turned her bowed head, back and forth. A pair of work shoes walked into her field of vision, prompting her to look up at two uniformed men.

"Mademoiselle?" One of the men squatted next to her. "Please don't move. We'll help you." He gently placed his hands on her upper back. "I'm a doctor with the Pompiers de Paris."

"I'm all right." She twisted her body and sat with her skinned knees bent. Anne's body ached and her scrapes stung, but she didn't think any bones had broken.

A throng of concerned faces encircled her.

"She was hit by a motor scooter," a French speaker said. "It sped off." Others nodded or murmured assent.

The doctor pressed competent hands along her limbs, "Do you feel any sharp pain?"

"No," she whispered.

"We need to backboard you. Protocol." He helped her lie back. "You should be checked at the hospital."

"I'm fine."

"We can't leave you here. I'll call someone. Whom should I call?"

"I don't know." Anne closed her eyes and fought tears. She didn't show weakness; she could cope with this alone.

"You're American. Are you visiting?" the doctor asked. The other attendant had retrieved a backboard and laid it next to her. It looked scary.

"I live here. I work at the American embassy."

"Whom do you want me to call?" The two men followed normal procedure for a possible spinal cord injury and before she could protest; the men had efficiently strapped her to the backboard.

"Stefania Ambrus." Anne was surprised she spoke her name although the woman lived near her. The medics lifted the backboard and eased her into the van. One attendant sat next to her and they pulled away. Listening to the sirens peal through Paris with her aboard, she closed her eyes. What would she do now?

After x-rays and a thorough cleansing of surface wounds, the hospital staff bandaged the worst scrapes and pronounced her sound. Informed she would need help home, Anne asked for her mobile to call her assistant. Jane would either come or send someone; Anne should have called Jane sooner.

"Anne. What happened?" Stefania asked. She breezed into the room and took charge with her presence. Wearing an orange shift dress and peach-colored sandals with heels, the outfit collided with her vivid hair and dark blue eyes. Her confident posture and shapely silhouette attracted attention; the men in the room fawned. Anne had forgotten she had given Stefania's name. It must be shock. Jane should have been her obvious choice.

"I take her home," Stefania said. A male nurse assisted Stefania with the discharge process and soon Anne was in a wheelchair bound for the exit. Stefania drove up in a borrowed car and in minutes, she was navigating Paris traffic with one hand punctuating her speech and the other hand steering. Anne shrank into the corner; her body assaulted by the shock of it all. Stefania intimidated her. Did she always wear orange? Why had she mentioned her name? Now she would have to deal with a relative stranger instead of the easy-going Jane. Stefania guided the car to the nearest entrance to their apartment building and jumped out, assisting her from the vehicle.

"Go to apartment. I come. I return car." Anne was thankful for the elevator; her body longed for her bed; and her bruised bones wouldn't lift her up the stairs. The elevator took forever to come, then forever to rise to her floor. Tears overwhelmed her just as the door opened; she hoped Stefania was gone.

Anne entered her apartment and her home soothed her at first and then she started to tremble. Her body was freezing and her teeth clattered. Anne leaned against the door. Her bed seemed a mile away and now weariness had engulfed her legs. When Anne reached her bed, and slid between the white sheets, she was still dressed in her torn and dirty workout clothes. She couldn't move her body again. Sleep came quickly.

"TIME TO GET out. You sleep enough." Struggling through layers of blackness, Anne shut out the distant words, dreaming she was in someone else's bed.

"Get out." The voice wasn't going away. Anne opened her eyes; sunlight streaked through partially closed blinds. Her bedroom. Dust particles danced between the window and the floor; however, it was too light to be early morning. How long had she slept?

"Breakfast here." Stefania hovered over Anne's bed with a tray in her hands: a chocolate croissant, yoghurt and a little crystal bowl with tiny strawberries and blackberries, a floral napkin and a pink rose. "I make coffee too."

Oh no, what have I done? Memories of Stefania's hospital rescue cascaded over her. "I'm fine." Anne lifted her head. "Go home."

"I here to help."

"I don't need help."

"You need friend. I am friend." Stefania swept to the blinds and lifted them; sunlight poured in. Anne whimpered.

"No." Anne shielded her face with her arm. "Please."

Stefania set the tray onto her bed and left. Anne hadn't had dinner last night and the food was irresistible She ate it all. When she licked the last of the chocolate from her fingers, Stefania brought her a Café au lait.

"Take shower. Get dressed." Stefania left again.

The shower revived Anne. She dressed in a yellow sundress and sparkly sandals, pulling her hair into a ponytail, avoiding the mirror. Stefania was back. Was she watching her?

Anne followed Stefania into her own living room and stretched her legs along her smaller white couch. Her skinned knees protested every movement.

Stefania sat on her other couch arrayed in a chartreuse midi dress that clung to her curves, grass green flip-flops hung from the toes of her crossed leg. A vibrant spatter against the white sofa, she leaned back with her arms spread across the back of Anne's couch.

"How you feel?"

"Well. You may leave. A motor scooter hit me; I have pavement scrapes, just need time to heal."

"It Sunday. I have all day."

"Oh." Anne longed to be alone; Stefania had been kind; and she should be considerate in return. But how? She had withdrawn from contact with others to protect her privacy and didn't respond well to friendship, the giving and receiving of social cues.

She had always been on the edge of social networks, whether she was in elementary school, high school, college or now in her workplace. No one to confide in, no one to trust. Melancholy overwhelmed her and huge tears spilled down her face, stinging when they reached her scrapes. She never cried.

Stefania sprang to her side and enveloped her in a hug so secure Anne felt safe, safer than she ever had. She quietly smoothed Anne's hair from her forehead, listening to her sob. Rarely touched, uncomfortable, Anne drew away, fleeing to her bathroom, pain twisting her gut—pain unrelated to the accident.

The mirror reflected her raw swollen face. Desolation enveloped her and all she wanted was to be alone. Stefania must leave. Would she go if she stayed in the bathroom? She sat on the toilet with her head down, tears plopping onto the creamy marble tile. She never cried.

"You okay?" Stefania tapped on the door.

"Yes." Anne washed her face with soap despite the stinging. She peered through the cracked opening in the door and saw Stefania. Curling up and hiding in her bed under the covers was not an option. Anne drifted into the living room where Stefania had perched on the arm of her overstuffed ecru-striped chair, her head drooping.

Stefania leapt op when she saw Anne. "Let's go for walk." But she appeared discouraged, less confident. Anne tentatively approached, then managed an awkward hug. They were the same height. Stefania was another tall girl. As they pulled away, shame settled inside, remorse for rejecting Stefania's innate goodness.

"I'm sorry, you've been kind."

Shrugging, Stefania suggested a walk along the Seine near Notre Dame Cathedral. "It Sunday." Anne nodded.

"I need get something from home. I come back in twenty minutes." Stefania pirouetted toward the door and dashed through, slamming it. Anne winced.

Anne took out the ponytail band, curled the ends of her hair, and applied ointment to her wounds. Strands of hair stuck to the goo so she redid the ponytail. Anticipation lifted her spirits, even without make-up. Did she want to accompany Stefania?

"I here," Stefania said, when Anne answered her knock. A large canvas bag hung over her shoulder. "We go."

They traveled on the Métro to the Cité station. Notre Dame Cathedral dominated the edge of the Île de la Cité, an island in the Seine River, one of two natural islands in the historical heart of Paris.

Legend considered the island to be home to the oldest settlement in the city, populated by Parisi Tribes in the third century B.C. Notre Dame's flying buttresses and rose windows usually enthralled Anne. Today, crowds of people littered the pavilion in front. An everlasting line of tourists wound around the side waiting to climb the tower to contemplate Paris just like Quasimodo—Victor Hugo's legendary hunchback.

"Want to go Mass? 11:30 is International Mass in English. Is early, maybe we get seat."

Anne studied Stefania. Why not? "Are you Catholic?" Anne asked.

"Yes. And you?" Wariness deepened Stefania's dark blue eyes.

"Maybe. Long ago. My Maman was sick, we didn't go to church."

The women entered, slipping into one of the uncomfortable hard wooden pews with upright backs and narrow spaces between the rows. Most of those gathered were either white-haired nicely dressed Parisians or casually dressed tourists—recognizable by their clothing, tennis shoes and camera gear.

While they waited for Mass, a continual line of visitors toured the church. The clicking of dozens of cameras intruded. Bus tour guides cautioned their guests to be quiet, respectful, no flash photos; but general disorder reigned. A line of priests processing the aisle to celebrate Mass ignored the hubbub. Then the exquisite music masked the chaos.

Anne closed her eyes, envisioning the millions of people who centered their lives on their faith and this church, sensing centuries of homage perfumed with incense, the smoke rising. Anne opened her eyes and the shadowy space—lit with candles and multicolored sparks of color from the windows— immersed her in an irresistible sense of reverence.

The medieval stained glass reflected the shimmering of innumerable hues of saturated color illustrating the story of Christendom for believers and visitors. The familiarity of the rituals resonated, perhaps unearthing a long-buried memory of Anne, a tiny tot, attending Mass with her mother.

Stefania joined the communion line, rejoining her before the service ended. Then Anne and Stefania toured the cathedral. The surreal church experience had unnerved her, combined with seeing André and the accident, her body trembled again, uncontrollably.

Stefania grasped her arm. "Are you okay?"

"I need to sit again." Stefania led her to the nearest pew, bystanders weaving around them. Even Stefania's presence had resulted in a paradigm shift; her predictable life had disappeared over the weekend. How should she respond?

They eventually exited through the immense doors of the West Façade that featured the Gallery of Kings, twenty-eight statues of Judean rulers who overlooked Cathedral Square. They walked along the side of the old cathedral, admiring the gargoyles and grotesques who inhabited the higher reaches of the building, black-stained and weathered, looking like they could topple at any time.

"I bring food. Let's eat." Stefania led Anne to a spot along the river, stooping to pull a blanket from her bag, spreading it onto the pavement. She unloaded a French baguette, creamy Ile de France brie cheese, a sliced hard cheese Fol Epi, and the flavorful blue cheese Cantorel Roquefort. Fresh veggies, grapes and two pastries completed the simple meal. "Sit." Stefania surreptitiously handed Anne a single-serving bottle of wine, holding her fingers to her lips, "Don't tell about wine, not allowed here."

Anne gingerly sank onto the blanket, her scabby knees cracking their displeasure, straightening her legs helped. The peace of Notre Dame soothed her like sheltering arms in the eye of a storm. Now calm permeated her, reassuring her, drawing her closer to Stefania.

She discovered Stefania was fluent in French, she had spoken English to accommodate her. When they switched to French, it was easier to converse; Stefania's French was exemplary.

Stefania shared stories of her many sisters and their giant families and didn't pressure Anne for confidences.

THE SUN SET over the Seine. They lingered on the banks that overlooked the bridge between the Île de la Cité and the Left Bank, watching the sky change, ranging from the palest salmon to peach and cantaloupe interspersed with pale gray clouds. The remarkable sunset reflected from the glassy still waters of the River Seine.

"I'm exhausted." Anne grasped Stefania's arm.

"I'm sorry, I should have thought." Stefania gathered her bag and hurried Anne away from the river. Darkness descended as the two women returned to the Cité Métro station. On the Métro, her body ached, but she was content. Stefania's presence signified friendship. Anne had visited Notre Dame alone; but in Stefania's presence, this historical and holy place had entered her soul.

Anne mattered.

Chapter XVIII André

THROUGH THE OPEN window, music permeated the clear morning air of his bedroom. The small band needed more practice, laughter accompanied the fitful starts and stops of the notes. André grimaced, pulling a pillow over his head. All over France citizens prepared for La Fête Nationale. Bastille Day.

The fourteenth of July approached like an out-of-control truck on a steep downgrade. His body tensed; the music soared, a bit louder now. The music stopped. He descended into a bottomless sleep that can arrive moments before one awakens.

He had walked along the edge, sometimes slipping into another time and place, at the brink of discovery, always stepping back—just in time. What was time? Was it a human construct? Humans occupied a short space in time, what was beyond? People spent a lifetime gaining knowledge, wisdom, and experience. What happened with the intelligence? There was a slight divergence between him and the seam to another sphere. Across the divide, he saw himself. Or was it his brother? They looked the same despite almost two passing decades.

Where did time go? He yearned for something. What? Where did seventeen years go? Was he afraid to love? Afraid to lose love? Time had continued at human speed for André— how had it moved for his brother? He would ask Pierre...when he woke up, after the parade.

André awakened, struggling from the clutches of sleep, its tentacles lingering. The music ascended again. He shook his head; he had dreamed of a parade. Now fully awake, he remembered a La Fête Nationale celebration his family had attended long before Pierre died.

His head cleared. It had been three weeks since he discovered *Miriam*. He and Collette had dinner plans with Michel and his date this evening. André intended to spend this Saturday at the Louvre.

The offending band lounged at an outdoor café drinking coffee, their instruments sitting drunkenly around their chairs. André observed the band members as he loitered at the same café with le chocolat pain and café au lait. Why had their merry practice session disturbed him? The dreaded La Fête Nationale had no power over him now. The catalyst of the fire had removed the fear usually centered around his Bastille Day birthday. He tossed a few Euro onto the table and walked to the nearest Métro station, anticipating a whole day immersed in paintings.

He entered the Louvre and it reminded him of the d'Orsay visit ten days before. Michel knew him well. The Italian Renaissance displays on the first floor of the Denon wing always beckoned him.

Each prince or family who ruled a region or city in Italy competed with the others in architectural style, massive building projects and the paintings that enhanced them. Different styles developed in different regions, with some painters renowned for their use of color, others dimension and perspective. Renaissance artists excelled at various artistic disciplines: painters, sculptors, and architects. Some wrote treatises on their works.

The development of the craft of painting intrigued André. Artists first painted flat figures, almost childlike in their simplicity. Proficiency expanded to include enhancement with gold leaf to shine in church candlelight. Over time artists acquired more skills, added dimension and perspective to their works, improved the realistic qualities of their figures. Anatomy played a role when artists dissected the human body and observed muscle, bone and skin. Movement added more facets to the figures and by the time of the early Renaissance, the pursuit of all types of art exploded, saturating Europe with an ever-expanding quest for perfection. The arts: architecture, sculpture, music, painting and literature experienced exponential growth.

Art history study satisfied André's quest for an explanation of life. Why humans exist. Why humans have the urge to create something which outlasts the frail body. He ambled through his favorite rooms.

André entered the Café Mollien located on the first-floor landing of the Mollien staircase. A perfect place for lunch and viewing the remarkable ceiling painting, *Glory distributing Palms and Crowns* by Charles-Louis Müller. Ornate architecture also enhanced the surrounding walls. André avoided the *Mona Lisa*, more famous for what happened to her than her debatable beauty.

Another painting in the same gallery drew him. In contrast to the tiny *Mona Lisa, The Wedding Feast at Cana* was the largest in the Louvre, more than thirty feet long and twenty-two feet high. The canvas painted by Veronese depicted a 16th century version of the first miracle performed by Jesus. The huge artwork portrayed multiple stories; one could stand in front of it and almost watch the figures interact. The main story focused on Mary, who prompted her Son to His first miracle.

Mothers—how could you live without them? Mary urged Jesus, "They're out of wine. What will you do?" An obedient son, he did what she asked. Wise mothers knew what to do when it mattered.

The first miracle involved food, wine and banqueting, very French-like although the artist was Italian. André lost track of time. Veronese chose to represent a wedding feast in 16th century Venice with all its opulence and some of its decadence. Veronese didn't paint a version of a poor wedding feast in Cana, where the bridegroom ran out of wine. Only Mary and Jesus wore simple clothing, most of the other figures flaunted ornate costumes of the 1500's. André hadn't remembered Mary's features in *The Wedding Feast at Cana*. Today, Mary resembled his mother. Paintings often spoke to the viewer in subtle ways.

Mary held an invisible glass that depicted the absence of wine; one hundred and thirty other figures celebrated at the biblical marriage feast. Mary gazed at her Son but only Jesus watched the observer. Historians equated much symbolism to this masterpiece, from the first miracle signifying the Eucharist, to the slaughtered lambs in a balcony above Jesus, signifying the sacrificial lamb.

André had just left the painting, when a large tour group surrounded him, intent on the *Mona Lisa*. He turned, his eyes caught the clear violet eyes of an attractive woman, holding the connection for a few seconds. Anne. Then his brother blocked her from view. Standing in front of him, he looked like André did when he shaved before a mirror. Beyond Pierre, the room filled with people who had arrived from different centuries, as if everyone who had ever been in the Louvre Castle had returned.

Pierre disappeared with the rest of the people from bygone eras, but not before he said, *"She is the one."*

Chapter XIX André

STILL AT THE Louvre and shaken by the weird experience, André's heart thudded as he pressed back onto the wall of the wide Mollien staircase, hands icy against the cold marble. People surged against him as they ascended and descended the stairs, some huffing through their chatter. A cacophony of languages swirled around him. He flattened further against the wall when two teen boys squeezed past; he must leave the stairway or risk getting trampled.

The last time André had seen his dead brother—before he saw him in the Louvre—had been seventeen years ago. Pierre came to his dorm room the night he met Anne at the college party. Pierre had said something to him then, a phrase he never remembered. He had forgotten about the it until Pierre appeared here in the museum.

His mind flashed to the harbor in Corsica. Pierre had slipped over the edge of the sailboat; he was dead. What was he doing in the Louvre? *"She is the one,"* Pierre had said today.

The woman in front of the *Mona Lisa* looked like the Anne he remembered. Was she a vision too? And the others in the room? People dressed like servants, aristocrats and monks— even a cardinal. What was real? Damn, he should have followed her.

André dashed down the stairway and back to the gallery of the *Mona Lisa* and *The Wedding at Cana*. He waded through people exiting the salon. Another busload of people arrived pushing into the salon from behind him. He scanned the room for a tall girl, his eyes darting here, there, searching. The thickening crowd closed in on him, he could barely move, a claustrophobic feeling overwhelming him. "Excusez-moi. Pardonnez-moi." Escaping into the hall, he stopped, and breathed deeply, settling his nerves, slowing his heart rate.

Once more he entered the fray, systematically examining each quadrat of the moving crowd. The statuesque woman had resembled an older version of the woman he remembered— very dark hair, translucent skin, violet-blue eyes. His futile search ended there, but he scrutinized each brunette woman's face as he left the Louvre. Coincidence would have to strike twice in the immense castle.

André entered the gardens and drifted through the plantings, hands in his pockets, shoulders hunched. Near a pond in the Tuileries Garden he sat on a bench, contemplating the still water, and questioned his sanity. He had just seen his dead brother. Again. Was Anne dead? She appeared dead in the painting but that was the artist's rendition. He left the haunted grounds but haunting memories lingered in his consciousness.

André believed in a higher being but sometimes the trappings got in the way, especially in this city of churches. Many French people raised as Roman Catholic questioned the rationality of organized religion. Perhaps this life was the end of being. There was no afterlife. What about his vision? What message had Pierre given him in Michigan?

The American woman must now be in Paris. André first saw the *Miriam* painting at the end of May and then one extraordinary event after another had occurred. Anne and *Miriam*. Were they connected?

Dinner. He had almost forgotten. Michel had made reservations for them weeks before at La Dame de Pic, one of the hottest new restaurants in Paris. Anne-Sophie Pic—awarded three Michelin stars—was the only female chef in France with the honor. The restaurant was nearby at 20 rue de Louvre, he would be on time if he hurried.

His friends were waiting. "Bonjour, Collette." He kissed her. "Michel." Nodding at Michel he waited, he had his arm wrapped around a new date.

"Violeta, meet André. This suave man is my boss. Remember, I saw you first." She laughed.

"You'll do," Violeta said. Her voice low she touched Michel's face, her other well-toned arm around his waist. Short blond hair blew across her eyes and she tossed it back in place. Not Michel's usual type.

The modern elegant interior of La Dame de Pic displayed an open kitchen with visible chefs. Square and rectangular tables—graced with pink Alstroemaria in vases—were clothed with heavy white table runners and white napkins. White interiors hinted at the palest hue of pink. Modern leather chairs conveyed a fresh up-to-date ambience. The restaurant offered three menus each based on different perfumes. The three menus presented three selections and a dessert selection. Guests sniffed perfumes to choose dinner; Michel had wanted to experience it.

"Not sure what to expect," Michel said. "Reviews are good; the concept is intriguing. Perfume and food—a strange combination, even in Paris."

An attentive staff seated them, inviting them to breathe fragrances on perfumed tabs created for the restaurant by a

Japanese perfumer. They were to choose a menu based on their olfactory preferences.

"I've researched this. Close your eyes and think about the chef's inspiration." Michel sniffed the tab with an angelic facial expression.

"Amber vanilla aroma, the sea and flowers aroma, or the sours bois and spices aroma." André read the titles. "The food will be unusual."

"We should each choose a different one. Experience them all," Violeta said.

Michel pointed two fingers at them. "You two agree?"

"Yes."

The server brought butter infused with aniseed and matcha green tea served with bread from a well-known bakery. André relaxed. Michel had drawn him into the light-hearted evening.

The courses included unusual combinations in complicated artistic presentations. The wine pairings exemplary, the two couples ended the evening in high spirits.

"Thanks for planning this," André said. The four mingled outside the restaurant, Michel and Violeta stroking each other's hair, a signal they should leave. "Au revoir." André clasped Collette's hand, slowing his stride to accommodate her petite frame. "Did you like it?"

"It's different." She shrugged. "The food was good. I like simpler fare though." They walked with hundreds of others on the wide avenue.

"I agree. Interesting experience." André preferred the odor of food when he ate. "Michel and Violeta had fun."

"Michel knocks you from your reserve. Were you a shy child?"

"Maybe. Pierre was the lively twin. It was easy to let him talk, scheme, whatever. I followed."

"Was he like Michel?"

"Not at all." How do you describe the other half of yourself? He and Pierre fit together, filling each other's spaces, two components of one whole. The weekend before Pierre died, he had betrayed his brother. The persistent memory still punished him.

André escorted Collette to their building. Her parents had come to Paris for a visit but she had kept the long-planned date.

"Let's talk for a few minutes." They found a quiet corner in the lobby and sat on a small couch. Collette was a comfortable companion. She needed someone who appreciated her, not one flawed like him. She nestled against him.

"My parents saw you at the retirement home. They had visited Grand-maman."

"Oh?"

"You're too hard on yourself. You overcompensate for your brother."

André sighed. What had they seen?

"My parents saw you with an older woman. You treated her like a queen. She was animated, sparkling." She leaned closer, touching his face. "Grand-maman told them you take women out who have no family visitors, for lunch, a movie, the theatre."

André stared at the floor.

"The women love it. They feel younger, valued. You are good to others, though you are stuck in the past. I want . . . I would like . . ."

André tightened his arm around her, nurturing the easy silence. Did Collette expect more? Was she interested in a sexual relationship?

"When did you begin dating these women?"

"A while. I handled the sale of a treasured painting for a woman. The painting was valuable, handed down from her family, and she was the last survivor. At ninety, she had outlived her son and his wife. Her granddaughter died young." André strived to shorten a long story. "I took her to lunch a few times while we conducted business. She anticipated them so much, she appeared younger. We continued our little outings, sometimes a movie or a play. Until she died." Collette's eyes glistened, a tear escaped.

"What a sad story." Collette touched his hand.

"A happy time for her. Rewarding for me."

"Did she need the money?"

"No. She wanted to sell it before she died so she could leave the proceeds to the Catholic Church—and control how it was spent. She was of that generation. People who centered their lives on the Church, and left money to carry on its work. She left her estate to the St. Vincent de Paul Society to care for the poor. We helped her invest the proceeds. The money will keep on giving."

"And now? The other woman my parents saw?"

"Another woman without family." He hoped she understood. He put his arm around her and pulled her to him. "You are the only one who knows." He kissed her lips. Relaxing in his arms, she responded. The kiss escalated. They were breathing hard and his heart pounded, her heart racing against his chest. When he lifted his head her eyes were murky, unreadable. "Will you keep my secret?"

She didn't know the worst, why he overcompensated for a failing he couldn't correct. The old misdeed resurfaced.

The week before Pierre had died he had tricked his brother, an overdue payback. He called Pierre's steady girlfriend, pretending he was Pierre, and made a date. They attended a classical music performance at an exclusive venue. He took cues from her and when she initiated a kiss, he kissed her. It went farther arousing both. He hesitated, she begged him to continue, calling him Pierre. She laid across him unbuttoning his shirt and stroking his bare chest. He had pulled away. She belonged to Pierre.

"We can't. I'm André. I pranked my brother."

"I know." She wrapped her arms around him, clinging to his chest, nuzzling his neck.

"What gave me away?"

"We never listen to classical music. It was so 'not Pierre'. And there were other reasons . . ." Her voice trailed wistfully.

"Why did you come?" Regret overflowed within him. "I'm sorry. Pierre cares for you."

"I wondered how alike you were." She tossed her long hair back. "He likes me more than I like him. I might like you better."

He apologized again and escorted her home. Should he tell Pierre? He had worried incessantly during those days leading up to their Corsica vacation, but he never approached Pierre. What could he say? When his family arrived in Corsica, it was too late.

The day they had rented the sailboat André and their two male friends invited some local girls to go sailing. Pierre shocked him, said he was not interested in the local girls.

"I have a new love. I don't want to mess around with girls here," Pierre had said. André's gut exploded as if Pierre had punched him. What had he done? The trick he played on his brother was not funny now. Pierre loved the girl, and she didn't seem appropriate.

Pierre's declaration hung over André all day—the last day of his brother's life. Then he was gone and he could never tell him he was sorry.

ANDRÉ WALKED COLLETTE upstairs and kissed her again at her door. Had their relationship moved to another level? On the other hand, was he using her? When he arrived home, André poured himself a drink and sat in the dark. The events at the Louvre came back.

He pinpointed the exact time something bizarre occurred. It had been when his eyes converged with hers. Then he saw Pierre with his eyes fixated onto his own. Beyond Pierre he saw a roomful of people in period dress, covering a great time span. When Pierre spoke, he and the others disappeared. He was a rational thinker. Why had he imagined what didn't exist?

Pierre had said she was the one. Did he mean Anne? André stood, pacing in the dark. Pierre had appeared to him twice—both times after he had seen Anne. However, before today, he had seen neither for seventeen years.

If he could only remember what Pierre had said in his dorm room.

Chapter XX Michel

MICHEL ANALYZED THE known facts and identified three key points in the *Miriam* case. One: the painting shouldn't be hard to locate. Someone with authority removed it from the Musée de l'Erotisme; it was unlikely a thief stole only that painting. Two: Monsieur Bertrand had painted *Miriam*, and per André, the model resembled a teenager he met in the U.S. Three: Monsieur Bertrand was their primary suspect.

The case centered in Montmartre since the Musée de l'Erotisme was in Montmartre, M. Bertrand had organized the exhibition, and he lived there. Since Bertrand had disappeared, his daughter, Charlotte, provided his best chance to find the missing artist. André had reluctantly passed him Charlotte Bertrand's mobile number, warning him to be judicious.

Michel had worked at the firm for five years and the aloof and efficient André always guarded his emotions. When Michel found the comatose André, and witnessed his pain—as raw as skin ripped from muscle—the shared experience changed them both. André's manner was now warmer and he was more approachable. Indebted to André for a past intervention, Michel had now returned the kind act. Evened the score a bit.

He called Nancy Legrand, manager of Bertrand's gallery. "Bonjour. I'd like to contact Monsieur Jean-Paul Bertrand."

"He's not available."

"Do you have a contact number?"

"No." The tone meant no.

"Thank you." Charlotte Bertrand's mobile number was in his contact list.

"Bonjour." A musical voice answered immediately.

"Bonjour. Michel la Roche." Surprised, he scrambled. "I...I work for the Gensonné family law firm. I would like to meet with you."

"Who?"

"Michel la Roche. I've met your father . . . Will you have lunch with me?" Michel closed his eyes, crossed his fingers, and prayed a little.

"Why are you calling?"

"Trouble with one of your father's paintings." It was just a little white lie.

"Papa has been anxious. You work for a law firm?"

"Yes." Michel winged it. "Do you want to meet at Evelyn's Café? A small café near the gallery where your father displays paintings. Today? Tomorrow?"

"Maybe."

"What is convenient?" Michel pressed her, too anxious. "I'm available any time." The words ricocheted out of his mouth.

"I can't tomorrow. Today? Maybe one o'clock."

"Perfect. Do you know of the café?"

"Yes. Is my father in trouble?" He cringed at the tremor in her voice.

"We'll talk later. Thank you. I'll see you at one."

Michel entered Evelyn's Café at twelve-thirty. Evelyn bustled to the door, her plump figure belying her energetic movements.

"Dining alone?" She led him to the table closest to the kitchen; he hurried to keep up.

"I'm meeting a woman." Michel seated himself in a chair facing the door. "A glass of your house wine please." She returned with the wine, a cup of mixed olives and dried bread sticks. "Merci."

The little restaurant filled with lunch patrons and Evelyn managed all twelve tables, six on each side of the long narrow room, greeting many by name. White daisies filled green jugs and emerald napkins rested on starched white tablecloths. The odors drifting from the kitchen smelled like Rosemary and Thyme—perhaps roasted chicken was on the menu. His stomach rumbled. Wisps of French dominated the conversations permeating the restaurant.

The petite woman wavering at the door was much younger than he had expected, silhouetted against the sun streaming through the window. She was scanning the tables as he hastened toward her. "Bonjour. Michel la Roche. Charlotte Bertrand?"

"Yes. I'm not sure why I'm here. Do you have a business card?" She read it thoroughly, and tucked it into her purse.

"Thank you for coming. Please, my table is here, near the kitchen." Michel guided her with his hand on her waist, seating her first. The tiny table implied intimacy.

Michel couldn't connect her features with Bertrand's face. He looked like a poster boy for the French art profession with his faded red beret and bony elegance; his daughter looked like an Irish lass. Charlotte's cornflower blue eyes appeared cautious, a dusting of freckles peeking through her make-up. She brushed her long strawberry-blond hair back from her face, it fell in thick waves around her shoulders.

Evelyn appeared with a wineglass. "The house wine Mademoiselle? Chosen to complement the day's menu."

"Yes, please." Charlotte touched it to his raised glass. "How do you like the wine? My friend Nancy and I come here often. She works at the gallery that sells Papa's work."

"Excellent wine. The kitchen aromas are intoxicating." Evelyn brought them a starter course. Cucumbers in square chunks drizzled with aged balsamic vinegar, and sprinkled with fresh thyme.

"Do you know my father?"

"A little." A swell of guilt surged over Michel. If she was aware he had intimidated her father, she would leave.

"I'm worried." She stared quietly at her plate. Other diners' conversions floated across their table as Michel fidgeted. Patience wasn't his best trait. Refocusing, her clear blue eyes met his and she blushed, startling him. Hard to fathom the young woman was the aged Bertrand's daughter. "Something happened a couple of weeks ago. Maybe three. He wouldn't answer his phone, doesn't own a mobile. When I finally got him, he sounded disoriented. When we visited on the weekend, he was thinner. He's with me now."

"And?"

"He'd rather be home."

"I work for a reputable legal firm." Michel handed her another business card. "We handle most legal issues, but we specialize in the art industry—on many levels." Would that reassure her enough? "May I speak about your father?"

"Yes." Charlotte took the second card, glanced at it and pushed the engraved rectangle away. Her lush hair had fallen forward, covering her small shoulders. Mistrust clouded her eyes. "I don't know; my father's business is his own. But if I can help?"

Michel zeroed in. "Do you remember if your father painted a woman lying on her back in the sea? She wore a red ball gown, had dark hair, fair complexion. Oils on canvas." Scrutinizing her face, she showed no sign she knew of the painting.

"I don't remember one. It would've been unusual, although he's very talented. He can paint anything. He has a large commission from an American businessman."

"Has anyone tried to contact him? In the past month?"

"I wouldn't know. I live away from. . . Paris. He has many cronies he socializes with. He's closer to them." Her pensive mood matched her sad face. "I moved away from Montmartre when I married."

"You said he's different. Any idea why?"

"I've asked, he won't say. Something strange happened last weekend. We went to the Parc des Buttes-Chaumont with my daughters. His grandchildren." Her eyes smiled like his did when her father had mentioned his grandchildren. She ate a couple of bites, and set her utensils down.

"Something unusual?" Michel prompted.

"I'd asked Papa to come for an extended visit. He wanted to stay home, paint around Montmartre. We enjoyed a delightful day in the park."

"He acted normally?"

"He did. Then, a short time before we left the park he said he was tired. Needed to get home."

"Was he with you the whole time?"

"I think so." Evelyn brought the main course of chicken stuffed with rosemary, rice, mushrooms, water chestnuts and onions. An herb-infused aroma wafted over their dishes. Michel started eating, but Charlotte was lost in thought, contemplating her cooling food. Michel controlled his urge to speak. Sighing, she finally picked up her knife.

"Remember the park. When did he seem different?"

Charlotte closed her eyes. "Later in the day, we went to the playground and the girls ran ahead. I asked him what was bothering him. He said he had had a problem. It was resolved. We sat on a bench, watching the girls play, and then he left to use the toilet."

179

"Did you leave the park afterwards?" Michel drank his wine; Evelyn had selected the perfect complement to the poultry dish.

"Yes. He was distraught. He tried to hide it, said he was exhausted. Papa hurried home so fast, my youngest daughter cried. He came out of his bedroom later with a packed bag. He has been with me more than a week. My girls love it. Grandpapa spoils them."

"Could he have seen someone at the toilets?"

"Perhaps." Charlotte distractedly gazed past Michel again. "Maybe he saw someone." Her blue eyes darkened. "It'd be a guess." She executed the Gallic move, appearing more French-like than she did before.

"I'm sorry to pry. Just searching for answers." They finished their main course. Many of the lunch patrons left, and the background conversation diminished. Michel detected soft music he had missed earlier. Evelyn brought two dishes of lemon gelato, drizzled with Limoncello.

"Monsieur la Roche?"

"Yes?"

"There may be something unusual about the American who buys Papa's work. It'd be another guess. Papa won't answer my questions."

"Do you know his name?"

"No. I may be able to find out from Nancy."

"You have my business card. You can reach me there. The bottom number is my mobile." He had planned to set up a meeting with the three of them, but caution overruled. Her father would remember him. Patience was hard, but essential, with Charlotte.

Charlotte put her arm onto Michel's, her creamy skin contrasting with his darker arm. "He's not happy. I mean, he's not happy at my home. He was at first; he painted with Simone, played with the girls." She pulled her hand back, and clasped them in front of her, squeezing them until her knuckles whitened.

"He misses Montmartre. He's fading, his vitality's gone."

Chapter XXI André and Jean-Baptiste

JEAN-BAPTISTE GENSONNÉ hastened into André's office at noon on Monday and stopped in front of his desk, unnaturally still.

"Bonjour, Grand-père." Grand-papa was not a word he usually used to describe his grandfather. When they visited the family firm as children, Grand-père had scared him and Pierre. More approachable at family events, he couldn't turn off his formal persona at the office. Now he and his grandfather shared a passion for paintings

"Bonjour. Do you have some time?" He put his hands in his pockets, shifting from foot to foot.

"Yes." André came around his desk, and kissed his grandfather. "Do you want to sit?"

"I want to go somewhere. Private, not here. Would you schedule in an afternoon?" His grandfather's face was set in rigid lines. He rubbed his temple, exhaling a shallow breath.

"Are you all right?" André hugged him, then gripped his arms, searching his familiar features. A hard man to understand, his grandfather had personally experienced war as a child, a tragedy beyond the present generation's comprehension. Those teenage years shaped his gruff character, though André felt deeply loved by him, and understood Grand-père's sometimes irrational fear for his only grandson.

"I want to spend time with my grandson."

"Tomorrow afternoon? We can eat lunch together." André moved to his desk. "I have appointments this afternoon."

"What about today? Do you have an hour?" His jaw was hard, his mouth a grim slit.

"I can leave now. I'll notify Maria." He hurried, fretting about Grand-père's uncharacteristic behavior.

"I'm leaving for lunch with my grandfather. I'll be back for my two o'clock. Call me on my mobile if necessary." Maria nodded and kept keyboarding. Back in his office Grand-père gazed out the window, his normally erect figure hunched, again as motionless as a statue. As if it was difficult to move.

"Where should we go?" His grandfather turned in slow motion.

"Anywhere. You choose." He appeared older and thinner than he had been. André guided him to the stairs, then switched direction, leading him to the elevator.

They walked companionably to the neighborhood bistro. The familiar proprietor moved his head toward their usual table in a secluded corner; the Gensonnés were frequent customers. His grandfather sat across from him.

"I'm eighty-five." Said with an authoritative air in a strong voice, André must have imagined weakness. His rigid facial features carved in granite lines implied strength. Black eyebrows curved over his brow-bone, wide as André's little finger, contrasted with his thick white hair, cut short. His grandfather usually appeared somewhat forbidding. What was different?

"A young eighty-five." André lightened his voice, hoping to dispel his grandfather's grave mood. Grand-père sighed with his whole body, head bowed. When he looked up, his eyes were steely black bearings boring into André's eyes.

"I need your help. You *will* keep this confidential." This man was a stranger. Hostile. Intimidating. He held André's eyes for seconds longer than was comfortable, André struggling to maintain eye contact.

"I have a fast-growing brain tumor. Three to six months without treatment, a couple months longer with radiation and chemotherapy. I took the three months." The terse words slammed into André, cold chills ran in straight lines down both sides of his body. His skin shuddered as a barrage of thoughts clogged his brain. Despite his grandfather's odd behavior, he hadn't suspected this baldly uttered pronouncement. He would not ask him if he was sure, his grandfather's craven face told the truth.

"I, I. Are—I'm sorry." Aware he didn't want to be touched, André shifted his gaze from Grand-père's hard dark eyes to the attentive proprietor. André summoned James with a hand movement.

"I don't want sympathy. The tumor has nothing to do with what I want. I have another request…you might say, a demand." Did he know this man? André cast around for appropriate words, he didn't have a vocabulary for this. He noticed James.

The proprietor waited, just beyond his grandfather's shoulder.

"Do you want something to eat? A drink?" André asked.

"No."

"I'll have the Beef Burgundy. Choose a complimentary red. Two glasses." Grand-père had ignored the exchange, continuing his conversation as soon as James left.

"You know some of my history. You can respond. Or not. Just listen." James arrived with the wine and two glasses.

"That's not my vintage."

"No, sir." James left with the wine and returned with a very fine wine, identifiable by its silver and gold label. André wasn't aware the bistro stocked the costly bottle. James popped the cork, and poured a measure into Grand-père's glass. He swirled, sniffed, swirled, finally tasting.

"Needs more air. André will pour. You may leave." André glanced sideways at James, whose lips twitched, just before he turned.

"The Germans occupied Paris from 1940 until 1944. I turned twelve-years-old on January first, 1940. My parents organized a big party for my friends, many of them Jewish. It was my best birthday." His best birthday? His 12th?

André's grandparents had spearheaded birthday celebrations for family members, often spending too much on extravagant presents. Now the expensive sports car made more sense. His grandfather's last gift.

"Hitler invaded France on May tenth, 1940 and it took them a month to reach Paris. The city fell with almost no resistance on June fourteenth, 1940. My father owned a successful law firm, so we stayed, even though 1.5 million of the 3.5 million people who lived in Paris, fled. Paris remained under German occupation until 1944.

Four years is a long time for a young teenage boy. When I was twelve, and thirteen, and fourteen, I thought we would live like that forever. On the surface, we tried to live normal lives, with German soldiers everywhere. Underneath those attempts at normalcy, Parisians walked a tightrope between collaboration, and resistance. No one trusted anyone."

What difference two generations made. André and his siblings had been carefree teenagers, until Pierre died.

"After I die, remember . . ." His grandfather grabbed both his hands. "Every choice we had was complicated, contradictory . . . and painful." His grip was hard for an old man. Neither had touched the wine André had poured. His face now kind, loving, he looked like the grandfather who had spoiled him every birthday and Christmas.

"When I was twelve and a half, I saw Hitler speak in Paris. Some say he came to gloat that he had captured the beautiful city of art, literature and music. I remember his uniform. I remember his black mustache. I remember the smell of fear. It's been more than 70 years . . . and I still remember." His grandfather's body sat opposite him, his mind was elsewhere. "All these years and I can still see his evil face." He pulled his hands from André's, his head bowed. An animal-like sound escaped his lips.

"Grand-père, you want—" André hurt deep in his heart as if he had been stabbed. Grand-père was struggling to explain war from a teenage perspective, one experienced by many older Europeans. His direct gaze intimidating again, he lowered heavy brows over his eyes, frowning, his lips a slit in his jaw.

"I resolved to protect what I could." He emitted the words with force, hurling them at André like a WWII grenade. His body tense, old anger raged. Then he wilted, the wrath gone. "It was a crazy scheme. I was twelve." His voice rose, almost question-like. "A boy. I didn't know what I had resolved to protect." Jean-Baptiste lifted his wine glass and drank a third of it. André contemplated the burgundy red liquid in his own glass. Still untouched.

"I was drawn to art, particularly paintings. The pure talent to create such masterpieces amazed me. Still does. I can't paint. I do recognize the aptitude of those who can, those with talent to explore the world and record it for the ages. I admire what they see, how they see it, how they draw the viewer into their vision." He lifted his glass and swirled the precious wine. "I had a propensity to recognize genius, even then. I refined the ability for seventy years. I became wealthy."

They sat for several minutes as his grandfather's mind went somewhere no one else could go. When he resumed speaking, his voice was a harsh whisper. "Life was unpredictable and we feared nothing. During the first year after the Germans came, we played boyhood games, cops and robbers, spied on German officers, and risked our necks for fun.

Our privileged lives had vanished. Adults focused on life-changing circumstances they sheltered from us. We felt isolated from events in our neighborhood, so we treated the occupation like a game."

Now André initiated touch. He caressed his grandfather's hand for a few quiet seconds, and then his grandfather gripped his hand as if it was a lifeline.

"All that changed the next May. In 1941, the Germans took Jewish families to the Winter Velodrome for processing, and then took them by train to Eastern European death camps. Some of my friends disappeared. Whole families. They were gone forever. We heard adults whispering, when they thought we were asleep. We shared what we heard from our parents, other adults. The Germans tightened control over daily life, barricading streets, patrolling.

We became daring, many of us were thirteen and fourteen years old. We were children, but we intended to save France's heritage, its history. So, we stole her art."

Tears ran down his face, tracing the deepened lines. André moved to his side, pulling his chair close and encircling him with his right arm. His thinning shoulders were fragile. He was his grandfather, his protector, his partner who had had his childhood stripped through war. When his grandfather spoke again, his eyes were soft and warm like a puppy's.

"You are the only person, the only one I trust." His grandfather sat with his head bowed, his words difficult to hear. "It'd be easier to die, let my secrets be found after I'm gone." Moments passed. Had he finished speaking?

"I can't hurt your grandmother or the rest of the family. If you make some of it right . . . provide restitution . . . maybe it will make a difference." He squeezed André's hand and whispered. "Maybe."

Why me? The questioned screamed inside André's brain.

His grandfather lifted his head. His hooded eyes sought André's, the wrinkled lids too heavy to show his eye color. "This is where my story starts."

André was World War II shell-shocked. How much more did he want to hear? His eardrums thudded.

"What did you say?" André asked.

"I'm so sorry." He took another shallow breath. "There's a lot more. It will shock you, but there's no one else. It involves passion, desire, craving, an appetite like no other. Desire almost destroyed me. It could destroy you." His intense words attracted the attention of a couple who had just been seated. His grandfather raised his fist. "Your father doesn't share what we have."

André body reeled. He couldn't comply with this, yet his grandfather needed reassurance. André leapt into the chasm. "Tell me the rest." Perhaps he could make sense of this, if he learned more.

"It will change everything. You will hate me. I hope my mistakes don't damage our family." His grandfather drained his glass. "I don't feel like eating." He dropped two hundred Euro on the table and shuffled toward the door. André followed behind. Just outside, he stepped closer to André.

"You have appointments today and . . . and, I'm not ready. After your birthday on La Fête Nationale, we will talk again. Let's celebrate the day without shadows from the past."

Chapter XXII Maximillian

WILD DARK GRAY clouds churned above the Paris sky. The swirling masses hanging so low the dome of the Basilica appeared to be battling them to retain its space on the Butte. The layers of steps swarmed with people carrying umbrellas; Paris never lacked for tourists and the stormy weather didn't deter them today.

The electric atmosphere stimulated Maximillian. He felt more alive in tumultuous weather, the rumbling thunder reverberated through his body, propelling him uphill.

The Basilica of the Sacred Heart of Jesus crowned the Butte with its majestic presence. A political and cultural monument completed early in the twentieth century, after nearly fifty years of construction, it represented the conservative moral order of those times. Maximillian didn't have much use for God; the Basilica was a convenient meeting spot. Last time he was here, a wedding couple had reminded him of Émilie's marriage proposal. She hadn't talked about marriage again. Most marriages he had observed were a disaster.

Maximillian spotted Beauregard before he saw him. He sat at the top of the steps watching Beau climb. He and Beau had a lot in common, they had been roommates before he met Émilie, their family backgrounds matched, and their attitude about what life handed them coincided. They had planned mischievous stunts over the years and more seriously, criminal capers.

Before Maximillian found Beau working at the café in the Place du Tertre, he had lost touch with him. Beau had married and stayed out of trouble. Just as living with Émilie kept him clean. However, his old friend had called him yesterday.

"Bonjour, Beau." His malleable face stretched into a huge rubber smile when he saw Max.

"Bonjour, Max." The friends had agreed to the nicknames when they were just boys. Others stuck to the parent-bestowed versions, it was Max and Beau between them. Unless they were teasing or serious. They walked away from the tourists on the wide verandas that overlooked Paris, moving to a far corner. The menacing storm held off. Paris looked dark and dirty, with hulks of uninspired buildings lining wide gray avenues, deep green trees swaying. The wind snatched at their clothing, much stronger here at the top of the Butte.

"What's up?" Maximillian asked. "The *Miriam* painting?" His words ripped from his mouth whirling away in the wind.

"Overheard something in the café." Beau looked around, huddling closer, before he continued. "Might be able to move the Elisée Maclet."

"You found a buyer?"

"I think so. Does it have any provenance?"

"I...I don't know. What do you need? The artist I hired painted over the original."

"Do you have photographs? Any proof of what's underneath."

"No." Maximillian's heart plummeted. He had nothing. The rat had taken advantage of him. A few heavy raindrops plopped from the leaden sky. They opened their umbrellas, the wind threatening to flip them inside out. They leaned close.

"Where is it?" Beau asked.

"Back at the frame shop. My sister Mimi threw a fit; I had to move it. I asked the rat to store it, and find a buyer." Tourists crowded close, boxing them in. Maximillian shrunk away, pulling Beau away from curious people.

Beau lowered his voice. The approaching storm grumbled and cracked in the distance, though it was moving closer. "I need proof of provenance, and then, I may have a sale." Beau grabbed his arm and droned in his ear. "Also, assurance the current painting didn't damage the Maclet."

"I'll get it. How much time?"

"Soon. Contact me at the café. I'm there most days."

"Thanks." He shook Beau's hand and turned, anger suffusing him. His head could explode.

"Max." Had he heard his name?

"Max." His ears caught it before the wind whipped it away. He rushed back to Beau. "I almost forgot." Beau held out a dirty rectangular envelope. "My wife found this under your old bed. After she moved in, she scrubbed the place. Guess we were bad housekeepers. I didn't know where you were, so I kept it. It's been a long time . . . I hope it's not important." Maximillian stuck it in his back pocket.

"Thanks." Max furiously ran down the steps away from the Basilica, heat rising in his face. People sidestepped him as he charged past, glancing away from his enraged face. He wove between slow-moving sightseers roughly bypassing the turtles. Time was short; he was due at Chez Philippe. He had only taken an hour off between the lunch and dinner trade. He must get back.

Damn, damn, damn. The rat got him again. He should have avoided the dishonest scoundrel. A hush fell over the Butte, and then the clouds expelled their load in driving rainfall slanting sideways in the revived wind. Maximillian was drenched in moments. His heavy rain-slickened workpants clung to his legs as he struggled with his unwieldy umbrella. It sailed out of his hands, tumbling and rolling along a now nearly deserted street.

When Maximillian saw the shop with the faded *Frames* sign, his anger escalated. He burst through the shabby door and waited for his eyes to adjust to the inside gloom. His clothing dripped, forming a puddle around his feet. Murky light struggled through the cloudy window in the darkened room. It appeared empty. He listened, controlling his accelerated breath in the quiet stillness. The door had been unlocked; he was here. Something rustled in the corner and he charged toward the rear of the shop. The proprietor crouched behind a workbench with his arms over his head.

"Stand up you scoundrel! You cheated me." His sodden clothing hampered him as he pulled the little man to his feet. "I was naïve, didn't recognize the value. You screwed me!"

"You got what you wanted." He backed away from Maximillian, circling around a worktable overfilled with junk, keeping it between them.

"What did I get?"

"An old canvas covered in white gesso paint ready for an artist to work on." He threw his shoulders back standing taller, defiant. "That's what you asked for."

"What about proof of the Maclet? I didn't know I needed proof."

"Calm down." His manner now more confident, he circumnavigated the worktable, moving closer to Maximillian. A musky stench overwhelmed Maximillian's senses, the rat smelled as if he had had his last shower a month ago. Max covered his mouth and nose with the crook of his arm.

"The Maclet was so striking, I couldn't paint over it. Gesso is hard to remove, takes an expert. I stretched the Maclet over the frame, and then nailed another old canvas over it. The Maclet is underneath. I checked when you brought it in last week."

"Why'd you cover it with another canvas?" Maximillian crowded close, threatening him with his size.

"I wanted the Maclet," he admitted. "I took photographs: of the stretched Maclet, of the white-coated canvas, of the finished painting. All proof of provenance. Before the buyer took possession, I planned to remove the Maclet."

"You double-crossed me." Maximillian held the man's bony shoulders in his hands, he could crush him, if he chose to.

"You would've been paid. The buyer would discover the loss later."

"You would have cheated the buyer?" Max asked.

"Yes."

"You're rotten and you smell horrible. I want Miriam back. With the Maclet intact." Maximillian shook the man, whose loose jowls flapped. "The photographs too." He nearly gagged as he waited for the man to answer.

"I don't have it. Gave it and the photos to a contact." The rat squeaked. "You wanted a quick sale." Maximillian threw him against the wall.

"Get it back. With the photos. By tomorrow." He tore through the frame shop, and thrust the door open so hard it crashed against junk piled behind it, and ricocheted back, hurling shut. Beau had found a buyer and the painting was gone.

He raced to Chez Philippe without an umbrella. He should've stolen one from the crook. The relentless rain hadn't slackened at all. How could he get any wetter? Every pair of eyes stared when he entered his kitchen.

"Get to work," he said as he entered his workplace, "what are you looking at?"

He snarled at his head sous chef next, and then the rest of his staff avoided him. Claustrophobic wet clothes impeded his food preparation. Hurling a large kettle across the counter, he didn't hear Monsieur Dubois approach, until he spoke.

"Maximillian." Dubois's voice was low and ominous, compelling Maximillian to strain to hear. He moved close behind him. "There are too many altercations between you and your staff." He lowered his voice further, growling just behind Maximillian's ear. "Control yourself. You have a job. Take care of business. We have a full house expecting excellence." Dubois expelled an exasperated sigh, and flapped his arms. "Look at me." The man dressed in formal black clothes pointed his finger. "Don't waste your talent."

Everyone was against him. Dubois usually tolerated a lot, aware genius often came with an ugly disposition. Maximillian was a fine head chef and Dubois needed him. Dubois was right, he must restrain his urges, contain his tendency to self-destruct. Old demons arrived in his head mocking him as he struggled through black waves of despair. He finally focused on Émilie's serene face. Without speaking to his staff, he mechanically finished his work as the evening snaked to an end.

He was exhausted when he entered their apartment and he bypassed his usual shower. No energy. Peeling off his wet clothes next to the bed, he stepped over them and snuck in. Émilie was asleep. He had fought the devil and simultaneously cooked exquisite food. Had he won the battle? Émilie awoke.

"I've been waiting for you," she said. She pulled him closer and stroked his body, fondling his head and ears, arousing him. After they had made love and she still held him close, she whispered. "I want to marry you." Damn. She hadn't let it go. What a day.

She, the baby, and his job should be enough. But for Maximillian, poor decision-making, and an irrepressible need to take advantage, always impeded rational thinking. Maximillian fell asleep long after Émilie did.

Maximillian had forgotten about the envelope Beauregard gave him. When he got up in the night to use the bathroom, his foot kicked something, but he was too tired.

It hadn't registered enough to remember later.

Chapter XXIII Bertrand

CHARLOTTE'S MODERN second-floor apartment stifled Bertrand and crushed his talent. His home sat on the ground tying him to the earth, and connected him to nature. Even if nature meant his familiar Montmartre street with its ivy-covered stone wall. The black ironwork of her balcony resembled jail bars; his spirit would die here if he couldn't go home. But how could he betray his daughter's kindness?

Bertrand hadn't told Charlotte why he had to leave Montmartre. When Maximillian shoved him into the park service area, he told Bertrand the *Miriam* painting disguised an original Maclet. He had committed a crime by painting *Miriam* over it. Although he had suspected Maximillian's intentions when he had commissioned the painting, the bald truth scared him. His role was illegal. After Maximillian confirmed his original suspicion, he had been too nervous to stay at home.

He pretended his visit was normal at first, a chance to play with his granddaughters. But he still couldn't sleep; the merry-go-round of worry circulated endlessly, night and day. The commissions slated for the American were only half-finished and his inspiration was gone. He couldn't paint a stroke. He must confront the *Miriam* issue.

Everything Bertrand loved—besides Charlotte, Nicole, and Simone—resided in his beloved Montmartre: his friends, his neighbors, his home, and the bistro. After a somewhat virtuous life (he was a Frenchmen), one poor decision had caused a misstep. By his calculation, Bertrand could move on with his life if he took responsibility for his part. Two troublesome men prevented him from going home, Maximillian and Michel la Roche. They had both confronted him.

Bertrand calculated he had two options. Maximillian would leave him alone if he helped him sell the painting. He just wanted the money. He was wretchedly bad; but he couldn't expose Bertrand without exposing himself.

Michel la Roche said his client wanted the *Miriam* painting. Was Michel aware of the Maclet? The Gensonné firm might bring in law enforcement, it was the nature of their business. He could call Michel la Roche, admit his role, and hope the disguised Elisée Maclet was a minor crime. If the original artwork was retrieved and unharmed, the penalty would be light. Perhaps a fine.

A brilliant plan had occurred to Bertrand last night. Sell the painting to Michel la Roche and pay Maximillian. Another idea occurred to him today; he could probably now afford to give the painting to Michel and pay Maximillian off. How much did crooks get for fenced art? Probably not much.

Where had Maximillian hid the painting? The last time he saw *Miriam*, Maximillian had stomped angrily through his doorway with it clutched under his arm. Bertrand could fix this and return to his idyllic life in Montmartre. He painted in weeks, and for an artist like him, to paint was to live.

"Papa, where are you?" Charlotte called, her footsteps echoing through the apartment. "I'm home early."

"On the balcony." It was the only view of the outdoors and he saw it through black wrought-iron bars edging the drop-off. Uninspiring.

"Why don't you go out into the neighborhood? To a park or to the shops?"

Bertrand hunched his shoulders. "I like it here."

"Papa, you're not painting. You did at first. Simone loved painting with Grand-papa."

"I haven't felt like painting." He avoided her worried eyes. Charlotte worked at a bank, plus took care of two children while her husband temporarily managed a multinational company in China. "I'll paint when I get used to it here."

She sat across from him, her knees touching his. "Papa, I had lunch with someone. I'd like to talk." Her cornflower eyes were filled with concern. Light freckles strewn like fairy dust matched the cloud of red-blond hair that framed an oval face, wavy ends grazing her elbows. His daughter was a stunningly beautiful woman.

"You look like your mother." He caressed her cheeks. "I should paint you." Hope briefly soared inside; his fingers itched for a paintbrush.

"Papa. Let's talk." He probably should tell her his problem, share the burden. But a father took care of himself. "I had lunch with Michel la Roche on Monday. He thinks you are in trouble. With a painting." Bertrand looked through the railing, noticing how the bars made each opening look like a long narrow picture, framed in black.

"What kind of trouble?"

"He didn't say. I'd like to help you, Papa."

"Did he give you a clue?"

"He said the painting was of a dead woman floating in a red dress. It was oil on canvas. I don't remember one. When did you paint it?"

Therefore, Michel (and perhaps others) surmised he had painted *Miriam*. Odd, he hadn't told Michel. Did he find Maximillian? "Someone commissioned it six years ago."

"Who was the woman? Why would she want to be painted like underwater?"

Humorous. Charlotte assumed someone had commissioned the underwater scene. Her eyebrows drawn together, her mouth firm, puzzled. He smiled, hoping to erase her serious expression. "She was a model. Sometimes my artists' group hires a model and we divide the cost. The model was lying on her back on an antique lounging chaise; my friends painted her in the chaise. My vision was an underwater scene."

"Did someone commission the scene?" She was too clever. Her eyes searched his, she tipped her head, and studied him through thick sandy lashes.

"He didn't care what I painted. He wanted a well-executed painting he could sell." He had to tell her now. He sighed.

"The person brought me an old canvas over-coated with white gesso. I painted the woman onto the prepared canvas. I suspected it could disguise another painting as the commission was an odd one. I lifted paint from the edges; I didn't see anything unusual."

He had told her the truth. He didn't find anything except an aged canvas.

"Remember our day in the park? The man who commissioned it was also there. He said there was a valuable Elisée Maclet painted onto canvas under the top canvas."

"That's illegal, Papa," she wailed. She jumped up and paced three steps, and back. "Why?"

"I didn't know, I should have. It's bad, It's bad . . . I can't sleep. Sometimes we just . . . make choices . . . without . . . without thinking. I made a hasty decision. I regret it."

"What can we do? What does Michel la Roche think?" Charlotte brooder over him, concerned. His image of fatherhood didn't include disappointing a beloved child; he dropped his head into the palms of his hands. "I don't know." His shoulders quivered. "I don't know." "We have to fix this." She pulled him up and hugged him tight. "We need you, Papa. Don't let anything happen." Her tears moistened his shirt as soft indrawn sobs escaped from her lips. Caressing her neck and shoulders, he wished her mother was still here. His wife had been much younger than he, although she had been very young when she died of breast cancer. He was now an old man with aching bones and a gimpy hip.

"I have a plan. I need to think." Should he contact Michel la Roche or Maximillian first? Bertrand wanted his old life back.

Maximillian wouldn't leave Bertrand alone until he disposed of *Miriam*, and got his money. He was afraid of Maximillian; but the compulsion to return to Montmartre propelled him past fear.

Retrieve *Miriam* first, even if he had to confront Maximillian. Michel la Roche said his client would pay well for the painting.

Chapter XXIV André

THE GENSONNÉ CLAN had converged onto the family home to celebrate André's birthday with a hopeful exuberance not present for almost two decades. The white-limestone house gleamed from its power washing, and freshly-washed windows sparkled in the sunshine. Maman said their home had needed sprucing up. But she had preserved the border garden of exuberantly unshaped shrubs. Two squatty, chipped urns flanked the front door, hanging onto tumbling yellow roses emitting a spicy aroma all passed through when they entered. André's childhood home was happy to host the upcoming festivities.

André's determined mother said they would celebrate La Fête Nationale the same way they did when her children were young, when her twin sons' birthday had been the biggest celebration of the summer. Maman appeared youthful, flitting among her grandchildren, delighted the whole family had gathered, the home expanding to encompass additional people. All of them slept beneath Vincent and Sophia's roof last night, although it had taken many threats (by their parents) and promises (by their grandparents) to dispatch the children.

Sophia had prepared an abundant breakfast. Croissants with jelly, fruit juice and yogurt, café au lait for the adults and hot chocolate for the children.

They were all there: Celeste, Dominic, and their three daughters Gena, Lyla, and Remi; Isabelle, Christophe, and their two boys, Corbin and Lucien; his parents Vincent and Sophia and his grandparents Jean-Baptiste and Marguerite, him and Michel. The children finished their breakfast, and once they left the table, the noise level escalated.

The excited children energized the living areas as a game of tag, initiated by Michel and André, grew out of control. His grandparents finally begged for quiet.

"I can't hear." Grand-maman clapped her hands over her ears.

"Quiet!" Grand-père demanded. "At least until the adults finish breakfast."

Michel had just captured Corbin who was wiggling to escape. "We didn't get included in the adults," he said. "We're having more fun. And you're it." He had let Corbin go, and tagged André.

Even when they were young children, it was not like this joyous collaboration, the family had been smaller, and there were more rules. Or perhaps his perspective had changed.

Celeste reduced the din by seating the children in the middle of the floor. "Michel, where's your magic cards? You have a captive audience."

"Be back in a moment," he said.

"Grand-maman, who is Pierre?" Gena asked.

"He's your uncle, your Maman's brother. His birthday is today, the same as Uncle André."

"Did he die?"

"Yes. We loved him very much." Sophia lifted Gena, hugging her quickly.

"I love him, too." Gena squirmed out of Sophia's arms.

"I love you, little one."

Michel entertained the little ones as his sisters organized the parade outing. Celeste and Isabelle doled out shoulder bags containing the day's necessities, and discussed who would oversee each animated child.

"Okay, Michel. You're off-duty," Celeste said. "For a moment. Then you're in charge of Remi." She gathered the three girls and two boys to explain the day's events.

"When we were little like you, we went to the military parade on the Champs-Élysées." The children clumped around, Corbin leaning against her, rubbing her arm. "And then we went to a park for a picnic. Just like we are doing today. Please listen to the adults. You may go outside now."

The clump separated in five directions.

"Uncle André, I want to ride in your new car," Corbin said.

"It's your uncle's birthday car, it's a two-seater. Not enough room for all of us," Celeste said. Rolling her eyes, she winked at André. "Your uncle hauls girls around in that car." André caught his grandfather's smiling eyes, and shook his head. Grand-père shrugged and joined the children, clasping Corbin and Lyla's hands.

"I'll give you a ride another time." André squatted, and held his hand for a high-five, Corbin slapped hard with his free hand. "We're traveling on the Métro today, better than braving street traffic." Celeste and Isabelle herded everyone toward the nearest Métro station.

"Will you carry me?" Remi tugged on Michel's shirt. He stooped, swung her up, and André picked up Gena. His heart constricted with emotion. Was he entitled to all this?

The family sat among others on the Métro; André took an available single seat and held Gena.

When they were children, André and Pierre's family, and extended families had celebrated annually, establishing an unbroken tradition. Until Pierre died just two weeks before their birthday. It wasn't the only reason. Family dynamics had changed. He left France to study in America and his siblings were teens, then young adults, and they partied with friends. It was time for a new start.

Gena's eyes drifted shut, and his mind wandered to another La Fête Nationale, when he and his brother had celebrated their ninth birthday at the parade.

TRADITIONAL MUSICAL FESTIVITIES and official ceremonies occurred all over France on this day, beginning with the oldest military parade in Europe, held in the morning of July fourteenth, on the Champs-Élysées. The parade passed by the President of the Republic, French officials and foreign guests, and thousands of Parisians and visitors.

Bastille Day was "celebrated with all the brilliance that the local resources allow," per the Minister of the Interior on 6 July 1880. It was La Fête Nationale celebration for the entire country.

The twins were nine-year's old and excited. He and Pierre had craned their necks to see the military airplanes soar over the parade route, the engines' roar splitting the air, so loud their small bodies vibrated. The French president reviewed the troops, an event that opened the parade. The twins darted around the wide sidewalks; tagging their friends and cousins while they waited for the parade to reach them.

The boys stared at the men and women in matched uniforms with real guns and colorful flags representing their units. The children's goal had been to get marching soldiers to look at them, or wink, acknowledge their antics. Sometimes, one or two soldiers did break rank, lips twitching. The parade ended with the Pompiers de Paris and then the entire family left to picnic at a park.

The cousins challenged each other to a football game, each side valiantly defending their goal. Promising fireworks later, their parents insisted they go home and rest. The cousins collaborated, begging for gelato. The adults laughed at their recurring scheme—the children proposed gelato every year. The nine-year old twins had been in the thick of the action.

André's earliest memories had been of birthday parties, his large family celebrating each person's birthday, individually. Jean-Baptist and Marguerite had hosted most of the events, throwing extravagant affairs with wonderful gifts. His serious grandfather loved birthday parties.

The greatest excitement involved two little boys who shared a birthday on the national holiday, when everyone in their world celebrated. When they were young, they thought they were the only ones in France with this birthday. Growing older, it was the best birthday a boy could have.

His brother died two weeks before their 18th birthday; and it became a melancholy day when Pierre's loss was keenly felt by everyone. When the French people prepared for La Fête Nationale each year, André' grew anxious, always relieved after the day had passed. This year was different, anticipation coursed through him. He felt like a boy again although he was thirty-five.

A new generation of children would experience the old traditions. Gena, Lyla and Remi and four-year old Corbin and eighteen-month-old Lucien offered hope. The family had properly grieved Pierre's loss. They would finally celebrate both birthdays today.

They left the Métro, Celeste still giving instructions amid streaming crowds of people headed for the parade route.

"Remember the meeting place." Celeste raised her voice above the noise. "If separated, we have our mobiles. Michel has told a woman to meet us there too." Her eyes sparkled; her hair pulled back from her face, she looked like a happy mother of three. Curls escaped from the hair band, some bouncing, some dampened by sweat. Celeste caught André watching her. "Happy birthday, André." She spoke over the children's heads. "Happy birthday, Pierre."

Parisians celebrated in huge numbers as blue skies and an eighty-degree temperature brought thousands into the streets.

The family wound through the masses, Celeste and Isabelle, directing and herding them along. André, Michel, Dominic, and Christophe each held a child or a child's hand. Celeste carried little Lucien.

"Want down," Lucien said. He wiggled, trying to squirm out of her arms.

"Not yet." Celeste held the baby tight.

"There she is. Crazy Violeta." Michel startled Remi, whom he held in his arms. André didn't see Violeta yet, but a huge grin transformed Michel's face. Michel quickened his pace, Remi's whole body bounced and she urged him along, giggling.

"Faster, faster. Run faster, Uncle Michel." Michel hurried to the same girl who had dined with them at Madame le Pic.

"A second date with the same girl?" André asked. He had kept pace with Michel. "A long relationship."

"If you only knew." Michel teased. He bumped against him. Gena screeched, pulling back in André's arms.

"Ouch. My ears. I'll tickle you now." André tickled her lightly, eliciting another screech. His ears rang. They had reached the blond woman in colorful close-fitting sports clothes. "Shush, let's meet Michel's girlfriend." Gena nodded. Michel had already air-kissed Violeta's cheeks, Remi smashed between them.

"Bonjour. Violeta, this is Gena." The little girl shyly buried her head against André.

"Bonjour." Violeta had Remi in her arms now. She gave her a twirl and set her down, keeping her hand in a tight hold. The others dropped their belongings onto the blanket Celeste had spread, and the children settled on it. Celeste established the boundaries for the five children, and gave him a new assignment. "You are responsible for Lucien, André." The baby, he would have to be vigilant.

Celeste bossed naturally, Isabelle naturally observed.

THE CHILDREN GREW restless before the two-hour parade was half over. "Let me buy them gelato," André suggested. Celeste had just chased Lucien back to the blanket.

"Good idea." She picked up the baby. "I'll go with you. You can't manage five of them."

"Uncle André is buying gelato. Who wants to go?" The little girls and Corbin jumped up and down.

"Me. Me. I do." They gathered around, Lyla and Gena each clasping one of his legs. Celeste imparted the rules.

"Lyla, Gena and Remi hold hands and walk between me and Uncle André. Corbin, you hold my other hand. André, you carry Lucien." Celeste handed Lucien to him. "Let's go." They crawled along the packed sidewalk, Celeste weaving through the crowds. It took longer than André expected though the children cooperated.

Lucien slept on André's shoulder, his head bobbing; his thumb stuck in his mouth. A line of people stretched along the block near the gelato shop, but the line moved steadily. Celeste took charge again.

"I'll take Corbin and you stay here while we stand in line," she said. "My girls listen, they'll stay close." She took Corbin's hand and left André under a Planc tree with the other four, Lucien asleep in his arms. Tourists approached him, smiling, some cloyingly close. He swayed slightly, rocking the baby; he could see Celeste moving along in line, talking to Corbin.

André's arm ached; the baby was heavy. He had shifted Lucien to his right shoulder when he saw two statuesque women leave the shop with cups of gelato. One, an animated red head, arrayed in bright clothing, talked with her hands, her gelato flying. The other woman was reserved, with a Mona Lisa smile, the dark-haired Anne; although he suspected he wouldn't have recognized her if, he hadn't been obsessed with the painting.

"Anne." André raised his voice. "Anne." Lucien stirred in André's arms; the three little girls gathered around his legs, Remi clutching his pant leg. "Girls. Hold hands." André clasped Gena's left hand and the other two locked hands. His hand trembled, his sweatier than Gena's little fingers. Would she see him? His heart raced, he wanted to run to her and sweep her into his arms, but they were full, his numb right arm held precious cargo. "Anne." She had to see him. He shuffled toward them with his charges.

Anne and the other woman turned, scanning the crowd. "Anne." He had raised his voice. He saw her glance around, a puzzled look flashed across her face and her eyes skipped past him. "Anne." What would he do if she moved away? He couldn't let her disappear this time. He ushered the girls ahead of him, dropping Gena's hand and shifting Lucien to his left shoulder.

She stopped and met his questioning gaze, hesitated, and then took a step toward him. He motioned to her, his sister was right; the girls listened and hovered near his legs. Anne moved her head closer to the other woman's bright head, murmured to her, then pointed with her gelato. He nodded, encouraging. The women walked toward him.

"André. Children. Here we are. Gelato." Celeste had just reached them with a loaded tray, Corbin clinging to the edges of her blouse. Anne and the red-haired woman arrived under the tree at the same time as Celeste and Corbin did.

"You were a good Papa, André. You didn't lose any of them," Celeste teased. "Oh. Bonjour." She motioned toward the other women with full hands, her gaze darting to make sure Corbin was close. "Friends of yours?"

"Maybe." André winked, Celeste returned it. "Bonjour. Anne?" André asked. She smiled. "From Michigan?" A quiet nod. The woman next to her was spirited, looking expectantly from him to Anne.

"This is Stefania." Anne motioned to her companion.

"Bonjour." Stefania said and then moved toward the children. "Let me help".

Lucien stirred in his arms, whimpered, and snuggled closer, then circled his chubby arms around André's neck.

"Can you wait?" Anne nodded again. "Give me a second to sort this out." André joined Celeste and her girls.

Meanwhile, the red-haired Stefania reached for the gelato tray and received a grateful look from Celeste. "Merci, I'll get them settled and you distribute," Celeste said. She pulled the blanket from her shoulder bag, spread it out, and directed Corbin, Gena, Lyla and Remi to sit.

She gathered Lucien from André's arms and set him down. Lucien babbled, rubbing his eyes and stretched his arms to André. "Up." The bright-haired woman gave him the first gelato. Lucien flashed her a wondrous smile. He bent his head to taste it and then looked up, nose and lips smeared with gelato. Celeste handed him a spoon.

"My name is Stefania." She pressed a cup of Spumoni gelato into each child's hands, stooping to their level, caressing Corbin's tousled head.

"I'm Celeste. Thanks for the help." They lingered near the children, eating their own gelato. André saw Anne a short distance away from the blanket, eyes flicking toward them and away, wavering. He didn't want her to leave.

"Celeste, will you watch the children? I'll be right back." André took Anne's arm and led her behind the tree. "I have a million questions. First, do you live in Paris?"

"Yes." Her voice was soft, her manner shy. He had forgotten how tall she was. "You have your hands full."

"I do." He drew a business card and handed it to her. "My contact information. Will you call me?"

She took the card and read it. "Yes." He glanced behind him; Lucien had pushed himself up and toddled off the blanket. Lucien was his responsibility; he turned and swooped him into his arms in mid-stride, Lucien's plump legs pumping.

"Please. Call me." He managed to hang onto the squirming sweaty baby.

She nodded and motioned to Stefania; they walked a short distance and disappeared among the revelers. Anne disappeared; Stefania's red and orange clothing was still visible when Lucien screamed. "Down." André put him down, holding his sticky hand.

"Who were those women?" Celeste asked.

"I'll tell you later." He guided Lucien back to his melting gelato onto the blanket, the other children had finished theirs. Celeste handed him a wet cloth and he squatted, wiping little faces. Then it occurred to him Anne might think the children were his. Had he said anything? Both tall women spoke accented French well. He stood, towering over the children. He had given her his business card; he hadn't asked for her surname, or asked where she worked. She would have to contact him. Damn!

IT WAS THEIR thirty-fifth birthday—and Pierre came to him again. He held out his arms, looking like the Messiah. For the third time since his death, he spoke to André, *"Happy birthday, brother. Talk to Monique."*

André didn't believe in ghosts, he'd convinced himself he'd dreamed his brother appeared. Monique could be someone his brain conjured. He considered himself a rational person; why he struggled with religion. For thousands of years, religion defined how people participated in the world. For him, the laws of nature defined the world and God was subject to the same laws. Young Europeans didn't practice the faith of their parents and grandparents and his family had fallen away from the church.

Pierre's death had hastened his disbelief in a God who had His finger on the pulse of His people. Michel still had faith; but he couldn't think of anyone else. He had seen Pierre's spirit again. Who would believe him? He was the grounded one.

Unable to sleep, he linked unconnected incidences. Each time he saw Anne, Pierre appeared with a message. The first time was in the dorm in Michigan; the second when he saw Anne at the Louvre. Pierre had said, *"She's the one."* He wished him happy birthday tonight and told him to talk to Monique. Who was Monique?

If only he could remember the first message.

Chapter XXV Anne

ANNE MARIE MORGAN dressed in a new blue and white striped linen sheath, and then tied a filmy red scarf around her waist. Looking in her full-length mirror, she then untied the too-bright scarf. She scanned the clothing in her closet. When did her wardrobe get so boring? Just before she left her apartment, she retied the red scarf and avoided the mirror.

"Do you want to attend the parade with me?" Stefania had asked. Anne just returned from a morning run and when she saw her, she stopped. Still hard to reciprocate Stefania's overtures, she forced herself to reply.

"Maybe. I guess so. I usually go——."

"Did you say yes?" Stefania asked.

"Yes." Her voice husky, she had just committed herself.

Bastille Day arrived, and the women disembarked from the Métro, joining hundreds of others who streamed toward the Champs-Élysées, the main avenue downtown leading to the Arc de Triomphe. Near the center of festivities, many of the Métro stations had closed for the day, so they wore comfortable walking shoes.

"I like your dress, Anne. Is it new?" Stefania sported a vivid orange blouse over an orange, red, yellow and white patterned skirt.

"Yes." Anne glanced at her dress, and touched the red scarf. The festive crowd heightened her excitement; the bright summer day held promise. The last few years she had attended the parade alone. They joined the crowds which lined the wide Champs-Élysées, standing behind children who sat on the curb. Military jets trailed red, white and blue exhaust, the colors of the French flag, opening the ceremonies to the cheers of thousands.

The woman applauded with the French, celebrating the storming of the Bastille, and the beginning of the 1789 Revolution. Colorful regiments of various military units marched the parade route festooned with the red, white and blue tricolor. Stefania grew restless about halfway through the parade.

"All those handsome men, and I can't flirt." She flounced away from the street. "I'm famished." Stefania had a metabolism she stoked regularly. Anne lifted her shoulder, she had been in Paris long enough to have mastered the expressive movement that covered a variety of communications.

"Let's get gelato at the last shop we passed." Stefania took Anne's arm. "Before the parade finishes, and it gets busier."

"I'm ready for gelato." They conversed easily in French.

"There it is. Hurry. Let's get in line." Stefania darted forward, securing a place at the back. The line barely moved. Stefania talked to others near them, asking where they lived, switching between French and English. They finally reached the freezers and peered in the narrow metal trays displaying confetti-colored gelato, swirled with lavish markings.

"I'm treating. What flavor do you want?" Stefania asked. Anne chose lemon and Stefania chose orange, and raspberry.

They left the shop, Stefania talking, and gesturing with her gelato-filled hand. Anne heard her name. Twice. A man's voice. She turned, searching for the speaker. She heard her name again. Her eyes found him. André?

André held a baby toddler in his right arm, and clasped the hand of a miniature girl with his left. On his right side were two more tiny girls, holding hands. The four children looked just like him. Mesmerized, she stared. "Anne," he said. He dropped the little girl's hand, and motioned to her.

She clutched Stefania's arm and directed her gaze to André. "I know him." Anne navigated around several groups. Stefania gasped, following closely, muttering under her breath. Just when they had reached the man and children, another woman hurried toward them, a little boy trailing behind, his hand clutching the tail of her blouse. He was a bit smaller than the three identical girls were.

"You were a good Papa, André. You didn't lose any of them," the woman said. Celeste was teasing him, but five children. All his?

HE HAD HAD his hands full, and the day had gone dark for Anne. Stefania had stepped in to help the mother distribute gelato and supervise children, while she had hovered at the margins of the happy spectacle. André had called her away from the group, but distracted by the small boy, had only time to give her his card.

She had hurried Stefania away from the picturesque family, however, she bubbled with questions. "Who was he? He's hot! Best-looking man I've seen in Paris. How did you meet him?" Stefania hurled question after question.

Anne's face warmed. They could probably hear Stefania. "He must be virile. Did you see all those kids? Those girls had to be triplets; they looked identical, and were dressed alike."

Anne grabbed Stefania's arm, putting her head close to her mouth, hissing. "They'll hear you." Anne still held the expensively engraved business card. "His name is André Gensonné. I didn't know his last name." She had been so young and inexperienced when she first met him; she hadn't understood his accented English.

"Who is he?"

"I met him at home, I mean the U.S. I was in high school."

"An exchange student?" Stefania was bursting with curiosity.

"No, maybe. I don't know." Stefania finally sensed Anne needed silence.

Anne concentrated on the card with his name, André Gensonné, attorney. The firm name and his, were the same. Stefania wanted more information; but an icy pebble formed in her heart and grew, she felt cold inside. She had dreamed of him since she was seventeen; his being had permeated every pore, transforming her. She couldn't share it with Stefania. Why did it feel as if her body was tearing apart?

It had been years since they had first met. She had known he could be married, probably was married, a striking boy, and now a handsome man.

The possible glimpse of him at the embassy, and the shared look at the Louvre intensified the old desires, nurturing possibility. Meeting him surrounded by children and a vivacious woman, quenched the dream. What had Celeste said? *"You were a good Papa, André. You didn't lose any of them."*

She tucked the card into her purse. She had forgotten to look for a wedding ring.

Chapter XXVI André

Monday, July 15, 2013

ANDRÉ ROLLED ONTO his back and folded his arms behind his head as the night gradually receded. The joyful chaos of exuberant children enjoying holiday festivities yesterday had been replaced by a melancholy mood; he should have spent this bank holiday with Maman and Papa.

Morning light dispatched some of the murkiness, revealing his brown and cream striped bedspread. When had he decided varying shades of muddy brown should dominate his home? Yellow might be nice—or red. The painting and the fire had changed him—he hadn't realized his life was brown.

André flopped into a supple leather chair in his salon; his favorite chair was chestnut brown. Red dresses were nice. Would red drapes be too dramatic?

The day brightened, promising sunshine and blue skies, and inside André's walls came alive. An abundance of oils and watercolors decorated the buff walls of the two-story salon, the deep hues of oils and softer hues of watercolors, in living color. The interior decorator had recommended a warm paint shade; the color enhanced his collection of paintings. A bright accent color would be a nice touch though.

Who was Monique? Pierre's apparition had told him to talk to her, but her name meant nothing. The name had nibbled at him, like a scavenging crow picking at prey. His dinner meeting with Grand-père also loomed, black and ominous. What his grandfather divulged might threaten his restored life.

He walked in measured steps, back and forth, across the living room, then moved to the massive window overlooking the city. The firm had closed today for La Fête Nationale. This Monday could not be long enough, or short enough.

André hadn't known his grandfather kept a secret which could destroy their generations-old law firm. Even his turbulent youth hadn't been shared with the family. Shaped by war during his critical teens, Jean-Baptiste had lived a complex existence as an adult. Sometimes he had played the role of paternalistic grandfather. But André knew him best as his formidable partner, often feeling fortunate he was on Grand-père's team, and not the opposition's.

Their primary connection had been almost a mystic connection; the two could spend hours in a museum contemplating a handful of paintings, discussing nuances of color, perspective, and light. A museum was neutral territory, Jean-Baptiste was neither partner nor grandfather.

André's propensity for discerning exquisite paintings, discovering new artists and recognizing masterpieces, eventually rivaled that of his grandfather.

He dreaded his dinner meeting with Grand-père; worried his situation might become incomprehensibility complicated.

Piled atop that worry was Monique. Perhaps his mother knew who she was, most of the people he associated with weren't aware he had a brother. Monique must be a friend of Pierre's.

"Bonjour." His mother answered immediately.

"Bonjour, Maman."

"André. So soon, are you all right?"

"I hope you can help me." André pictured his mother in her kitchen. Yesterday had been full of activities; they hadn't spoken much. Had it been only yesterday? His restless night had taken its toll. "Do you remember someone named Monique?"

"Monique? Maybe. Pierre's old girlfriend? She's the only Monique I know. Why?"

"Now I remember." He tapped his forehead. Nikki. "I knew her as Nikki." The girl he had taken on a prank date the week before Pierre died. His stomach knotted. Guilt, and regret, engulfed him. Pierre had said he was in love with Nikki, the reason he didn't want to dally with girls in Corsica.

"It was long ago. What's wrong?" His sensitive mother was astute.

"Where does she live?" André closed his eyes, please don't ask too much.

"I can find out. She married an acquaintance's son. I haven't spoken to her in years, but if they are still married, she would be the one to ask."

"Thanks, Maman."

"Will you tell me more?"

"Not yet. I didn't remember her name." André lightened his tone. "I'd like a telephone number."

"I'll try. I'm curious. I didn't think Pierre was serious about Monique. Before he died, he told me they'd broken up. He said it was mutual."

"Did they date long?"

"It was a summer thing. Mothers aren't always informed. She did call herself Nikki for a time."

"I knew her as Nikki. If you find her number, let me know. Au revoir Maman. Thanks." He broke the connection.

He sat on his couch, leaning forward, head in his hands. His mother was wrong. Pierre had said he was in love that day. It must have been Monique. The night of the disastrous date, Monique told him Pierre liked her more than she liked him. It was why she participated in his charade. Even when she knew it was him.

His mother located Monique's mobile number within fifteen minutes. André called her immediately.

"Bonjour." A beautifully modulated voice answered.

"Bonjour. I don't know if you remember me. My name is André Gensonné, the brother of Pierre Gensonné."

"I remember . . ." Her voice was fainter.

"This is awkward, the last time I saw you, I was a foolish seventeen-year-old." He closed his eyes; his actions had been despicable.

"We were young, all of us. I'm sorry about Pierre."

André struggled for the right words to approach Monique. He had initiated the fateful date, and the reopened wound hurt.

"Are you still there? André?" His name hung between them, somewhere in space. They probably had landlines then.

"I'm so sorry for—," André spoke quickly, pausing, unsure.

"I wasn't honest that night, about Pierre and me. I've regretted the lie. Pierre ended the relationship before we went out. And then he was dead the next weekend." She swallowed a sob. "You family was grieving; I dared not call." Her voice softened, he strained to hear the next words. "Then you went to the United States."

"I went to school there."

"Why are you calling?" The question ballooned large—and then receded. Why had he called? Because Pierre told him to?

"André?" He hadn't spoken for several seconds.

"About this phone call, it may be easier to meet."

"I'm married, Pierre is gone. What difference would it make?"

"I'm sorry I intruded. Will you answer a question?" André anticipated a refusal.

"Yes." Her lovely voice was kind. Before he could ask, she continued. "I loved Pierre; he didn't love me. It took a long time to get over him, even after he died. Pierre's choice was so extraordinary, so unexpected. It hurt so much." André wished he could soothe her, but no words came. "Now, what is your question?" He couldn't remember; he ruffled his hair. What did she mean by extraordinary choice?

"What choice? Before we went sailing that morning, he said he had a new love. I assumed it was you."

"It wasn't me. It was the Church; he felt called to priesthood. He said he cared for me, but felt chosen."

"My brother?" Time stopped and his mind floundered, unable to imagine Pierre—a priest. How could he not know? Such a life-changing decision. Unshared with his twin. Maman couldn't have known.

"That's why I knew it wasn't Pierre when you called me; he had broken it off. I threw myself at you, wishing you were he. It was over, my dreams gone. I thought . . . maybe . . . you could replace him. You looked alike."

"Monique. I'm so sorry. I didn't know; I'm sure my parents didn't know. Poor Pierre."

"I'm not sure, but I think he wanted to tell your family during your vacation. All these years, I thought you knew. Your family priest guided him, perhaps he knows more."

The family hadn't been faithful to the Church. When they were younger, they had usually attended Mass on Sundays, and he and his siblings participated in all the expected Sacraments. Maman had been the only committed Catholic, and hers had originally been Greek Orthodox. After Pierre died, no one went to church. A vocation to the priesthood and Pierre? Incompatible

"Are you sure? Pierre was incorrigible, a trickster, we all suffered from his exploits. A priest?"

"I believed him. He seemed sincere; but it was shocking. Young men in France rarely choose the priesthood."

"I feel worse. I asked for a date, pretended to be Pierre, after he left you."

"I told you then, I knew it was you," she said. "But I didn't tell you until the evening ended. I regretted my lie."

"We both hurt you. I apologize, for everything." André wished he could hug her.

"I could understand another girl, but the Church. I couldn't compete with that." He heard her teenage anguish.

"We humans can mess things up, so much time lost, so much guilt. Thank you for helping."

"Did I answer your question?" she asked.

"I don't remember. Thanks for your honesty."

"How are the others? Your parents, sisters?"

"We've adapted, adjusted to life without him. Pierre and I were thirty-five on La Fête Nationale."

"I know. Was it a good birthday?"

"Probably the best since, since he died." André's mind drifted to Pierre. Monique may have been right for him. "Are you happy?"

"Yes. I fell in love again. I have a full life, and children. And you?"

"I'm still looking; I may have found her. I'm ready now."

"We do our best. Forgive yourself, André. Au revoir." Monique disconnected before he said goodbye.

His body was numb. Pierre died without sharing his vocation. Did Pierre think the family would reject him? Grand-père and Papa may have given him a rough time, they were harder men then, they had mellowed. *I'm sorry I was not there for you, Pierre.*

Hours loomed before dinner with his grandfather. The Monday from hell. He was weary, his birthday celebration, the chance meeting with Anne, the message from Pierre, and Monique's bombshell. It had begun in the Musée de l'Erotisme.

Why hadn't he asked Anne for her telephone number yesterday? He needed a woman.

Chapter XXVII André and Jean-Baptiste

ANDRÉ PACED IN front of Le Grand Véfour with his hands in the pockets of his navy Cifonelli suit. The interminable wait for this meeting would soon be over. André checked his watch.

Grand-père had revealed his brain tumor two weeks before, and André had adjusted to the catastrophic news of his impending death. At Grand-père's age, death could come anytime, but was hard to explain. What about life? His grandfather had lived through a precarious, even dangerous adolescence, yet had lived a long time. His eighteen-year-old brother had died after a short, relatively carefree life.

André had made dinner arrangements at the same restaurant where he and Papa had welcomed Grand-père back from a holiday. The Palais Royal setting on a quaint Parisian street suited his grandfather, the restaurant reflecting bygone days. It had opened in 1784 and reflected timelessness. Last month had been a light-hearted reunion.

Grand-père was late. He walked closer to the street, peering each way and walked back to the restaurant. Was death permanent? It was in the physical world. What about another sphere? Many used God to explain the unknown; however, André was unsure of an afterlife.

Conflicting emotions of sorrow, regret and hope competed in his thoughts as he anticipated this meeting: Sorrow for his dying grandfather, regret he hadn't understood his grandfather better, and hope his moral code didn't cause irreparable harm to their relationship. How would his role evolve?

A black limousine motored to a hushed stop in front of André and the driver exited. Opening the back door, he offered the passenger his hand. Grand-père pulled himself up, appearing more diminished than he had just yesterday. He shuffled to André and clutched his arm. André opened the door, his heart heavy, as his grandfather moved slowly, dragging one foot.

Grand-père lifted a stiff arm to the Maitre d' and shuffled past him. The familiar Maitre d' hurried ahead, escorting them to their customary table. Grand-père dropped into his chair.

"Bring the red wine I ordered." The Maitre d' nodded, returning promptly with the restaurant's sommelier, who expertly opened an exclusive bottle of wine, swirled it, sniffed and presented it to Grand-père. The Maitre d' and sommelier waited attentively. He nodded, and they left. "I ordered our dinners too." André eyes met his grandfather's defiant ones.

"Thank you." Grand-père's selections would be exemplary, although his behavior was inexplicable.

"My life is nearly over. In retrospect, I'm fortunate. I had some notice, I can prepare." He sipped his wine and pulled one hand through his thick white hair. "This is hard."

"We have time." André took his hand. "Talk when you can."

"No time . . . the pain . . ." Grand-père bowed his head. André massaged his veiny hand. The atmosphere trembled with foreboding; André's was motionless outside, disordered inside.

"A weighty decision. . . Was it better for the family to discover my indiscretions now, or later?"

"Your decision, Grand-père." His physical condition alarmed André.

"Remember? I told you I turned twelve on the first of January 1940? That birthday was my last carefree memory, my childhood ended a few months later. Paris fell to Hitler in June 1940, and the Allies didn't liberate France until 1944. Children heard things but we didn't comprehend . . . Many Parisians left the city. My father refused to leave the firm.

I ran the streets with my friends whose families also stayed. I was still twelve when I saw Hitler revel in the capture of Paris. He emanated evil. The way he looked, his mustache, his uniform, burned into my brain. I can still see him.

I promised myself I would thwart the Germans in any way I could. I was young and the decision flawed. I held onto that youthful promise my entire life. I need help."

His grandfather's head still hung low, his words had been soft, directed down. André leaned toward his grandfather, willing him to look. It was important he see his eyes, his face. André grasped his forearms. "I feel inadequate. Perhaps someone not connected to family? Grand-père ignored him.

A waiter approached and André waved him away. His grandfather's eyes fixated on André's arm.

"I collect paintings. You've seen some of them." The words were weighty, abrupt. His grandfather paused, glaring over André's shoulder.

"Our offices are filled with your paintings." André said, compelled to fill the silence. His grandfather grew agitated.

"There is more. A lot more. No one knows of the others." His grandfather's reddened face and tight mouth frightening, he banged his right fist on the table. "No one."

"What are you saying?" André's stomach rolled, a sour taste filling his mouth. He drank half of his mineral water. "Grand-père?"

"I have underground storeroom filled with paintings. Most I have purchased. Some date to the war."

"From the 1940's?"

"Yes." He nodded. "My friends and I were merciless. Hitler stole European art by the train carload. We didn't know it then, but we knew they took art from Parisians. When we could, we would steal one back. The Germans were careless— at first." His eyes were black now, his dark brows slashed over his eyelids, veering to a point over his nose. His voice deepened. "Sometimes we entered small museums and stole paintings. We were protecting it from the Germans."

André focused on the ornate furnishings beyond his grandfather, beyond this stranger. Motionless.

His grandfather grabbed for his arm. "André." His tone deep, urgent. André pulled back, crossing his arms across his chest. Grand-père's hand clutched nothing, opening and closing.

"What did you do with them?" André asked. His grandfather withdrew his hand, toyed with his wineglass.

"We put them in the basement where father had his offices. So many people had left Paris; there were places to hide things. Germans soldiers always patrolled the streets, barricaded some of them, but they partied a lot too, got drunk on our fine French wine. We fooled them though." His vacant eyes softened and he relaxed, chuckling. "We had nothing to lose, so we were brave, great fun for teenage boys."

His face serious again, he continued. "Sometimes, I feel like I'm still there. I could wake up and find Germans on duty in my beloved city." Grand-père's eyes focused on nothing. "There's one left."

"One?" André dreaded his answer.

"One of my friends from the war. He's my age." His grandfather's mind was kilometers away. "Still lives on both sides of the law." His grandfather grimaced. "His name's Luc

Portier. We had the apostle's names: Matthieu, Marc, Luc and me, Jean. It was funny, named after the apostles, and stealing."

André's mind jumped from one slippery stone to another, trying to navigate the shallow river of truth, justice. He had never suspected this. His perception of his grandfather had been uncomplicated just last month. An older, still handsome, successful, wealthy man still involved with daily work in the firm.

However, the gift of the two-million-Euro sports car had uncovered extreme wealth. The purchase had been obscene. Poverty existed worldwide; millions were hungry and many Parisians struggled. Even the wealthy couldn't afford such excessive luxury, apparently, his grandfather could.

Remorse engulfed him; he shouldn't have accepted the unjustifiable gift. It was immoral, especially now he knew of Grand-père's background. André jerked when his grandfather spoke.

"Life was complicated. In occupied France, people had to cope to survive. Some collaborated with the Germans; others assisted the Resistance. No one trusted anyone. Every person was subject to suspicion. I trusted my friends; they trusted me. We rescued each other from near captures."

"And now?" André prompted him.

"I still have the art we saved, or took. And a lot more I acquired over fifty years."

"How?"

"A lot of it was due to the vagaries of war. War is uncertain, erratic. Sometimes the best-laid plans don't work because people are involved. People are unpredictable. Sometimes even a kid could bribe a German soldier. We had no plan; the other boys fed off my defective vision. Unexplainably, our stash was never discovered."

He had confessed he was an art criminal. The family firm had upheld the law for decades and secretly harbored an art thief. French museums had made reparations for years, returned art to its rightful owners and received back confiscated art. Who owned Grand-père's hoard? Would the family experience the same scrutiny as that surrounding the art stash discovered in Munich? Worldwide publicity had proliferated on the internet and in other media coverage. How would they endure it?

"What do you want from me?"

"Beyond the stolen art, there are many more pieces. Our law firm has been successful. You are the fourth generation to partner here. It afforded me a lucrative lifestyle I enhanced with paintings. Before art became a commodity traded in world markets, I recognized exemplary workmanship. I bought legitimate works that subsequently gained in value. Some of my legitimate art is priceless." He emptied his glass.

"Where are the paintings now?"

"I had underground storage designed and built beneath our home decades ago. No one is alive who worked on the project. Even your grandmother doesn't know." Grand-père refilled his glass and set the bottle down. He absently swirled the wine counter-clockwise. His dark eyes peered into André's eyes.

"I'm not asking for judgement; I'm asking for advice. This would have surfaced after my death. You have the same passions; I believe you understand.

You didn't experience war, though you did experience profound loss. Pierre's death devastated all of us; however, my guilt was immense. God took Pierre because of those paintings I coveted, and then idolized. To covet, one of the seven deadly sins, maybe. I know it's one of the Ten Commandments. Thou shall not covet."

"Do you think God is a punishing one? God would kill Pierre for your sins? If there is a God?" His rational grandfather had disappeared; perhaps it was the tumor.

"I don't think God has his finger on daily life." André lifted his glass, staring at the red liquid. "And I'm also guilty of deception."

In the depths of Grand-père's eyes, André saw the complexities of his grandfather's soul. He was a defective man with flaws, and now in old age, frailties.

What had Socrates taught? Virtue is a necessary requirement for happiness. Was his grandfather happy? Was he happy? He had to get away. André arose from his seat. His grandfather pushed his hands against both of André's forearms, compelling him to sit.

In an urgent monotone, he spoke. "It is more than the stolen paintings from wartime. I developed an obsession. I would see a painting, and had to possess it, despite the consequences. I did some unsavory things." He held tight to André's arms.

"You made choices." André said. His grandfather's grasp was strong. "We all make choices, sometimes we cross a line, a moral line, certainly. For some, perhaps a criminal act. We are fortunate if our decisions don't harm others." What had Grand-père meant by unsavory things?

"I'll show it to you. This diagnosis accelerated my eventual confession, to you, you were always the one. Pierre is gone; your father has no knowledge of my deceit." His grandfather pulled his arms away, seeming to gauge his possible reaction, before he spoke. "My son Vincent . . . your Papa. He's not like us."

Like him? When hell froze over. How much more illegal activity? André kept his face expressionless, a thousand demons bombarding him. His grandfather had destroyed his view of family.

As a fourth-generation partner, he was a member of the firm who practiced integrity in the changing world. The firm's adherence to a moral code reflected honesty in what they thought, said and did. His grandfather's actions were anathema to that moral code. How would this undermine the firm's reputation? André's world unbalanced.

"What do you expect from me?" André asked. He couldn't look at the man whom he had loved, and revered.

"Forgiveness." His grandfather touched him. "André?"
André looked at him.

"Perhaps, understanding." His grandfather pulled his hand away.

"I don't know what—" André buried his head in his hands. "Grand-papa." The word escaped—an involuntary wail. The burden of Pierre's death was off his shoulders and now his grandfather's revelations jumped onboard.

"Don't hate me. I know my past . . . my behavior, shocks you." His grandfather signaled the waiter, at his side in an instant. He ordered another bottle, and waited for him to leave.

"I'll try to explain. Art is emotion. A way to connect to our past, and a way to leave something for succeeding generations to know we existed, we were alive. That we loved, lost, and overcame hard times: war, hunger, despair, heartbreak.

It's hard for twenty-first century young people to comprehend, but when I was a teen, we had no hope, no definable future. The present became the way to cope and protecting our French art heritage seemed plausible, a way to preserve our past. If our heritage disappeared, France would fall. Art defines where humanity begins, and now I'm dying, where we end."

André lifted his head and searched for words. "Grand-père, do you believe in God? Do you think man is capable of pure faith? Or are we men of reason?"

"It's hard to believe in God when your life is overturned at twelve," Jean-Baptiste said. "I'm not sure. Any faith I had disappeared. On the outside, the Gensonné family appears to be elite. André, you've experienced the real situation, the grief the family suffered, and now, my indiscretions." The waiter brought the first course and discretely left. His grandfather grew more animated.

"Art is a conduit, a way to bring the vibrancy and energy of life to those who come after. My collection took on a life of its own. Like an alcoholic I had no control over its growth, except to monitor it, safeguard it." His weary eyes considered

André's, his gaze so intense, it burned. "You are the caretaker now, for the future of our family, for the future of France." He put his elbows onto the table and rested his head in his hands. "The headaches are worse."

"Grand-père, what about the illegitimate part of your collection? I can't be part of it."

"When I'm gone, do what is right. I've attempted to dispose of some of it over the decades; I can't, without damaging the family. You can, André. You stand alone, the one person with the wherewithal to accomplish what I cannot."

"No." The food sat between them, untouched, the no, harsh, uncompromising.

"You love paintings as I do. You're unconnected to my crimes. You can do what is right—morally, legally, ethically."

"You ask too much." The waiter brought the main course, efficiently placing a plate before each of them. The waiter lifted his brows, Grand-père nodded; he filled his glass.

"What I have acquired legitimately, is worth millions, sell those paintings to make reparations. Return the stolen pieces to the rightful owners. There is enough money, help me fix this." His grandfather began eating. Seconds later, André picked up his knife and fork, but his stomach recoiled.

"I feel ill." André excused himself and left the restaurant.

DEATH WAS A PARADOX; it could be contradictory. Death was final in many ways; but in others, people lived on in photographs, in the memories of people they left behind, in the genes of their descendants, in the good they did, and the harm they promulgated.

The death of his twin had shaped his past. His grandfather's final request would define his future.

Chapter XXVIII Maximillian

Monday, July 15, 2013

MID-MORNING SUNLIGHT streamed between the orange linen curtains, brightening the ecru walls of their eclectic studio apartment, highlighting the primary colors in the décor.

Émilie was preparing breakfast; he could see her through the opening in the ecru wall curtains separating their bedroom from the rest of the large room. If she was cooking, she would want him to get up. He hadn't had a shower in two days; he'd barely managed to keep working. Shutting his eyes to block the brightness didn't work; he pulled a pillow over his head.

Émilie snuck in and kissed him on the lips. Grasping his hand, she pulled him out of bed and led him to their bright yellow table, where she had placed a steaming cup of café au lait.

"We need to talk." Émilie wore a white cotton batiste nightgown edged with lace; she appeared to float like an angel.

Pregnancy enhanced her beauty, the slight swelling of her abdomen just visible beneath the translucent fabric. She brought his breakfast to him, and seated herself, where an identical breakfast rested. Her tranquil demeanor unnerved him; she was overly calm.

She stroked the handle of her coffee cup, and then lifted her chin, her voice trembling. "You're angry about something." She moistened her lips. "I don't like how you talk to me." Her tone strengthened, remaining controlled. "You've shut me out, what's wrong?"

It had been several days since Maximillian met Beauregard at the top of the Butte. He had seethed inside since he learned the rat tried to steal the Maclet. Maximillian had been back to his shop twice, hurtling threats, boiling with rage, demanding the *Miriam* painting and the required provenance of the Maclet.

"Nothing." He shoved the blue plate with a fresh croissant, a cup of French yogurt and a sliced peach, across the table. It crashed against her plate; she caught them before they landed in her lap. "None of your business." A dirty white envelope rested beside her plate. Recognition flickered, and then disappeared, when Émilie said in an evenly modulated tone.

"Max. Stop!" She straightened her plate and dining utensils, placing his in the center of the table. "I won't have this. I respect myself. And I'm worried about our baby." She bowed her head, her arms enfolding her abdomen. "You've changed. Is it the baby?"

"I love you. And our baby." Maximillian put his elbows onto table, threading greasy stringy hair through his fingers. "I'm sorry Émilie."

"Sorry isn't enough. I'm ready to leave." She clasped her coffee cup. She sounded like one of his schoolteachers, lecturing, lecturing.

Maximillian folded his arms, and plopped his head on them, his face hidden. "It's my problem." Maximillian had alienated everyone.

His job was in jeopardy at Chez Philippe. Monsieur Dubois said Maximillian caused havoc in the kitchens, disrupted staff who worked under him, and his behavior compromised food quality. Everyone was against him. Damn. Damn. Damn.

"It should be our problem. Are you in trouble?" She didn't raise her voice. "You can't yell at me every time you come home. We share, or I'm done."

Maximillian leapt to his feet, overturning the bright chair she had meticulously painted in the early days. He stomped into their bedroom, dressed, and stormed out of the apartment, taking the steps by twos, jumping down onto each landing. Every part of his life was in jeopardy; it was the rat's fault. He would strangle the smarmy little rodent, now, before he went to work.

Maximillian jogged several blocks to the *Frames* shop where he had taken the *Miriam* painting after Mimi failed him. Mimi should've have kept it longer; he might still have it. The old man waited outside his shop, his beady eyes half-closed, his sawed-off back teeth contrasting with the protruding front ones. Maximillian had forgotten how disgusting he was.

"We sold it, I have money." He scurried back and forth. Agitated, his eyes gleaming, his facial hair sprung from his cheeks, stiff and wiry. "Not all of it, yet. Enough." He shooed Maximillian through his doorway. It creaked ominously just like it had the first time he opened it. Max glanced at the faded *Frames* sign and shuddered at what had happened since he first passed under the grimy signboard. The man scuttled to the back, rustling through papers, and emerged, money in one hand.

"Your share is 5,000 Euro. €500 now—the rest in two weeks." He shoved some Euro notes at him.

"I should trust you?" Motioning at the stack of worn money in the rat's outstretched hand, Michel half turned his body away. His life ruined for €5,000.

"This or nothing. Take it." He threw the money at Maximillian's feet, and shuffled off. Grungy paper Euro fluttered to the dirty floor.

"Who bought it? How will I get paid?" Maximillian shouted at the retreating man. He turned. Maximillian could barely see him in the dim light.

"Strict secrecy, buyer's demand. I'll have cash two weeks from Monday. Now get out of here." He was gone. Maximillian scooped up the scattered Euro and left the door open. Two more weeks.

Bereft, Maximillian wandered through the streets of Montmartre. The quest to profit from his serendipitous find had consumed him, robbing him of the life he and Émilie had established. He was a victim of his greed.

He should have thrown *Miriam* into a dumpster. The last two years with Émilie had been his best, except for the last few weeks. She was too honest, too pure. If he left now, she would be better off. He had tried to change, but he was flawed, and the flaws were too deep for Émilie to polish away.

Maximillian called his employer and told him he was sick. He must talk to his sister, Mimi. He was out of control and had alienated everyone else.

He arrived at the Musée de Montmartre too early. Draping his legs over the armrests of a too short bench, he waited, the hard boards uncomfortable against his back. He shifted his body down, so his knees hung over the armrest. The morning sun warmed his face, soaking into his skin, releasing some of his rage.

"Maximillian?" Mimi stood above him, pressing her left hand against his shoulder. She smoothed her right hand down the side of his face, touched his eyelids.

His eyes flew open. Mimi was radiant, the light was behind her, swathing her in a luminous aura. The glow from within— shimmering through her eyes—compelled him to sit up.

"I was waiting for you, I fell asleep." He sat hunched over on the bench, aching and stiff, trying to banish the lingering wisps of a bad dream.

"Did you come to see me?" She moved away, her hand fluttering over her abdomen. "I have news. I'm pregnant too. It happened for me, Max." She rushed to him, grabbed his hands to pull him up and enfolded him in her arms. She pulled back, her eyes shining. "Oh Max, our children will be the same age. Isn't it exciting?" She clutched his hands. "Maybe our family can connect again."

Maximillian held her small hands. She was lovely, light as air, and he had a cold black heart. Unlovable. What should he say to his joy-filled sister?

"How wonderful! You'll be a great Maman." It had taken huge effort. This time he engulfed her, his long arms encircling his petite sister. "You are beautiful; pregnancy agrees with you." She glowed like his Émilie, embodying sereneness. "Mimi, I must go home. Congratulations. I love you. I'll call soon."

Mimi remained in front of the museum, a puzzled expression on her tranquil face.

"Men." She lifted her shoulders. His eyes captured hers and he shrugged too.

Émilie still sat at the yellow table in her nightgown, both plates of food untouched, reading a strange-looking letter. A brittle old envelope lay between the plates. She lifted murky eyes to him, shining with tears, although none had fallen. Émilie appeared unapproachable as if she had planned which didn't include him.

A painful tightness moved from his stomach to his throat. He wanted to embrace her, kiss her sad eyes, but his legs trembled.

"You always run, Maximillian. It hurts." The tears spilled. Comforting her wasn't an option, she didn't want him. The pain in his throat tightened, constricting his breathing.

"What does this mean?" She held the folded sheet of heavy paper. "Is this why you're acting crazy?"

Maximillian dragged his chair to sit next to her. "I don't know what it is." The letter smelled musty.

"You expect me to believe you? I found it under our dresser when I cleaned. You must have hidden it."

"Damn, I forgot. Beau gave it to me the last time I saw him. His wife found it, she had cleaned too."

"Is it yours?" Émilie thrust the paper at him, folded in half along its time-sharpened fold.

"Maybe . . . yes . . . I don't know. Beau said she found it under my old bed, stuck between the woodwork and the wall. We were bad housekeepers." He reached for the letter. "Did you read it?"

"Yes. It's hard to see the writing and the French is old-fashioned." Her eyes looked old, the wise kind of old. "You need to explain." Her tone resigned, she expected an explanation.

If he told her about *Miriam*, she would leave. This was it. Maximillian lifted the top of the old paper. It crackled open; the stiff paper smelled like ancient dust. Fine cursive lettering scrawled across the thick paper, faintly visible; some of the ink missing along the fold. A dried insect stuck to the top corner. Maximillian turned the paper toward the light.

I'm writing this letter for whomever finds it and the accompanying painting. I'm hiding it in the wall where I'm staying in Montmartre on 12 July 1920. I was lucky. In 1881, I was born a gardener's son and expected to remain a gardener. Fate, or God, intervened. The local parish priest was a painter and through him and other good fortune, I went to Paris to study. Montmartre is my favorite place to paint, although I have painted in many places. I have known the great Impressionist painters of my time and due to patrons, enjoyed much commercial success.

I want to share my good fortune with you, the finder of my painting. I ponder how long it will remain hidden and think about who will find it, a tradesman, a poor man, a wealthy man.

I, Élisée Maclet, being of sound mind and thirty-nine years old today, leave this painting to the person who finds it first. It is yours. To sell. To cherish. To destroy. To allow it to destroy you.
Élisée Maclet the Painter of Montmartre 12 July 1920

The letter dropped from Maximillian's hands. He arose from his chair, head bowed, his shoulders sagging. He trudged to his shoulder bag, opened it and turned it over. Dirty money scattered to the floor. He dropped the bag and left their apartment. Émilie called after him, he continued down the stairs, one hand holding the rail, sluggishly descending one step at a time. Despair overwhelmed him. Every decision he made was poisonous, he would end it, everyone would be better off.

He was the legitimate owner of the Maclet, of two paintings, because he had also commissioned *Miriam*. Both were gone, for a miniscule amount.

When Maximillian reached the street, one line in the letter resonated. *To allow it to destroy you.*

Chapter XXIX Bertrand

BONJOUR, MICHEL LA ROCHE?" Bertrand had kept the business card Michel gave him, and had now dialed Michel's business number. "Monsieur Jean-Paul Bertrand here. Is your client still interested in the painting?"

"Yes. I can meet you today." Michel sounded bossy; Bertrand wouldn't let Michel bully him this time; he counted to ten.

"Next Tuesday, the sixteenth."

"Almost a week." A note of exasperation filtered through. "I'd like to meet sooner."

"On the sixteenth. At the same bistro. Twelve o'clock." Bertrand hung up.

Bertrand had controlled the conversation, arranging the meeting on his terms. Fear had taken a back seat to his need for home. Why had he let Michel intimidate him before?

He must possess *Miriam* before he met Michel. Maximillian had tried to force him to take it twice, it should be easy to retrieve. Michel said his client would pay well for the painting.

Bertrand plan was to get the painting, sell it to Michel la Roche and pay Maximillian. His own obligation would be over.

Everyone benefitted.

BERTRAND HAD CALLED Maximillian Broutin twice a day since July tenth, every morning and every evening. It had been five days since he had made an appointment with Michel la Roche. For tomorrow. He must find Maximillian. He had either ignored his calls, met bad luck, or changed his mobile service. The mobile reported to a non-personalized message. Maximillian lived in Montmartre; it was time to go home and find him.

He impatiently waited until his daughter left for work, tucking a note into her dresser mirror. He walked the girls to school, hugging them extra tight, experiencing a wishful moment. His granddaughters had been happy with him here. But painting sustained his soul. And Montmartre . . .

Buoyancy lightened his body, the worry of the past weeks evaporating like raindrops on hot pavement. Searching for Maximillian meant progress toward his goal. Idleness was worse than fear and he had had enough of both.

The morning rain had dried off the streets and now sunshine brightened his mood. He listened to the tinned voice announcing the Métro's familiar stops, each bringing him closer to Montmartre.

The village-like arrondissement defined him: neighbor, painter, friend. Bertrand recalled past events by the markers of the neighborhood: The door jamb where he and his wife had measured Charlotte's growth, their favorite places to kiss, the smell of paint supplies that permeated his workspace, clothes, and belongings. He yearned to paint in Montmartre as he did before his works sold for real money. And how could he describe his favorite hangout? The neighborhood bistro had been the pulse of everyday life.

He was akin to Élisée Maclet, the painter of Montmartre, early in the twentieth century. Believing he was the twenty-first century counterpart to Maclet was easy, Maclet had loved Montmartre too.

Taking an unscrupulous commission, once his worst decision, felt like a spiritual connection to Élisée Maclet who could now guide him toward resolving his predicament. The lack of response from Maximillian had tested his new resolve. The unknown frightened him, brought back the nervousness that had ruled his life.

Bertrand's steps quickened when he neared the bistro; he paused to gaze around the familiar block. Red geraniums, yellow daisies and blue lobelia exploded from flowers boxes, hanging purple-hued flower baskets swayed in a light breeze. The sky was Cerulean blue painted over with bleached white clouds by nature's artist. Did the birds always sing in Montmartre?

Monday was the day his cronies habitually met, from twelve until mid-afternoon. They mingled in an everchanging mixture of men and schedules the other days, but Monday was special. He had missed the Monday gathering twice, and his old body moved faster than he thought it could. Even his knee cooperated. Anticipating a fine lunch and camaraderie with his friends, he burst through the door. His friends were seated in the usual place.

"Jean-Paul! Bonjour." One of his friends spotted him, and two others leapt from their seats, greeting him, ushering him to their customary table.

"We missed you, old man," the youngest said.

Georges, retying his apron, hastened over to shake his hand. "Monsieur Bertrand. How are you, friend? Welcome." He sped away and returned with un pichet de blanc. Bertrand settled into the vacated seat at the head of the table.

"Do you want the special? Quiche Lorraine, with truffle oil today."

"Bring it on." He rubbed his hands. Bertrand basked in the warmth of his friends and the ambience of the bistro. His vision blurred. He blinked hard, observing his friends' faces: painters, writers, pensioners, hangers-on. "It's good to be back." He lifted his glass. "Cheers!" They echoed him; the roar attracting attention from other bistro patrons.

"Where were you?"

"Why did you leave?"

"Are you here for good?" Questions arrived faster than he could answer. His cronies gathered around a long table formed by shoving smaller ones together. He had missed them: missed their teasing about who sat at the cracks, missed the food, missed Georges. Best of all, it smelled the same.

"Just a visit with my daughter and granddaughters," Bertrand said.

"You didn't tell us. We thought you died." His friends' jostled elbows, murmuring concern. They had worried about him; he had made the right decision to come back.

Lunch with his cronies had been what he needed. Friends and Montmartre, what could be better? He had met and wooed his wife in Montmartre, raised Charlotte, and worked his craft. This bistro was part of his way of life, illustrating why he had brought Michel here, to his favorite place.

Lunch with Michel la Roche had reignited his problems with Maximillian. When Michel found him, and asked probing questions; suddenly, the painting wasn't an ordinary commission. It was vital to someone.

He motioned to Georges and ordered the local wine for everyone. He lifted his glass. "To all of you. My friends. You inspire me. You invigorate me. You brighten my life. Thank you."

"What happened to you?"

"Why so maudlin? So, sentimental?" His friends' questions peppered him.

"It's great to be back in Montmartre." He drained his wine glass.

Georges set his food in front of him with a flourish. "Voila." He inhaled the rich aroma of eggs, cream and the subtle fragrance of truffles, gathered in his France, and brought to his table by the gods. He would find Maximillian. Montmartre was still a village, though incorporated into the city of Paris; it was hard to hide here.

HE LEFT THE bistro at two o'clock. Warmth permeated his body, either a result of plentiful wine or his friends. He nodded crisply at people on the street, and punched Maximillian's number—one more time. A sobbing woman answered.

"Bonjour," she said, swallowing a sob. "Is that you, Maximillian?"

"This is Monsieur Bertrand. May I speak with him?" Soft hiccups answered. Not Maximillian. "Maximillian gave me this contact number."

"He left. He's gone." She wailed.

"Mademoiselle, please, calm yourself."

"I think; he's reached his limit." It was what he thought she said. Fresh sobs had masked her words.

"Please help me." She pled now, desperate. Perhaps he could help.

"Where are you?"

"Home." She had paused. Had she hung up?

"Are you able to meet somewhere?" No answer. "Mademoiselle?"

"Yes?"

"Do you want help?"

"Yes."

"You pick a place, a bistro, a café. I'll come." Bertrand encouraged her to choose a place near her home. She named his bistro. He told her he would be there soon, he was just a block away. Serendipity? He re-entered the nearly empty bistro.

"Monsieur." Georges hurried to him. "Did you forget something?"

"I'm meeting a woman. We need privacy."

"Sit where you want, the lunch trade is over." The waiter swept his arm across the bistro. He chose a chair facing the entrance.

Within ten minutes, a woman was vacillating near the door, glancing around the small bistro. Small-boned. with dark hair pulled back, her long neck exposed, she wore sunglasses, but no make-up or jewelry, well put together despite her distress. Bertrand met her near the door.

"Mademoiselle?" Bertrand asked. She lifted her head, removing her sunglasses. "Are you Maximillian's . . . friend?" She shifted a floral handbag she carried over her shoulder, the strap caught on the sleeve of her navy dress, and she pulled it higher. Her puffy eyes reflected the devastation he had heard in her voice.

"Yes. He's my boyfriend." She looked down at her abdomen, and back at him. A tear straggled down her face. "My name is Émilie." She bowed her head. "I'm afraid."

"Of him?"

"Not of him, for him, I'm afraid of what he might do . . . to himself." He nodded toward his table, accompanying her without touching; flight was possible. He didn't want to frighten her.

"Please sit, Émilie. Would you like a drink?" He held a chair, she melted onto it. "Or something to eat?"

"Maybe something to drink." He seated himself across from her. Georges hovered in the background, and approached at Bertrand's signal.

"Will you bring the lady the special?" She probably needed food. "And to drink?"

"Mineral water," she said.

"Coffee for me." The waiter left.

"How can I help?"

"Do you know Maximillian?"

"Business only, he commissioned a work from me. I'm a painter."

"Oh, you must think—." Fresh tears filled her dark eyes, spilling onto her cheeks. "I'm not usually like this, so teary. Perhaps it's . . . the baby." Using a napkin, she patted her wet face.

"Maximillian's?" he asked. He reached across the table to touch her wrist. She nodded. "Tell me why you're worried."

"He got a letter. I mean—he—I found—" She groped in her bag. She pulled an envelope out, held it tight against her breasts, protecting it. It was dirty, antiqued, the paper weightier than most paper envelopes. "This must be why he's behaving—why he's changed." She set it on the table. "I don't understand. He won't tell me anything." She pushed it toward him, then gingerly pulled it back. "Can I trust you?" The pain in her eyes distressed him. She reminded him of Charlotte. This dark-haired woman didn't resemble his blue-eyed, strawberry-blond daughter, but her naïve manner pierced his heart. She was like a daughter asking her trusted father for help. Bertrand's kind heart responded.

"I have a daughter about your age, and two granddaughters. I love them more than life." He took her hand. "You can trust me like a father." Tears threatened, he removed his hand.

"I don't know how to start." She glanced away, and then met his eyes again. "How do you know him?"

She was fragile; he had to be careful. She loved the man. Maximillian was a crook and dishonest, though even the worst people had good qualities, and others loved them despite their vices. "We had a business deal."

"What kind of business deal? He's the head chef at Chez Philippe, here in Montmartre. Is it related to that?" She asked, a hopeful note in her voice. She found a handkerchief in her purse.

"It was something else. I told you I'm a painter." Perhaps she had forgotten Maximillian had commissioned a painting.

"Oh, I forgot." She held her hand over the envelope. "This letter is about a painting." She pushed it toward him.

"Do you want me to read it?"

"Yes." She blotted the corner of each eye.

Bertrand lifted the letter, slipping the heavy paper from the thick envelope. "Have you read it?"

"Yes."

"And?"

"I don't know what it means. Perhaps you will know more, a painter." Bertrand motioned to Georges; he brought the day's specialty, deftly placing it front of her, refilling her mineral water.

Bertrand opened the letter. The script was faint, written with a fountain pen. He read deliberately, allowing the woman time to eat. "This is good," Émilie said. She took small bites, assessing him. When he had deciphered the letter, he held it up.

"This is a valuable letter. Where did you get it?"

"I found it yesterday under the dresser in our bedroom. I was cleaning. I thought Maximillian hid it there. I wanted to ask at breakfast, but we argued and he left like he does when he's angry."

"Is he angry often?" Bertrand asked.

"Now he is. He changed. He's upset most of the time. Not at me, I don't think it's me. It's something else."

Bertrand held the letter toward her. "Did he read this?"

"I assumed did, and that he hid it from me. After he ran out, I read it."

"Why don't you think he read it before you did?"

"Maximillian came back later, and I asked him about it. He said his friend Beauregard gave it to him, his wife found it. Said he didn't know what it was."

"Where is Maximillian now?" Bertrand asked. He pushed the letter back to her.

"I don't know. After he read it, he threw a pile of money onto the floor and left. He always runs away. He wasn't angry this time. He looked horrible. He left without—even saying good-bye." Fresh tears streamed down her face. "I'm afraid." She wiped her face, blew her nose. "I'm sorry, Monsieur."

If the letter was authentic, its contents stated the accompanying painting belonged to the finder. Did Maximillian find the painting? Alternatively, did he steal it from someone else who found it? Maximillian had hired him to disguise the Maclet. So, he hadn't known of the letter six years ago. Émilie said he had first read it the same morning she did.

"Émilie." He leaned toward her, picking up the letter. "This is very important. Safeguard it." She nodded. "I'll help you find Maximillian. Do you know where he might go? Does he have family, friends?"

"He's not close to anyone, except his sister Mimi. She works at the Musée de Montmartre. He has a huge family, doesn't get along with them. He had some friends; he lived with one of them before we moved in together. I don't know them." She had stopped crying. "It's been just us. And now, now I think he'll hurt himself."

"Why?"

"I told him I would leave him, take our baby away if he didn't tell me why he was so angry." She straightened in her chair, her manner determined. "I had to protect my baby."

"You did the right thing." Émilie had difficult problems. Love was like that; it sucked you in, then controlled you.

"I love him. I don't want him to miss his child's life. I just wish he was like he was before."

"Do you have somewhere you can go?"

"Not in Paris, my family lives in the south of France. You don't have to worry about me." Émilie fumbled for her handbag.

"Please stay a moment." What should he say? "I have an interest, it won't help you to hear my part, yet. We need more from Maximillian. I'll help you find him." Bertrand motioned for the bill, paying Georges.

"I'm meeting a private investigator tomorrow. We'll consult him about Maximillian."

247

Chapter XXX Anne

ANNE WANTED TO hide under her covers and withdraw but she had forced herself to get up. Her body resisted, aching inside and along her bones. Only essential employees were required to work at the Embassy on this bank holiday; she could have slept in.

Exercising invariably improved her mood, just getting out into the streets of Paris often renewed her, chasing away melancholy, but old demons chased her home today.

Bastille Day had been enlightening. She had enjoyed the pleasurable day with Stefania and had finally found André. He possessed a real surname and he lived in Paris; she hadn't conjured him to escape reality. However, a tiny flame of girlish hope had fizzled and died. She had expected a man like him to marry, but imagined other possibilities. Her girlish dream had reawakened when she saw him at the Louvre.

Anne reexamined her list from the diplomatic event, and found his parents Vincent and Sophia Gensonné had been the invited guests. Researching his background proved easy, there was much media attention surrounding the prominent family. André was the wealthy scion of an old French family, therefore, out of reach.

Knowing his family was prominent brought on the sense of worthlessness. Anne's family was not good enough, wealthy enough, or of a high enough social class. She had grown up poor; dependent on charity in the form of public support, an ocean away André Gensonné's privileged life.

Her quest for conversion began the night she met the worldly-wise cultured young man, with an aura of vulnerability. It had been a catalyst for transforming her life, one measured step at a time. Beneath complex layers of her personality lay a seed that germinated that night. She had persevered, and nourished hope for a long time. It was gone.

André had asked her to call him. Impossible. Underneath, after all those years, she was still the ill-nurtured child who lacked confidence. Stefania called her crazy; she would have contacted him last night. She pressured Anne this morning.

"Did you call him?" Anne had met her in front of their building. Anne shook her head. "Why not? Anne!" She turned and flounced away. "You want be alone your whole life?" Reverting to English, she tossed the English words over her shoulder.

Did she want to be alone? She lived as if she did. Stefania had helped her in a myriad of ways, although Anne had not divulged her secrets; she never would. Stefania had forced Anne to respond to her overtures and she would be forever grateful. Having just one friend had made a difference in her solitary existence; Anne felt like she belonged to something, although she couldn't yet define what it was. Perhaps a greater connection with others.

An only child of an only child; her mother's death when she was barely eighteen meant she was without a family.

Mother had refused to discuss her father. Family had no meaning.

Dependent on her own resources, friends had been hard to cultivate. She hadn't anyone to depend on as she matured, so she had no relationships with people attached to one another by affection or personal regard. But Stefania was persistent.

Humans lived in communities and to be friendless was to be alone, ostracized from the group, on the outside. Her lifelong experience. Anne hadn't disengaged from her past long enough to sustain a friendship.

Working at the embassy was her life and it had been enough, but she was lonely today, different from being alone. She could cope with alone. Two things had changed: Stefania had barged into her life and she had discovered André was married.

Anne ate yoghurt and strawberries and dressed. Monday would have been a workday and now she had nothing to do. What would she have done before? She would have visited a museum or attended a movie. Restlessness kept her from attending alone because she could now discern the difference between alone and lonely.

André's business card listed his personal mobile and his workplace number. He had asked her to call him, it should be easy to key in his number on her mobile. What about his vivacious wife? She slipped it back in her purse.

Friday, July 19, 2013

THE THICK EMBOSSED business card was mangled pulp by Friday; Anne had mishandled it for days. The numbers had been memorized; she even imagined she pressed them into her iPhone, and he answered. But she had not found the courage to call. The card was now under her pillow.

Anne conceived countless scenarios over the years. The fantasies never included a wife and five children; just kisses and love scenes which were now an adolescent dream. Her embassy work suffered as she had been unable to keep her mind on her responsibilities. Her clothes sagged.

"You should call that handsome man before you blow away." Stefania yelled at her that morning. Dramatic Stefania, she watched for her in the mornings now, sometimes rushing to catch her; her burnt henna hair, posture, and wild outfits, identifiable long before Anne could see her features.

Friday night arrived at last. Anne donned her nubby white bathrobe, nestled into a comfy chair, and turned on the television, opening a single serving portion of sparkling wine.

Half an hour later, rambunctious knocks startled her. When the door opened, Stefania swept through, wearing a body-hugging dress with blue peacocks, red poppies and greens plants splayed across white fabric. An oversize sparkly green purse completed her ensemble. Stefania was party-ready. Talking on her phone, she waved her free arm at Anne.

"Do you want to go out for drinks?" Stefania dropped her bag on the nearest chair.

"No . . . I couldn't."

"Why not?" She said goodbye to an unknown person and plunked down onto the sofa. "Some friends are meeting at a club, you're invited."

"Maybe next time. Why didn't you call?"

"You'd have said no. It'll be fun. Let's find you a dress." Stefania dragged Anne to her bedroom, flung open the double closet doors and gasped. Anne's clothes hung on white hangars, nestled in color-coordinated hues of neutral colors. "These are boring. All your clothes are black and brown. You can wear one of mine."

"I'm not going." Stefania slid hangers along the rod, pushing Anne's clothing back and forth; a couple of blouses slithered to the floor.

"Too neat, how do you find anything?" She picked up the blouses and handed them to Anne.

"Wear this." She held a simple midnight blue dress Anne had never worn. Each time she tried it on, she immediately took it off. Besides being too short, it was too revealing. One shoulder was bare and midnight blue rosettes hugged the curved neckline, from the top of the covered shoulder across the bodice around the under arm, and across the back.

Stefania maneuvered Anne out of her robe and into the dress. Nudging Anne into a chair, she turned her away from the full-length mirror. With a few twists and turns, she coiled Anne's hair around her head in a crown-like roll. "You are ready. Make-up?"

"No, and I can't wear this dress."

"Let's go. Wear comfortable shoes and bring party shoes in your bag." Anne located two pairs. "And don't look in the mirror." How did Stefania know she had peeked?

She looked racy, sexy in the tight dress and piled up hair. Before the Bastille Day parade, she would never have agreed to go out like this. She deftly applied light make-up over her still healing face. Butterflies assailed her abdomen and her legs turned to jelly. She'd rather stay home, but she had had a lonely week.

Anne cautiously entered her living room. Stefania stood near the door, iPhone at her ear. "We need to leave." She swung her purse toward the doorway. "Go."

Seated on the Métro, Anne cringed at the attention they generated. "Who else is coming?"

"Depends. Sometimes three or four, sometimes ten or more. Whomever feels like dancing. It'll be fun," she repeated.

"I won't be dancing. Just a cocktail for me."

"Maybe." Stefania still talked on her mobile, arranging details, interchanging French, Hungarian and English. How did she get involved with a character like Stefania?

Chapter XXXI Michel

MICHEL HATED WAITING. He got things done, found the most direct route to resolve an issue, and then made it happen. The call from Bertrand was a gift, a gift with a "do not open" tag. Bertrand had insisted on meeting him at his bistro in six days—way too long. But he had no choice.

Bertrand had been different on the phone, decisive, even breaking the connection. Unusual behavior for the nervous painter with the eye tick whom he had bullied in Montmartre. Now he was curious—and impatient. Why had the old man changed?

Tuesday finally arrived. Michel barreled down the Montmartre street near the bistro, and almost ran down an old man, with his head bent toward a young woman. He slowed, recognizing the faded red beret, and the man's distinctive artistic mannerism. Monsieur Bertrand murmured into the young woman's ear. She leaned toward him, her left hand resting on his forearm. She appeared to trust him, though the woman was not Bertrand's daughter Charlotte, with her cascade of blondish red waves.

This woman had pulled her shiny dark hair back with a black hairband, her long neck delicate, creamy white and unblemished. She wore a bright pink sleeveless dress with matching flat-heeled shoes. An oversize black and white zebra print handbag weighed upon her slender shoulder. She looked chic and from what he could tell from behind, she was a striking woman.

Michel strained to hear. No words were audible. He lingered, watching them converse, their heads still close. It appeared this woman was invited to lunch. Who was she? She had enlivened the bony old man with the elegant carriage. Monsieur Bertrand had a confident air he lacked the last time Michel shared a table with him. Bertrand stepped forward to pull the door open, and stood back to let her pass, guiding her through. They disappeared inside.

Michel considered what Bertrand had said in the short telephone conversation. Bertrand asked if his client was still interested in the painting. He said yes; but Bertrand held him off.

Fortunate for him he had seen Bertrand and the young woman together. Michel opened the door. It smelled the same, good food and the ambience of an old man's hangout: stale cigarette smoke, board games, and musty comfort. His mouth watered, the meal had been memorable. Bertrand and the woman sat side-by-side, at what must be his regular table. When he approached, Bertrand stood.

"Bonjour, Monsieur la Roche. Please." Bertrand indicated the opposite chair. "This is Émilie." His intuition had been right; she was gorgeous, with shining gray eyes, thick, short eyelashes and full lips painted bright pink.

"Bonjour, Monsieur Bertrand, err . . . Émilie." No surname supplied, he awkwardly repeated her first name. Despite the make-up and stylish clothing, she appeared vulnerable, sitting with her long legs pressed together and her feet squarely on the floor, like a schoolchild. Her hands clasped the sides, but she put them on the table when she noticed him assessing her. As he sat, Georges appeared with pitcher of white wine, two wine glasses, and mineral water for Émilie.

Pouring this time, Bertrand lifted his glass toward Émilie, then Michel and took a drink. However, he didn't initiate conversation. Michel hesitated, then plunged in.

"You asked if my client was interested in the painting. I assume you mean the one that hung in the Musée de l'Erotisme, and then disappeared." Bertrand nodded, absently swirling his wine. "He's interested. Where is it?"

"I don't know," Bertrand said. He glanced at Émilie.

"Can you get it? Do you control access? I mean, are you the owner?" Bertrand shook his head no.

"Circumstances have changed since I proposed this meeting."

"You don't have it?" Michel asked. He prepared to leave.

"No." Bertrand's voice was strong; his eyes compelling Michel to stay seated. There was no evidence of the tick. "Émilie and I," he placed his hand on her forearm, "need legal help. We want to hire you, and expect confidentiality." Émilie silently pleaded with her eyes.

"I'm not a lawyer, I'm a private investigator. I work for the Gensonné family; I can arrange a consultation."

Bertrand questioned Émilie with raised brows; she nodded, giving tacit approval. "We need an investigator more; however, we do have some legal questions." Bertrand motioned to the waiter. "Let's eat lunch. Georges will bring the daily special. We'll tell you what we know, perhaps you can advise us." He peered at Michel, his raised brows wrinkling his lean forehead. Michel assented to lunch and more.

Georges immediately brought the starter, marinated Salmon rolled in sunflower and poppy seeds on a bed of greens. "Merci." Bertrand nodded at the waiter. "Please, eat." Michel picked up his knife and fork.

"What has changed?" Michel asked. M. Bertrand controlled this meeting, and had no reason to hurry. Bertrand forked a morsel into his mouth, took a drink of wine, and asked Émilie if she liked the Salmon. She smiled.

"Émilie and I met yesterday. We share parts of this story, mostly through Maximillian Broutin. We don't know all of it. When I called you last week, I thought I'd possess the *Miriam* painting, and I planned to sell it to you. The proceeds would be given to Maximillian, Émilie's . . . boyfriend."

Michel gazed from Bertrand to Émilie, and back to Bertrand. "You met yesterday?"

"Yes," Bertrand said. Émilie confirmed with a tiny movement.

"And now?" Michel asked.

Bertrand finished his Salmon after Michel and Émilie did, and summoned the waiter for the next course.

When the main course arrived, Georges flamboyantly placed a plate before each of them. "Voila!" Guinea fowl with crispy golden skin, served on a bed of caramelized sauerkraut with silky mashed potato. Bertrand winked at Georges.

"We each need legal advice. I was involved with a questionable commission, not knowing it was illegal at the time; although the project was suspicious. I'm prepared to deal with my responsibility." He held out his hand; Émilie reached into her handbag, pulling out a soiled envelope, and handed it to Bertrand.

"After I read this, and talked to Émilie, and analyzed this last night, I . . . I believe no crime was committed. At least regarding the *Miriam* painting."

"What are you saying? My client wanted to purchase a contemporary piece of art displayed in the Musée de l'Erotisme. It hung among other pieces that were for sale. All this cryptic talk." Michel waved his hands. "Means nothing."

"I wanted to get the legal issue established first. I'll give a quick overview; you may ask questions." Bertrand continued to eat without comment as Michel and Émilie waited.

"If the food wasn't so good, I'd leave." Michel was tired of this. "If you don't have the painting . . ."

"Enjoy your lunch. You'll hear what we know." Bertrand ate slowly, setting the pace, controlling the silence and thereby, controlling the conversation. "I was painting in the Place du Tertre, when I was approached by Maximillian. About six years ago."

"I know the place."

"He wanted to commission a painting, and I agreed. He brought me an old canvas, painted white; it had fissures and lines running through it, painted canvas cracks for many reasons. The canvas could be old, or exposed to high heat. It's standard practice to re-use expensive canvases, especially when you're not selling much."

"Continue."

"I needed the money then, for—well . . . I beat down my reservations. My artists' group had hired a model. She was lying on a chaise lounge; I painted her underwater, floating on her back in the ocean. It was one of my best works. When it was finished, I called Maximillian; he paid me and left with it. I didn't hear from him again for five years."

"How did you know Maximillian?" Michel asked.

"I didn't. He had approached me, in the Square. Early this past June, he came back, pounding on my door, wanted me to store the *Miriam* painting. He couldn't take it home." Émilie sighed, disconcerted when they both glanced her way.

"I had regretted the commission, and didn't want any association with it; he threatened to expose me, or to harm my family. I took the painting, and I placed it in an exhibition I had organized for the Musée de l'Erotisme. Not a wise move. It drew so much attention—I got calls from people who wanted to purchase it—I removed it, brought it home. This time I insisted Maximillian take it back." Bertrand leaned toward Michel. "Then you showed up."

"Sorry for the rough treatment. I thought you were the culprit."

"Understood." Bertrand touched Émilie's arm. "I didn't hear from Maximillian until I ran into him at the Parc des Buttes-Chaumont. He asked me to find a buyer. I refused, and then, he told me the painting covered an original Maclet. I was culpable, too. He threatened me. I was frightened and left Paris. Spent time with my daughter."

He lifted his wine glass, gesturing around the room. "I wanted to come home." Bertrand set his glass down. "Therefore, I planned to acquire the painting, sell it to you and pay Maximillian. I would be free of the quagmire. When I couldn't contact him, I came to Montmartre to search. I arrived yesterday."

"How did you meet Émilie?"

"She answered Maximillian's mobile. He had thrown some money at her and walked away, without his mobile or the money. He didn't come back." Bertrand eyes softened as he looked at Émilie. "Do you want to tell him the rest?"

"No, please." She leaned toward Bertrand. "There's not much more. I'm sorry I've wasted your time."

"I'm interested," Michel said. "What's the rest of the story?"

"We met here. Émilie told me she found this letter, but she thinks he read it for the first time just yesterday. This morning, we went to visit his sister Mimi, and she said he had asked her to store a wrapped painting. She stored it a few days, and then asked him to pick it up. She doesn't know where her brother is." Bertrand pulled the letter from the envelope and pushed it towards him. "Read the letter now."

Michel read slowly in the dim light, deciphering the faded handwriting which was hard to read. Written with a fountain pen, there were spots where the ink ran thicker, obliterating some letters. "I'm not a lawyer, we don't know if or where Maximillian found the Maclet. He could've stol—taken it." Michel didn't look at Émilie. "I can investigate. Where is he?"

"We don't know," Bertrand said. Émilie's gray eyes watered; she turned away, searching in her bag, pulling out a handkerchief. Tears overflowed and Bertrand put an arm around her. "She's worried about him."

Michel took Bertrand's contact information, said he would call, and wished them a good day. He dialed André's private line when his shoes hit the street. He broke the connection before André answered, spun around and re-entered the bistro where the disparate couple still sat at the table.

"May I ask a question?" Michel was breathless. He had almost forgotten why André coveted the painting.

"Yes, what is it?"

"Who was your live model for the *Miriam* painting? Do you know her name?" Michel asked.

"Someone else hired her. I believe she was an American."

Chapter XXXII André

PEOPLE WERE A bundle of vices and virtues and what unraveled often depended on chance. One decision or choice could alter one's life—sometimes irreparably. Life was a crapshoot and its unpredictable nature hard to fathom. How did God fit in the seemingly randomness of the world?

"Got a minute." Michel dithered near André's open office door. Energetic and exuding vitality, the man didn't stress; he was one of those people who made others feel better when he entered their orbit.

"Bonjour. Come in." André half arose from his leather chair. "Please sit." He motioned to a chair, but Michel plopped onto his desk. André sank into the soft leather again; his shoulders slumped.

Monday had been hard. His conversation with Monique had lingered; she was a lovely person. Her voice still reflected heartbreak and broken hopes at Pierre's long-ago rejection, and her pain had deeply affected him. Endless thoughts of Pierre circulated in his head. Another letdown regarding his brother. Pierre must've felt he couldn't trust him with his priesthood vocation.

But family expectations were high for both. Especially then. Would he have been able to face their father and grandfather with his decision?

Tuesday dragged into Wednesday and became Thursday. He worked long hours and went home alone. Friday crept by, Anne never called.

"You all right?" Michel asked. He sat on the front edge of the desk, with his upper body twisted toward him. "You look like hell."

André straightened his body, resting his head in his hand. What could he tell Michel? His grandfather was a crook and his brother a priest. Those words still shocked him. "Working too many hours. Do you need something?"

"I've had some progress on the *Miriam* case." Michel's direct gaze dared him. "Bertrand contacted me last week. Asked if we still wanted the *Miriam* painting."

André stood. "And?"

"I said I'd come right away. But he held me off."

He moved closer and leaned on his desk next to Michel. "What does he want?"

"To sell it."

"You said yes?" André leaned toward Michel; his heartbeat accelerating. They had been at a standstill, nothing new.

"Of course, but he doesn't have it. A man named Maximillian does, and he's missing. Lots of interesting twists." Michel detailed the timeworn letter, Bertrand's role in the Maclet fraud and Émilie's problem with Max.

"What are the chances it's a genuine Maclet? Have you checked the missing paintings registry?"

"There's one missing, although the story and letter suggest it's an unknown Maclet." Michel slid off the desk.

"Bertrand thinks the dimensions are consistent with his work, but only Maximillian has seen it."

"Is anyone looking for Maximillian? What's his surname?" French society interconnected in multiple ways, it was hard to be invisible in Paris.

"Maximillian Broutin. I've searched all week. He's one of nine siblings and he's estranged from most of them. He's closest to his sister Mimi who lives in Montmartre. She and Émilie have exhausted every lead." Michel walked to the end of the office and back, stopping in front of André. "His pregnant girlfriend's afraid he'll harm himself."

"Any other ideas?" André asked.

"I've investigated most of the Broutins, there are dozens of extended family members. I interviewed his co-workers. No one has heard from him. The women called several police units and some hospitals—a huge task. We are all meeting on Saturday at the bistro in Montmartre. Just wanted to update you. I have plans tonight."

"Wait. That's it?" André asked.

"I haven't found him, I will. Don't be so serious." He slapped André's arm, a wide grin split his face, and his hair waltzed around his head. "I'm going to work another hour. Call me before you leave."

"You said you had plans."

"I do. Call anyway. You need company."

He should invite Collette Dupris for dinner; he had put her off earlier this week. But his mind had been on Anne; he had dreamed of her again last night.

He worked another hour, checking stolen art databases for a Maclet painting. One was missing, about the same size as *Miriam*, rather a small painting. Logging off, André contemplated the street and contemplated calling Collette. If he didn't, it would be another evening at home alone

Switching off two lamps, he left his office. Michel had had interesting news; the missing *Miriam* disguised a Maclet. What were the legal implications of the letter?

265

He nearly collided with Michel. "Whoa! You must have a deep thought," Michel teased. He grabbed his arm and strode along with André. "I was headed your way, forgot something. Bertrand said he did use a model for the painting. He thinks she was American. Could be your Anne."

André stopped, turned to Michel and grasped his shoulders. "Michel. It's been a crazy week. I saw her at the parade. When Celeste and I went for gelato with the kids."

"Why didn't you tell me?"

"It . . . it's been the week from hell." He pulled his arms away from Michel, and rubbed his palm down his face. "I didn't get her name. I gave her my card and asked her to call. She hasn't, but she said she lives in Paris."

"André, let's go out tonight, just guys. I'll meet you at your place around ten o'clock."

Time with Michel would improve his mood. "Sure." I'd take less effort than calling Collette.

Michel laughed. "You don't sound sure. I'll see you then."

MICHEL WAS AN hour late and by then André had changed his mind. The nightclubs fired up late, and he was not in the mood for that scene.

Michel finally rang in and André used his remote to click open the outside entry door.

Michel knocked once and André opened the door; Michel still had his hand up. He was in high spirits; perhaps he was full of spirits. André felt dizzy, after following Michel's exuberant movements. "Did you begin partying early?"

Michel slapped his shoulder. "Just dinner and drinks with Violeta. She has other plans. I'm all yours." Michel looked like he had won the lottery.

"I'd rather stay home; I don't want to socialize tonight."

"You need to go out." Michel waited by the door, pointing through it and bowing. "Let's go." André reluctantly followed. Michel pulled out his mobile and arranged a meeting with someone at one of the bars in Saint-Germain des Prés.

André listened; Michel talked. He was excited, his eyes sparkling, bobbing around in his Métro seat like an antsy child. Anticipation shone from his face. His behavior irritated André; he must have had a great time with Violeta. They exited at the Odéon Station and Michel blazed through the station and up the stairs.

"Where are we going?"

"The Alcazar Bar."

"Why?"

"You'll know soon." Michel strode down the street, zeroing in through the door of the swank restaurant and bar, André had been there many times, as a younger man. The building had been a royal tennis court in the 17th century, and had served a variety of purposes since. An odd choice for tonight.

Michel whispered to the Maître d' who led them to the Mezzanine at the back of the bar lounge where two people sat at a corner table. A tall woman with bright orange hair and a vivid multi-colored dress leapt up, waving wildly. Aah, the woman with Anne at the parade.

Michel met her at the table, kissed her cheeks, and turned to André with both arms extended to a woman in a dark blue dress.

"Voila!" Michel took the woman's hand and lifted her from the chair. "This is Anne Morgan." Michel gently pulled her toward André, and placed her right hand in André's hand.

"I believe you two have met?"

Chapter XXXIII André and Anne

ANDRÉ CARESSED THE hand of the woman he had thought about on and off for most of his adult life. His brother's words resonated inside his head, near his right ear. He half-turned, expecting to find Pierre behind his right shoulder, it was Michel.

André had just remembered the words his brother spoke when he visited him in his dormitory; the night he had first met Anne.

Anne is your future, the one you will love. Be patient. Patient? Seventeen years was a hell of a long time. Anne was now poised in front of him, his right hand holding hers. She trembled, or was he the one shaking?

"André." Michel's voice echoed from a distance, though he stood close. "Stefania's invited me to a party. Call me later." Michel took Stefania's arm and circumvented André and Anne.

Anne withdrew her hand. She glanced at the floor, then at him and then away. She clasped her hands around her middle, and then dropped them. She moved away from him, the look in her eyes suggested flight.

"Anne. Please . . . stay." He touched her forearm, holding her wary gaze with his, and raised his eyebrows. "Please." Her head moved. He guided her to the table, and sat in the chair Stefania had vacated. "Did you know you were meeting me?" She shook her head. "I thought not."

"And you?" she whispered.

"No." He smiled. "We've been set-up." The Mona Lisa smile lingered over her lips. He hadn't remembered the young Anne was this beautiful. "Where do we start?" She sat silently, her eyes deeper blue, uncertainty in them. He couldn't look away. The dark blue dress hugged her curves, one shoulder was covered, and the fabric disappeared under the other graceful arm, her bare shoulder glowing above the dark dress. Her elegant neck held her head high, the dark hair encircling like a crown, her eyes captivating him. He reached for both of her hands, he felt them quivering.

"What will you have, Anne?" Saying her name beguiled him. He waited for her to answer, anticipating the sound of her voice. He had reacted like a teen-age boy; he *was* a teen the last time they spent an evening together.

"Sparkling wine? You choose, please." She spoke French. Her lyrical voice charmed him; he hadn't remembered it. She hadn't talked much that night, or at the parade.

André ordered for both. The waiter edged away, his steps silent.

"Where do we start? It's been so long." A tiny shrug rippled her bare shoulder, a French movement. She lifted her hand from his and tugged her skirt lower.

"Why are you in Paris—?"

"Your wife—."

They had spoken together. Wife? Aah, the parade. The last time he saw her, he was with Celeste and the children.

"Is that why you didn't call? I was with my sister, and my nieces and nephews." He reached for her hand again. "I'm not married."

"Those children? Not yours?"

"No. No children." He grimaced, remembering the sticky gelato adventure with five tots. "I've never married."

"I . . . me . . . either." Traffic had picked up in the bar, and the buzz of others' conversation overshadowed her words. The silence lengthened, she toyed with the stem on her glass. He leaned forward, putting one finger on her index finger. It tingled.

"Where do you work? Your French is fluent." She spoke French with a slight American accent.

"The American Embassy."

"How long?" The waiter reappeared with their drinks. "Merci." André thanked him.

"Five years."

"You've been in Paris five years. And didn't contact me?"

"I didn't know your last name." Anne stared at his chest, lifting her eyes to his face. She had acquired more sophistication, though unsure, her movements were refined. "Your accent was difficult. I'd had no experience with foreign—other languages." She sipped her Champagne. "I understood your first name and that you were French. I was a naïve seventeen."

"My English improved." He lifted one eyebrow, crinkling his face. "Where did you go? I looked for you the next day. No one knew you."

"I didn't attend school there. A friend had invited me for the weekend. I went home the next day."

"Like Cinderella?" André took her hand again. "Anne. This is important; it will make sense later." He clasped her other hand too. He hoped she'd understand. "Did I tell you that night my twin brother had died?

"No. I'm sorry. When?" Her hands fluttered under his. "How?"

"A boating accident, a couple of weeks before we turned eighteen. It's why I went to the United States."

Anne covered his hand with her free one. "You must miss him terribly."

"His death defined my life." He drank from his fluted glass. "And you? Why are you in Paris?" A confluence of emotions skimmed her features, slight fleeting movements.

"I don't know. Perhaps luck, or taking advantage of . . . opportunities."

How awkward. Anne had consumed him all week, and intermittently for the last several weeks. Since that fateful visit to the Musée de l'Erotisme. Why so clod-footed? The painting! He should have asked her sooner. Perhaps she could solve the mystery.

"Anne. I saw a painting in a museum, the Musée de l'Erotisme. The model in the painting looked like you. Did you pose for it?" Her eyelashes fluttered and color washed over her face, her pulse quivering on her exposed neck. She pulled her hands away, her right hand touched her ear; she pulled a strand of hair behind the pink shell, where three tiny pearls nestled in the lobe.

"I . . . I don't—. What portrait?" Her voice was huskier.

"You, a woman, was lying on her back in a red ball gown." She twirled her hair with her fingers; her face grew rosier. "Did you pose for it? Do you know who painted it?"

"I'm not sure. I . . ." She partially arose from her seat, then sat again.

"It's late, I need to leave." Anne grabbed her handbag, and flew across the hardwood floors. André pulled Euro from his pocket and flung them onto the table. He wound through the tables of the now-packed bar, and down the mezzanine stairs to the restaurant. Patrons observed him as he dashed past their tables, entering the foyer, he dodged those amassed in front of the door. He overtook her just outside the entrance where people also awaited access to the popular restaurant and bar. André grabbed her wrist.

"Not this time, Cinderella. You're not disappearing again." He held tight to her arm, she struggled a bit. "Please, let's talk. I won't mention the painting."

"I . . . I . . . need to go home." She pulled against his hold. He did not mistreat women. He dropped his hand and she rushed away, disappearing among the nighttime revelers. He remained where she had left him, tall, erect. People flowed around him like water in a stream, moving around imbedded rocks.

"André. What's up?" Michel asked. He and Stefania walked arm in arm, happy and engaged. "Where's Anne?"

André shrugged.

"I shouldn't have left," Stefania said. She dropped Michel's arm. "It was hard enough to get her here."

"I thought we should leave them alone, to talk about old times. What happened?" Michel asked.

He shrugged again. "I don't know. We talked a little, she seemed uneasy. I asked her about the painting. She bolted."

"That was dumb." Michel jostled his arm, jumping around. He pulled both hands through his curls. "You were supposed to woo her."

"Too late now, I'm going home."

"We're not. The night is young. See you Monday." Michel took Stefania's arm and waved.

André stuck his hands in his pockets, head down. He blended in with the other walkers on the street. He had read her body language; he should have realized she was apprehensive, nervous. That *was* dumb. The visit to the Musée de l'Erotisme had altered his staid life, beginning a succession of bizarre events. When he remembered the painting, it had been imperative she know. The *Miriam* painting had brought them together.

Anne Morgan, American Embassy employee, could be located. André's friend, the American Ambassador to France, would probably open the Embassy door himself.

THE LAST TIME SHE had panicked like this, running, an immense green door stood between her and freedom. It was so heavy; she couldn't move it at first, she was so upset. She had tugged and tugged, afraid they wouldn't let her leave. She wore an inappropriate dress then too.

The heels of Anne's shoes impeded her travel on the wide streets, as did her dress. The short tight skirt hampered movement and the low top attracted unwelcome comments. She stopped, glancing around, leaning against a building to rummage through her bag. She balanced onto one foot, then the other, changing into flat-heeled shoes. She tossed a wide scarf around her shoulders and rushed ahead, her heart pounding; her breath came in short bursts. Stefania had deceived her, her one friend.

She hadn't been prepared to meet André. Not yet, and dressed like a whore. Tears threatened, smearing black mascara on her hands when she swiped at them. She had trusted Stefania. She was ruined.

How had he known she had posed for those artists? Had he seen the painting? She felt the blood rush to her face again. The modeling job still haunted her, one of those horrifying experiences that she had buried. However, she still feared discovery, worrying her indiscretion would steal her hard-won life.

It had begun when a colleague at the Embassy suggested a way to enhance her income. Anne had worked at the Embassy in an entry-level position, and she budgeted strictly, lived frugally. However, her co-worker earned extra money "under the table, tax free" when she modeled for artists. Anne could model too, and she could refuse any job if she was uncomfortable.

She had modeled for the same group of Montmartre artists for a few months, when they asked if she would model in a ball gown, lying back onto a chaise lounge. The job lasted for weeks, every Saturday. One terrible day, she had asked to view their work. One artist left out the chaise, painting her floating underwater. Others painted her as depicted. She understood artists never painted the same scene, the renditions varied every time.

However, the last artist had painted her on the chaise, with the bodice of the red gown ripped off her breasts, shreds of red fabric dangling from her upper body, her face ecstatic, her body writhing, her legs spread. The image obsessed her, branding into her brain. She feared someone at the Embassy would see it. She would lose her position. She would have to leave Paris.

Now someone *had* seen it. The man she had loved for years. In what museum did he say he saw the painting? Oh God! The Musée de l'Erotisme.

When she reached a seat on the Métro, she remembered she told him she took advantage of opportunities. She sank onto the hard plastic, tears finally slipping, staining her expensive blue dress.

What must he think?

Chapter XXXIV Michel

MICHEL'S MOBILE RANG. He didn't recognize the number. "Monsieur la Roche? This is Émilie." Her voice trembled. "I'm afraid Maximillian is floating in the Seine or lying in an alley. Alone." He heard her sniffle. "He's been gone two days."

"I'm sorry he's still missing, Émilie. Most people who disappear come back safely."

"What else can I do? I met with his sister Mimi and we made a list of Broutin family members. We've called them all. She said he had a couple of close friends."

"Did anyone see him lately?"

"No, except for Mimi, he didn't speak to most of them. He told me he had a . . . horrible childhood. He wanted to forget." She blew her nose.

"And the friends? Did you contact them?"

"No-o-o. He lived with Beauregard Pascal before he met me." She swallowed hard. "I think, I think he's a bad guy . . . a criminal, maybe." She blew her nose again. "I'm afraid . . ."

"I'll talk to Beauregard."

"I think, maybe, he was the friend who gave Maximillian the letter."

"We'll find him, Émilie."

"Thank you, Monsieur la Roche."

"Michel."

"Okay." Émilie's voice strengthened.

Michel again checked with nearby hospitals and the police. He called Beauregard a second time, asking for names of other friends. No one had seen Maximillian.

Five days had passed with no new information. He was tired, had less bounce than usual in his gait. He had been out late with Stefania last night. What a party. She was something. However, he had agreed to meet Bertrand, Émilie and Mimi on Saturday in Montmartre. The two pregnant women loved Maximillian. He hadn't met Maximillian yet; however, he had a lot to say to him.

Bertrand wanted to find Maximillian too, for equally mysterious reasons: fear, hate, maybe revenge. Bertrand did seem to care for Émilie, treating her like a daughter.

The ambience of Montmartre seeped through his skin. He greeted aproned waiters stationed at outdoor café tables, inviting passersby to dine. Bertrand's favorite bistro had become his favorite, anticipating lunch restored his good humor.

Michel was whistling now and pondered the Saturday special. The owner didn't require a menu; his daily offering satisfied everyone. The food prepared on-site, unlike many smaller eateries, was fresh, creative, delicious and well-priced. His mouth watered. M. Bertrand, Émilie, and Mimi waited at the customary table.

"Bonjour." Michel responded to their greetings. He sat in the vacant chair, reached underneath, and scooted forward. Georges had poured the house wine, and Michel tipped his glass toward Bertrand. The pregnant women lifted their mineral water.

"Have you found any trace of Maximillian?" Michel asked. He set his glass down and pulled a notebook from his shoulder bag. They shook their heads. "Sometimes, no news is good news." Émilie rolled her eyes. The little bistro filled up, most of the incoming patrons acknowledged Bertrand in some way, some with a nod; others stopped at the table and greeted him.

Michel consulted his notes. "I contacted his employer at Chez Philippe; he called in Monday and has not worked all week. He didn't socialize with his staff or colleagues beyond work hours. He told his boss he'd be gone awhile."

Émilie wrung her hands. "I . . . I . . . called Monsieur Dubois. He said he was a good employee, had worked his way to head chef, then he changed. M. Dubois didn't like the change." She bowed her head. "I want the old Maximillian back."

"I've visited his friends. He hasn't contacted them since he moved in with Émilie, except Beauregard Pascal. He's a childhood friend, and a cohort in other . . . activities." Michel noted Émilie's bowed head. Her silky hair fell over her shoulders, hiding her face. How much did she know of Maximillian's past? He had uncovered a short rap sheet which included boyhood pranks, petty crimes.

"Beauregard Pascal said he saw Maximillian a couple of times in the last three weeks. He hasn't seen him since Monday. I think Beauregard knows him best. Sorry, Émilie." Michel grinned, lifting his glass toward her.

"I'm not offended. I just want to find him." Émilie's crossed arms protected her abdomen. Mimi hugged her close with one arm. "I talked to the owner of Chez Philippe again yesterday. He said, he said—. "He'll take him back if he behaves."

"We'll find him. Maximillian was excited when he told me about the baby," Mimi said. She touched Émilie's abdomen. "He cares."

Georges brought broiled onion soup topped with breadcrumb-crusted goats' cheese, serving the women first, returning with two more bowls. Michel savored the pungent caramelized onion and cheese aroma. "Monsieur Bertrand, I'm forever grateful. I love this place." He dipped his spoon into his bowl. "Any news about the painting?"

"Nothing new. We need Maximillian," Bertrand said. He dropped his head to breathe into his soup bowl and wafted the steam forward with his hands. "Smells great, Georges." The women were quiet, each enjoying the tasty soup.

"Why is the painting entitled *Miriam*?" Michel asked. Bertrand looked up, startled, eyes darkening.

"How did you know that?" He shot the question at Michel. "You said you didn't see the painting."

Michel lifted his shoulders. "Don't know, heard it somewhere. Why?"

"The plaque wasn't there very long—three or four days. I had replaced the plaque a short time before I had to remove the painting from the exhibition." Bertrand bent his head, lifting his spoon.

"André must have said something." Michel searched his memory. "Yes, when he first talked to me, he said the painting was entitled *Miriam*, he was sure the plaque was new, it hadn't been there the first two times he visited the museum." Bertrand's body language had changed.

"I'm sure I called the painting *Miriam* the first time—. The first time we met," Michel said. The women looked from him to Bertrand, questioning.

"Yes. Yes. Probably. I'm old, forgetful." Michel sensed he withdrew, pulled himself in. Had he offended the aged artist?

"Maximillian didn't want a painting with my autograph," Bertrand said. "She looked vulnerable, exposed to the world, lying still in the water. I named her *Miriam.*"

"Miriam? From the biblical story? The older sister of Moses? She saved him from the water, from the Nile." Michel spewed the words, enthusiasm animating him. Most French people didn't believe anymore and didn't read the bible stories.

"I like that, Bertrand. *Miriam.* How appropriate." He refilled his glass and reached to fill Bertrand's glass. "Inspiring."

"I believe in God, Monsieur la Roche. I know the biblical story of *Miriam*," Mimi said, her voice low. "I wish I had seen *Miriam.* I didn't know it then, but I hid the painting for Maximillian. I should have helped my brother more."

"No regrets Mimi, we only look forward." Michel looked at each face around the rectangular table. "When we finish eating, let's visit Beauregard at the café where he works." All nodded.

Georges brought four plates of Trout Amandine, replenished their wine carafe, and brought a fresh bottle of mineral water. An hour later, the four had a plan.

Beauregard had to know something; he had met with Maximillian for a reason.

Chapter XXXV Maximillian

MAXIMILLIAN HAD GONE underground, deep underneath the city of Paris. In the old days, he had been part of a mischievous group of troublemakers who haunted the underground passages and tunnels of the city of light. Adventure-seeking (mostly young) Parisians explored, partied and hid in a world unbeknownst to most other Parisians, or tourists.

A world inhabited by rats, insects and the dead, the Catacombs occupied long stretches of the underground passages. The tunnels had resulted from limestone harvested to build the great stone structures of the city during the 17th and 18th centuries.

Maximillian and dozens of others used the underground caverns as a secret place to hide when their escapades attracted police attention, or when they just wanted to hang out, undisturbed by life on the top. They had created sanctuaries in concealed spaces along the tunnels, bringing furniture, blankets and other comforts to modify their hideouts.

Maximillian hadn't been underground in years, though he remembered the route to his favorite hiding place. He had left his mobile and customary shoulder bag behind, but had money in his pockets. He bought cheese, apples, baguettes and beer, and disappeared into the dark. He couldn't tolerate the sunshine.

Émilie was of the light; she belonged in a virtuous wholesome world, one he didn't think existed for him— or for most people. He belonged in the dark, and it is where he stayed for days.

He slept for long stretches, dreaming of snakes. Writhing, swarming, creeping snakes. He ran and ran, but they were everywhere. Piles of baby snakes nestled against rocks. He tried to pass; they swarmed across the only way out. He changed direction, hid under an outcropping; larger snakes slithered from above, blocking the opening. They were coming, coming to choke him, squeeze the life out of him.

He deserved death; no one cared about him anyway. Except Émilie, and he was too rotten for her.

"Max. Wake up." Someone gripped his shoulders and shook him hard. The snakes receded; he could still see their glowing eyes all around him. One had a huge white eye. It was close to him, too close. He screamed.

"Max. It's Beau. Wake up." Maximillian dragged himself from the nightmare. The white eye was Beauregard's lighted helmet. "How long have you been down here?"

Maximillian struggled upright. "I don't know. What day is it?" The light hurt his eyes. "Turn that damn light off." He heard a click and the welcome blackness shrouded them.

"It's Saturday. People are looking for you. Émilie hired an investigator."

"Why?"

"She loves you, Max." Beau turned his helmet light back on. "Why are you hiding?"

"I'm rotten. No one cares."

"Max, listen. No one knows I came. When the investigator Michel la Roche found me, I said I hadn't seen you." Maximillian looked at Beau, his face illuminated by the light that encircled them. "I figured you'd be here."

"Don't look at me. That damn light hurts." Beau moved so his light cast its beam away from Maximillian. "Who is la Roche?"

"I don't know. Émilie hired him." Beau shifted farther away from Maximillian, sat back with his knees bent and his feet flat on the stones. "Max, I have a confession. First, promise me you'll go home to Émilie."

"Can't do it, she deserves better." Maximillian moved farther from Beau, waiting for him to speak. Beau sat with his legs outstretched, staring at his feet. His feet created huge shadows in the surreal light.

Beau glanced toward Maximillian, his headlamp illuminating his face, and Maximillian turned his head. "Shit Max, you're filthy. You have crap stuck to your beard." Max slid his hands down his rough cheek, and grimaced.

"Émilie needs you; don't let her and the baby down." Beau's words echoed in the recesses beyond the light. Maximillian didn't respond. He hurt too much, not only his body, but also his soul. A despicable piece of nothing. So Émilie had told Beau about the baby. Maximillian didn't care, the baby was better off without a Papa like him.

"Max. Got something to tell you. The man you call the rat is my uncle." His voice was low and rattled, his words disappearing in the cavernous space. "He was my contact for illicit art—and other stuff." Beau propped his head onto his hands, elbows on his knees, the light angled down. "That was in the old days. He's ruthless, Max." Beau reached out to grip his arm. "I hate him. I've steered clear for three years. Until you contacted me about the Maclet."

Maximillian rolled away from him. Curled in a fetal position, he put his arms around his head and ears. No, not his friend Beau, his roommate, confidant, fellow conspirator, betrayer, Judas.

"Max?" He heard Beau, couldn't answer. "Max!"

"Go away." Max curled into a tighter ball, making himself smaller. He was mad now.

"It's not what you think. You told me you took the painting there, I tried to intervene. He's my maman's brother, my uncle. He's cruel; he's cheated everybody, even me." Max sensed his old friend move closer, not quite touching his body. Maximillian didn't retreat. "I visited him and we argued about you. My uncle pulled a huge knife on me and chased me out of his frame shop."

"You expect thanks?" Maximillian said, his voice muffled in his arms. "Thanks for nothing."

"There's more. My uncle said the painting sold. You would get your share."

"Yeah, got it. Ten percent and a crook's promise."

"I feel really bad, Max. Yesterday, I found out—." Max heard Beau gulp, a sob-like sound escaping his throat. Maximillian sat up, ducking his head when Beau's lighted head swung toward him.

"Damn that light. What else?"

"My Grand-père died yesterday. My maman called us to visit . . . err . . . see him . . . before, before the end. Just a few of us were there, my sisters, a couple of cousins and me. Maman let my uncle come into the room too. She hadn't talked to him in decades, but Grand-père was his father too." Beau's halting tone contradicted his normal bravado.

"Sorry Beau." Maximillian uncurled his body and twisted toward Beau. "Is he the Grand-père you liked?"

"Sometimes. He was old, eighties, I think. Gruff, retired for years, never knew what he did for a living; he always had more money than most of my relatives." Beau put his hands onto his knees and dropped his head down. The crazy light beamed straight down, left Maximillian in the dark. Beau was silent a long time. Maximillian shifted on the hard floor, the mat was too thin. His friend was overcome. Was it grief?

"When my uncle came into the bedroom," Beau said. "He hustled in like he owned the place, ignored the rest of us. Strode to the bed, and said, 'We did it, Papa, one last deal.'"

Beau choked, swallowed his snot and mumbled. "Grand-père said, 'It was a Maclet'. Those were his last words; he didn't wake again."

"Sorry, Beau. What was his name?"

"Luc Portier. He always told war stories about a gang of friends who hoodwinked German soldiers during the 1940s. They stole stuff too: food, art, anything they could find. Boasted they were naughty teenagers, named after the apostles: Mathieu, Marc, Luc and Jean."

"Your uncle *and* your grandfather cheated me."

Beau looked at Maximillian, blinding him with his headlamp. "Sorry, Max. I come from a long line of crooks, didn't know Grand-père was in the business too." Beau stood, his light beam bouncing around the cave.

"My wife's waiting, I need to go." He scowled in Maximillian's direction. "Max, don't throw everything away. Émilie thinks it will work, trust her."

"No." Max felt weak. He didn't have much energy. His food and beer ran out yesterday and he wished Beau would leave.

"Have it your way." Beau scuffled a few steps, and stopped. "You've always made the stupidest decisions, thought you'd changed. I thought Émilie—." Beau took a few clumsy steps. "I was like you; but I gave up the bad stuff for my wife." He turned again, focusing his light directly into Maximillian's eyes. "It was worth it."

"Not for me." Maximillian mumbled.

"Rot in hell. You are too stupid to realize what you're throwing away."

Beau's light traversed down the long corridor, occasionally highlighting gruesome bones. He was in the dark again. Drip. Drip. Drip. Water leaked just beyond his head. He hadn't noticed before. It was black again; so black it was possible he didn't exist, he could have melded with the darkness.

He laid on the mat and dozed. The snakes arrived, all sporting the rat's face. The biggest oldest Grand-père snake slithered toward him; he wasn't afraid. Death didn't scare him.

Beau's words echoed in the dark: Max, the man you call the rat is my uncle.

"MONSIEUR BROUTIN." He heard footsteps. Was Beau back? Didn't sound like Beau. "Broutin." The stern voice grated. "Get your stuff together, you're leaving with us." Maximillian struggled to sit. Two men loomed over him; one was Beau. The other grabbed his arm and hauled him to his feet. "You're a sorry mess. Got anything good down here?" The man looked around. "Doesn't look like it. Beau brought sandwiches and water; you can eat while you walk."

"Who are you? Why should I listen to you?" Maximillian whined.

"Because two beautiful pregnant women love you. Quit feeling sorry for yourself. Act like a man." The stranger gripped his arm so hard it hurt; he stumbled. "Émilie talked to your employer, he's holding your job, and apparently, they've missed you, but you've got to behave."

"Beau, say something. What day is it?"

"Still Saturday. I came this morning before work, worked all day. Now I'm down here again. You owe me. Here's your sandwich. Eat it." He grabbed Maximillian's hand and slapped a wrapped sandwich in his palm. "You're disgusting. Wait until Émilie sees you. She'll probably change her mind." Beau reached into his bag for the water bottle. "Drink. You'll feel better."

"Don't know what she sees in me," Maximillian mumbled.

"I don't see it either," the other man said. "She hired me to find you, and searched everywhere since you disappeared. Name's Michel la Roche. Now shut up until we get out of here, too damn dark for me."

Chapter XXXVI André

ANDRÉ TAPPED HIS knuckles against Anne's closed office door. He winked at her assistant, and waved. Jane had been his accomplice since he and the Ambassador had asked for her help. With the Ambassador's blessing, Jane had cleared Anne's Monday schedule. She remained behind her desk and lifted her hands, both fingers crossed, her dark eyes acknowledging they were conspirators. André gave her a thumb up.

"Come in," Anne said through the closed door, her voice faint. He willed her to open the door and come to him. The doorknob turned and the door swung inward; he was ready.

"Mademoiselle. My name is André Gensonné." In her heels, she was nearly as tall as he. Her questioning expression changed to a confused one. "And what is your name?"

"Anne. Anne Marie Morgan."

"Anne Marie Morgan. Pleased to meet you. Let's start over again." Jane had joined him, standing near his elbow.

"I've cleared your schedule," Jane said. "The Ambassador insisted." Anne's eyes moved to Jane's and back to his, her shoulders ultimately moving in an easy Gaelic shrug.

"I'm pleased to meet you André Gensonné." She held out her hand, her smile radiant.

Raising her hand to his lips, he kissed the veins on top. "Please, spend the day with me." Her face colored. She attempted to pull her hand away, then stilled it. What would she say? Her face reflected her decision.

"I will." The radiant smile returned. "I'll collect my bag." She returned wearing flat-soled walking shoes.

Jane returned to her desk. "Enjoy your day off, Anne. I will handle . . . whatever." Jane bright eyes were blinking rapidly.

André took her arm. "Will you agree to one rule for today, applicable to both of us?"

"What is it?"

"Just for today, we live in the moment, no talk of yesterdays or tomorrows."

"Love it. I agree." She appeared more at ease than she had at the parade or at the disastrous blind date. Many of Anne's colleagues managed to watch their progress through the embassy, with curious interest.

André and Anne meandered to the Concorde Métro station without planning a route. "What do you like best about Paris?" André guided her to a seat, nestling his legs alongside hers.

"Just about everything. I've behaved like a tourist since I've arrived." She smoothed her hair back from her face, brushing against his arm, heightening his awareness of her. "I explore every weekend. I didn't know how long I'd live here, so I wanted to experience everything."

"Any favorites?" André held her hand, rubbing his thumb along hers.

"I love museums. I love the grandeur of the buildings. I love the differences in the neighborhoods of the arrondissements. I love the markets, wandering through them, tasting unusual foods, watching the diversity of the people who visit them." She placed her other hand over his. "And you? What do you love about Paris?"

"Fair question, let me think." He tilted his head back. "Hmmm . . ." He lowered his head toward her. "I'm a native Parisian so my perspective is different. Paris is the background of daily life. Does that make sense?"

"It does, my hometown is boring." Anne laughed.

"My fun-loving friend has tried to change me. Michel says I don't appreciate my surroundings." He almost said she had met Michel last Friday night, but he had originated the rule. "I love art, especially paintings. And I confess, I have a loose plan for our day."

He looked at the map of the Métro lines posted along the top of the car. "We get off at the Opera Métro Station." André checked his watch. "Look for the people in the pink vests at the top of the main steps, in front of the Opera Garnier."

They arose simultaneously, just before the doors opened. "Parisians love to walk the streets. It's one of our favorite pastimes. I've booked the Paris Landmarks Right Bank Tour at 10:30." André spoke too fast, anxious to please.

"DiscoverWalks. I haven't done this in years. I didn't have much money when I first arrived, these were inexpensive." Her eyes sparkled.

"A good way for us to discover each other." André finished in a rush, hoping it didn't sound trite.

"There they are." Anne pointed to a young man and woman in fuchsia purple vests. "Anyone can join the tour, walk-ins are welcome."

André had done well. He hadn't chased her off yet and she seemed happy to be with him; though he had surprised her at the embassy.

Twelve people had gathered by ten-thirty; the others were foreign tourists. André and Anne trailed the group within hearing distance. The knowledgeable native guides walked them from the Paris Opera to the Concorde, where the "guillotine took the life of King Louis XVI and Marie-Antoinette, and where nowadays the Tour de France stages its finale."

Highlights included the Arc de Triumph, Eiffel Tower, Champs-Elysées, and a walk along the Place Vendôme – where the world's wealthiest shop. The guides pointed out the Louvre, d'Orsay and the l'Orangerie – three of the world's greatest museums.

When the guide mentioned the Louvre, André longed to ask Anne if she had been there the Saturday he had visited; his rule intervened. The tour was to last ninety minutes; he slipped the guide a one-hundred Euro note after an hour and whispered to Anne he had booked a table for an early lunch.

André took Anne's hand as they strolled to Le Clos Bourguignon, a family-run bistro popular with the locals. The cozy, unpretentious ambience fit his plan—to avoid obnoxiousness. He had offended Anne on Friday, and he wouldn't repeat that blunder. She had played tourist along with him, pointing out details he had missed.

The Maitre d' directed them to a crisply clothed table for two. She had covered herself today, wearing a long-sleeved creamy striped blouse with a knee-length black skirt. Her dark hair was loose, longer than it had been in the painting, grazing her shoulders. Remarkable eyes were her best feature, today a violet blue with a darker blue rim surrounding the pupils. Looking at her this close across the table sent him back to the fraternity house party in Michigan. "Anne, do you re—." The rule, she smiled without commenting. "I suggest we order their special. It's always outstanding."

"Please order for me." She set her menu on his.

André placed their food order with the attentive waiter, asking for wine suggestions, then choosing a moderately priced bottle.

"You should choose our venue after lunch. Perhaps a museum?"

"The Musée de l'Orangerie is close." The server brought their wine asking André to sample, then pouring for her first. "I still can't believe I live in Paris." She combed her hair back with spread fingers. "It's a dream for someone like me."

Her last comment surprised him "We'll go to the l'Orangerie this afternoon." He lifted his glass.

"I'd like that." Her tone was soft. She touched his glass.

"To us and today—just today." André toasted. Conversation about their jobs established neutral ground and two hours evaporated. They ordered coffee.

Anne was intrigued by his friendship with her Ambassador. "I can't believe we haven't run into each other through him. Oups, is that off limits?" Anne covered her mouth.

"Who knows? We only have one rule, perhaps we need more."

"For one day? I don't think so . . ." she warned.

André's vibrating mobile interrupted them; work hadn't intruded since this morning; he had asked Marie to hold all calls. A quick check indicated the call came from his father's private mobile. "It's my father, it must be urgent."

"Please, answer."

"Bonjour."

His father spoke immediately without a greeting. "Papa collapsed at the office." Vincent's voice was agitated, distraught. "He's in the hospital. He insists you come, repeatedly calling your name. He can't be calmed. I'm with him; the rest of the family is on its way. The Hôpital Claudius Régaud at the Institut Curie." His father broke the connection.

His mind raced. Had his grandfather told anyone of his disease? His sluggish arm dropped to his lap. He stared at his mobile; his grandfather's confession overwhelming him, its significance now more critical. His core turned to ice, the cold spread to his limbs and froze his brain. Time stopped. How long had it been since the diagnosis? His grandfather said he had months, had time to plan. He grabbed his abdomen; the food he had eaten nauseated him.

"How are you?" Anne whispered in his ear. She had come around the table and had placed her arm around his shoulder. "Are you sick?" He shook his head no. Except he was, he had to leave, now. He staggered upright and the waiter appeared. Anne opened her purse, handing the alarmed waiter a pile of Euro, and escorted André through the restaurant. They attracted attention from other patrons as they passed. When they reached the street, he vomited. Anne held his arm and waited without speaking. Fumbling in her purse, she found a napkin, placing it in his hand, folding his fingers over it like he was a child. "How can I help?"

"I need to get to the Hôpital Claudius Régaud. Grand-père. Emergency."

"I'll find a cab." She guided him toward the corner. "We need the main street."

Anne procured a cab, taking charge, relaying the hospital name in fluent French. She helped him into the back seat, and sat close to him, her body heat comforting. She rubbed his arm, the shock dissipated some, and his body warmed.

Anne communicated with the cab driver, apprising André of their progress, the cab ride stretched interminably. They finally arrived at the emergency entrance. His grandfather must be critical; doctors on mobile units handled most emergencies, responding quickly to medical needs at the patient's home or workplace.

Anne asked him his grandfather's name, and relayed it to a staff person who assigned someone to escort them to his grandfather's room. Most of his family had gathered outside the door although his sisters hastened to him when he arrived. Surrounded by his loved ones, his eyes darted around the room. Where was Anne? His father latched onto his arm. "He insists on seeing you. Alone." André cringed, his insides constricting, feeling nauseated again.

"Papa, wait." André pulled away. "Anne."

"André, she's here with me." Celeste had placed her arm around Anne.

André gathered her close and hugged her, folding her against his chest. "Please stay. Don't leave me." She nodded against his neck, her soft breath comforting.

"Go to your grandfather, I'll stay." He reluctantly released her; his father already gripped his arm, urging him toward the door. André looked back at Anne. She waved her fingertips. He faced the room. What would he find beyond the door?

His grandfather rested, his eyes closed, appearing shrunken. He approached the bed.

"Grand-père? It's André." His grandfather's eyelids blinked slowly and he opened his eyes. His stare pierced through André, dark circles, hard and focused.

"Come closer, I want to see you." His voice was raspy. André leaned his head next to his grandfather's face. "Remember our talk?" André squeezed his hand. "I thought . . . I had . . . more time." His voice faded and he winced. "This thing in my head, spread fast, no time left." André smoothed his veined hand.

"You've lived a long time, Grand-père."

"A longer life, than I expected. Listen. Go to my study. Now. I locked what you need in my desk. The key is taped . . . under the mantle." His grandfather closed his eyes for several moments. Had he gone to sleep? He opened them again, staring into André's soul. "No one else must find it. Go now or the family is ruined." Grand-père had dismissed him; perhaps he was already gone.

Then he stirred, half-opening his eyes, "The Caravaggio . . . I almost . . . had a . . . Caravaggio." His eyes drifted shut and his head seemed to shrink even more, his breath becoming more labored, and there were longer stretches with no breaths.

André studied his face, emotions bombarding him. What did he feel? Greif, pity, hate? His grandfather had just cast his filthy net over André.

ANDRÉ RELUCTANTLY WALKED through his grandfather's hospital room door into the midst of his distraught family. Everyone had arrived: Grand-maman, his dear Maman, Papa, Celeste and Isabelle, and their husbands, Michel, his best friend. But he had never felt more alone, the bearer of the family shame.

"Was he able to talk?" Vincent asked. André nodded.

"I'm his executor. He had a request."

"Probably a demand," Vincent said. "I know my father."

"Yes, Papa." André hugged him, then Maman, Celeste, Isabelle. He walked to Anne; she wavered uncertainly just behind his sisters. He had looked for her first through the doorway, aware of her before he passed into the room. Before his family saw him.

He took both her hands in his. "Thank you for getting me here." He folded her within his arms. "Grand-père gave me a task. I'd like you to come." It occurred to him most of them hadn't met her—only Celeste, on La Fête Nationale.

He faced his family, drawing Anne close to him. "This is Anne Marie Morgan. We met in the United States. We've . . . discovered . . . each other . . . again." Each of them greeted Anne, some with hugs, some with double cheek kisses.

Maman hugged Anne, and then hugged him. She pulled his head down, whispering in his ear, the one farthest from Anne. "She's the one, isn't she?" Same thing Pierre had said when they were eighteen. Mothers were gifts.

THIS TIME, HE hailed the cab. "I need to collect something from Grand-père's house. I'll need my car." He directed the driver to where he stored them, the old beater—an ancient mini Mercedes, and the Bugatti Veyron. No male Parisian owned two such disparate vehicles.

When they reached the cars, André pointed. "Those two are mine. The old one isn't comfortable, the other . . . well. I don't like it. It was a gift from Grand-père."

"What is it?" Anne asked. "I don't know anything about cars. I don't drive much."

"A very expensive sports car. I suppose I should drive that one." He walked to the passenger door and assisted Anne onto the soft leather seat. He sat behind the wheel, turning toward her. "Only my grandfather and Michel have ridden in it, you're my third passenger."

"I'm honored, Monsieur Gensonné."

"Me too," he whispered. He turned the key, the engine responded as if it had been waiting just for them.

The sun disappeared, twilight took its place and then night descended half an hour later, their first journey through the lights of Paris. Anne seemed attuned to his mood, sensing his reticence. Wariness cautioned his thoughts. What had Grand-père hidden? For now, he was content in this protective cocoon with Anne, not wanting this ride to end. An uncertain future for himself and his family threatened them from beyond; he would savor these precious moments with her.

André killed the engine and faced Anne when they reached his grandparents' home. "My life may change beyond what I can control, stay with me now. I need you." He took her face in his hands and kissed her; he wanted to connect with her, be in her, part of her, assuage the intense loneliness of his spirit—bereft of his brother, his honor, his integrity. He deepened the kiss, she responded, opening to him. The kiss ended when his mobile rang. Vincent Gensonné.

"Bonjour, Papa." He knew.

"He's gone, André. He thought he had more time." His father's somber voice choked with emotion, grief.

"Did you know?" André had contemplated telling Papa about Grand-père's diagnosis.

"He told me shortly after he told you."

"I'm sorry, Papa. He was your father, your partner. He'll be missed."

"He will. He wouldn't have wanted to linger." Seconds elapsed. "It's a shock though. Love you André." He heard his father disconnect. André sat with his head bowed.

"Anne?" He turned toward her.

"I heard. I'm sorry." She placed her hand along the side of his face. Her eyes were dark in the cozy interior. The windows had steamed in the small space. When she removed her hand, he missed its solace. How would he let her go after tonight?

Grief settled over him; it had happened so fast. Grand-père seemed vital until just recently, still went to the office almost every day. He had been his soulmate in many ways, more like him than his father or Pierre. They shared a spiritual connection with paintings and artists and the creation involved with applying paint to canvas. What would he find? He took Anne's hand again and placed the other along her face, noting weariness around her eyes.

"Anne. People are complex, a bundle of vices and virtues. Sometimes . . . a choice, a spontaneous one or a well-thought one . . ." He caressed her face. "I'm trying to say." He moved his thumb along her jawline. "Choices change lives." He moved back against his seat and pressed his right hand to his temple.

"Everything will work out." She caressed his hand, running it along his arm.

"I'd better go in, please come." He opened his door, unfolding his long legs, and hurried around the car.

André helped Anne from the low seat. He held her hand, guiding her along the dark walkway, the doorway shadowed. He coded the digital combination and held the door. She passed him and he followed, flicking on the hallway lighting, and led her through the semi-dark house, to his grandfather's study.

André pushed open the paneled wooden door and walked in holding her hand; he fumbled for the light switch with his left hand, unfamiliar with this room. He had been here rarely, it had been off-limits when they were boys, and later hadn't been a priority.

The switch clicked and only turned on dim sidelights that hung above paintings attached to the walls. It was probably light enough for his errand. André led Anne farther into his grandfather's sanctuary. Anne's hand slipped from his and she fainted.

Two illuminated paintings graced a corner, rich colors glowing beneath incandescent oblong lamps. The same dimensions—the same ornate frames.

One a Maclet. The other—the missing *Miriam*.

AUTHOR BIO

Lorraine Baushke grew up in Fountain, Michigan and currently resides in Bowling Green, Kentucky.

Her interests include traveling the world with her husband, cooking, gardening and quilting.

Writing is her third career. She co-owned a flower shop for twenty years with her mother, then re-trained and taught American Government at the junior college level.

Please contact her at rainebaushke.com

SIXTY MORTAL SINS

The sequel entitled Sixty Mortal Sins will be published in July 2017.

The first two pages follow this page.

If you enjoyed my book please leave a review on Amazon, Goodreads or Barnes and Noble.

Chapter One André

Saturday July 27, 2013

PARISIAN ATTORNEY ANDRÉ Gensonné had battled his conscience for the past week, sorrow and anger competing with duty. As his family assembled to celebrate Jean-Baptiste Gensonné's funeral Mass, he regrettably succumbed. Heat warmed his body, gluing his shirt to his chest Anger—an emotion he despised—edged sorrow.

If hell existed . . . but André didn't believe in hell. Or heaven. The funeral Mass celebrating his grandfather's life would be another media spectacle, but it wasn't the hardest task imposed by Grand-père. He had left André a quagmire of problems relating to illegal activity, anathema to André's moral code . . .

THE STRETCH LIMOUSINE conveying the Gensonné family stealthily approached Notre Dame Cathedral in Paris and inside, quiet conversation faltered. Mayhem had overtaken the historic square. Grand-maman pressed closer to André her body quivering beneath her dark suit. A herd of camera-laden paparazzi jostled for position on the steaming sidewalk, snapping dozens of photos even before the family exited.

A somber group of formally-dressed friends and colleagues waited in front of the cathedral, dwarfed by the 800-year-old Gothic façade weathered by time and marred by ideology. Scantily-clad tourists speckled the plaza, heads swiveling from the black limo with its police escort to the scrambling newshounds.

"Are we ready?" André patted his grandmother's hand. Six other serious faces watched his, waiting for their cue. He had become their protector during the last few days. However, shielding them from this relentless scrutiny wasn't possible.

"I'll accompany Grand-maman." André opened his door and stood in one movement, assailed by intense sunlight and humidity. He waved. A cacophony of shouts, cackles and hoots accompanied the staccato clicking of cameras. He snatched his sunglasses from his pocket, bent to assist Grand-maman and faced the crowd from behind his Chevalier shades. His grandmother clasped his forearm.

Other doors opened and his parents and siblings exited, and were intensely photographed as the three couples sedately walked toward the massive doors, dividing the newshounds into two camps. All had remembered their sunglasses.

"André!" He turned toward the voice, sheltering Grand-maman against his side. A sweating man hefting a professional camera with an enormous lens snapped a close-up. André had twice hurried past the same man ensconced outside his grandparents' home since news of Grand-père's death rippled throughout Paris. The camera clicked a dozen times before police shoved the man back, away from his family.

André's arm was seized from behind as an envelope was pressed into his hand. He glanced over his shoulder and caught a brief glimpse of a balding man wearing a black suit. André pocketed the weighty envelope.

"ALWAYS ATTEND THE FUNERAL," Grand-père had said. "Your presence matters more than your convenience." André envisioned his austere face and courtly manner. "They will never forget you came." Prophetic words. Mourners filled the pews of the main sanctuary of Notre Dame.

In André's mind, the consecrated space mocked his family's presence. Only his twin Pierre Gensonné rightly belonged and he had bailed by dying. The rest of them sat in order in the front pew as if a nun from their childhoods had dictated the rules: Grand-maman, his parents Vincent and Sophia Gensonné, he was next, Isabelle and Dominic, Celeste and Christophe.

Pregnant with countless worshippers of firm faith, the ancient cathedral swelled to welcome them. Because Grand-père had given generously to the Church he merited an extravagant funeral.

CPSIA information can be obtained
at www.ICGtesting.com
Printed in the USA
FFOW03n1750061117
43384477-41972FF